PROTECTING TOVA

HAVANA WILDER

Protecting Tova
Havana Wilder

Protecting Tova is an original work of fiction. Names, characters, places, organizations and incidents either are the product of the author's imagination or are used fictitiously. Any resemblance to actual persons, living or dead, events, businesses, companies, or locales is entirely coincidental.

www.havanawilder.com

Edited by: Jes Geisler for CamRei Editing

Formatted by: Shanna Swenson

Cover Design: Christian Bentulan
https://coversbychristian.com

1

TOVA

A sharp, glistening knife follows and stops short of embedding into my skull when the shadow moves.

My eyes slam open as I inhale a desperate breath. I sit up straight in bed, breathing so rapidly my lungs burn. Sweat isn't just beading down my spine, it's pouring down in rivulets and soaking through my shirt. My hair is so saturated I can wring it out like a wet washcloth. I draw my legs in as close to my chest as possible. With shaking hands, I wipe the tears from my cheeks and whisper, "Stop hyperventilating. It was just a dream." But God, for the life of me, I can't stop seeing it. The vision was so vivid.

Unable to shake yet another nightmare, I take a shower and wash away the perspiration that saturates my hair and body.

There's only one thing I can do to escape these nightmares, and that's to run.

The beating of my heart and pounding of my feet are the only soundtrack to my cadence. My feet hammer down like thunder as I take out my frustration and fears, battering the pavement beneath me.

I shift my attention to the fence surrounding the track, taking a quick scan of the wilderness beyond the high protective barrier that encloses our entire territory. You learn quickly around here to always be vigilant and keep an eye out for predators—animals and humans alike. On more than one occasion, I've seen a Lynxwolf or two. These beasts are the largest canines alive. They're beautiful from a distance, and that's what I intend on keeping them—at a distance.

I love having the chance to run on the track; the only drawback is the roving band of alpha male types that always seem to hang around. The last thing I want to put up with while running is a bunch of burly Protectors and trainees, no matter how easy on the eyes they may be. I run to release stress, to try to outrun the demons that plague me every night, and in the moments of tranquility, focus on my impending choice. I come here to clear my mind, relax, and find a sense of peace and freedom. I am certainly not looking to hookup, find some arm candy, or wanting to bond. On more occasions than I'd like to count, one of those muscled meatheads has come up, meeting my stride step for step and trying to grab my attention. Their charms never get to me, though, and are always met with my polite "No thanks."

Smiling, I reminiscence about the day a few weeks ago when I got this bright idea after yet another run-in with one of the alpha brutes. I made my way back to the cabin where they house all of us Deciders, those of us yet to decide which occupation to take on to become an asset to society. When I got to the beautiful cabin made of massive old oak beams, I made my way around back and found some twine among some random supplies. Braiding the section, I tied it on the fourth finger on my left hand. This symbol is the traditional mark of betrothal in our society, and one I hoped would keep most of the brutes at bay.

So far, the fake ring has done its job and offered me at least some measure of solace during my workouts. I've also started getting to the track earlier to focus on my training and not focus on the testosterone that seems to permeate the air when all the big brawny men show up. Don't get me wrong; they are fantastic to look at. Even though I appreciate some eye toffee, I have no intention of doing anything other than concentrating on myself and my training.

Great, the guys are now approaching the track. There my peace and quiet goes out the window.

Muffling a laugh, I notice the scrunched-up faces of the testosterone gang when they see the braided twine. Well, all except one of them, that is. There's a new face in the crowd today, and I wish I could say that's the only reason I notice *him*. This six-foot-tall drink of gorgeousness captures my attention immediately, and I feel the heat creep up my neck, warming up to my already rosy cheeks. Thank goodness I've been running for about forty minutes already, so my cheeks can't betray my blush. This guy seems different. He doesn't come off as feral or as brutish as the rest. I get the feeling there is something more to him. There's a sudden burning sensation blazing through my veins as his eyes meet mine, followed by an overwhelming sense of comfort. He simply gives me a quick smile, flashing his blinding pearly whites as I pass by. I'm fairly sure I've stopped breathing, which isn't a good thing, as I am already gasping for air with four miles under my belt and more to go. Forcing myself to look away, I stop my gawking and pass the group of guys getting warmed up for their exercise.

Hustling toward the next turn on the track, I quickly sneak another glimpse at the group. Again, the handsome guy is there, stretching his arms above his head. As I round the curve, he must hear my pounding footsteps because he surreptitiously glances in my direction. Against my will, my heart speeds up, my eyes wander to him, and I can't breathe again. So inconvenient. I need dark sunglasses or something to hide behind because I'm sure my eyes give me away. Checking him out, I do my best to get my lungs to inhale. Breathe in, breathe out, I repeat to myself in quiet, controlled breaths.

Shaking my head, I wonder what it is about this guy. I've never had an instant attraction or interest in a male before. Damn, he's good looking. My wandering eyes trail over his skin that is sun-kissed, arms are ripped, and I can tell he has six-pack abs when his shirt is pulled tight as he lengthens his torso in a stretch. His thick dark chocolate brown hair is just long enough for the waves to catch the wind. His dark brown, almost black, deep-set eyes pierce my soul as they catch mine. I can't help but notice his strong jawline and the perfect smile he lets slip when he sees me examining him. My body betrays me, and I let a small grin escape my mouth as well. A fire ignites my veins as we lock eyes and throws me off balance slightly. Correcting my stride, I'm forced to redirect my attention down to my feet, ensuring I don't bust my ass in front of this gorgeous Johnny-come-lately.

As I start my cool-down laps, the group of Protectors begins their training. After a couple of laps of walking, I make my way out of the track area through the large fence topped with razor wire designed to keep predators out. I tell myself I'll just come here earlier tomorrow so I can get my entire ten-mile run in with no distractions. Elongating my muscles, my eyes keep deviating to that sexy, dark-haired, dark-eyed newcomer.

Breaking my train of thought, I attempt to rein in my roaming stare, but no sooner than I do, he glances in my direction.

Look away! Look down! Break eye contact, Fungus!

Finally, I'm able to snap the trance I'm in as a blaze burns up my neck. Looking down to assess my shoes, I hope they've somehow gotten the power to drive my feet to move at the speed of light away from this guy who now seems to hold a very intriguing part of my mind. Hurrying to the gym, I toy with the idea, determining that, yes, getting here tomorrow at the crack of dawn is vital. No distractions. Just me and the wind in my hair in the morning.

2

PIERCE

"Well, let's get this done and over with," I whisper to myself as my alarm blares me to life from a deep sleep.

Groaning, I plant my feet on the cold, creaky wood floor beneath me as I vigorously rub the chill bumps along my scarred arms. The cold sends shock waves reverberating throughout my entire body. Good God, if that blasted alarm didn't wake me up, this cold certainly would. The worst feeling after leaving behind warm blankets is the freezing floor on my bare feet.

Alright, get up, I mentally scold myself.

I shuffle to my chest of drawers, pulling out a set of shorts, t-shirt, and socks, before reaching for my best running shoes. After brushing my teeth and hair, while getting fully dressed, I head out of my room and down the stairs of the massive wooden cabin built for the Protectors.

About a century ago, our world almost came to a crashing end. However, some survivors made it out alive after a power-hungry dictator tried to take over the world, leaving only death and destruction behind, including getting himself killed in the process.

The planet was ravaged by a Dust that Dictator Teivel had his "genius inventors" create that would quickly spread through airborne transmission. They concocted the Dust to be easily distributed to key infection points across the globe. From there, it was released into the air to quickly spread through the population, bringing Teivel's Extinction Event to fruition. History books state that:

Dust Extinction Event: Dictator Teivel and his self-proclaimed genius inventors established secret factories scattered around on each continent, totaling over a thousand factories. Dictator Teivel, being the proud man he was, let his ego get the better of him. He deemed himself one of the several people to survive an attack on the entire human race. The world refused to give in to his dictatorship. Teivel and his inventors attempted to build up a tolerance by slowly exposing themselves to this Dust in the hopes they wouldn't succumb to the Dust's effects. These effects varied widely, but the most common and severe resulted in the complete loss of lung function in the affected body. The Dust had the potential to wipe out the majority of life on earth in a matter of minutes. Not even animals and sea creatures were safe because when the Dust dissolved into the ocean, it changed chemical properties in the water, killing most aquatic life. Conversely, there were small pockets of human, animal, and marine survivors that did not die from the Dust. It did not affect the survivors how it did the majority of humanity for reasons still unknown.

A large portion of the survivors lived here in our territory, known as Iron Mountain. It's thought our ancestors more than likely survived because the Dust was not as thick in this mountainous area, primarily covered by impenetrable forests. But just because they didn't die doesn't mean they weren't affected.

Slowly, we are starting to see the Dust has altered many of those who survived and continues to change each subsequent generation. Mostly, the changes are not noticeable, and no one really likes to talk about them. Still, for others, the modifications are more prominent. You can see the evidence in the animals.

Shudders rack through my body every time I think of a Lynxwolf. The memory of a decapitated hunter we happened upon last month while out on a hunting trip flashes to the forefront of my mind. The teeth marks marred on his body revealed eight canine teeth, four on either side, penetrating the shoulders of the unsuspecting individual as the beast ripped off their head. There is a chance the creature was protecting his domain, or maybe he just enjoys having skulls for snacks.

When our territory was established eighty years ago, it was determined residents must take on a responsibility and become an asset to society at the age of eighteen. This practice of 'Deciding' prevents freeloading and encourages the pursuit of useful training. Someone can pick several tasks they'd like to learn, but must master the primary one first.

When my first turn as a Decider came up when I was eighteen, I had chosen to farm with an additional study in naturopathy. I was happy with those choices for the first two years, but it quickly became apparent my skills would be better served elsewhere. Now twenty, and in a position to take another turn as a Decider, I feel my calling is to become a Protector. So, now I'm in training for that.

As a sworn Protector, I must ensure my mind, body, and skills are appropriate for the task. Protectors are sworn to protect the citizens of our broken-down civilization, if you can even call our little community that. I take my responsibilities very seriously and train accordingly. I must learn intermediate skills in paramedicine, master firearms, handheld weapons, and force my mind and body into pristine shape with my new role. All while helping to keep history from repeating itself.

This means breakfast before dawn and early morning runs. It's then off to the arena to practice shooting firearms, bows, knives, and ax throwing. I was fortunate enough to be assigned training in my top four weapons of choice this go around. After weapons training, I'll head to lunch, then spend the afternoon studying paramedicine.

Gaining the needed skills in the medical side of our training involves an intense amount of study. Hours spent pouring over what few books were able to be salvaged from before the Extinction Event, all culminating in an incredibly lengthy exam. Our society's only hope for survival is to ensure we have the skills to ensure our citizens don't die from the few things we can prevent with our limited resources. As a civilization, we are attempting to rebuild the population. Our ability to survive is the only thing keeping us from complete annihilation. There is no way of knowing how many others survived across the world. Still, all we know is that there are precious few people in our region, and every life is necessary for our survival.

Some animals survived, but because of the Dust many have mutations, they are as much of a threat as the Savages. The ravenous Savages were ostracized from society and survive independently in the wilderness beyond our walled mountain forest that encompasses several hundred-thousand acres.

Our settlement is in the southeastern part of what used to be the United States. At one point, this area was the state of Georgia and is still known as the "Boondocks" to the other territories. The old state lines no longer exist; everything is broken up into smaller regions now. Some are near the ocean, where we travel for fish. Some are southwest of us and provide fuels and other necessities. While we may have contact with the other regions, we keep our trade to a minimum. We only need enough fuel for tractors, small ATVs, and machines deemed essential by the Supreme Seniors.

We're fortunate in Iron Mountain that some of the most highly capable people in our region survived the Dust. The natural-born leaders, many with military training, farmers, and naturopaths that survived, all came together to create a new society to ensure our survival. Each new generation's ability and the necessity to grow in knowledge, strength, and capability ensure life will continue without facing the potential of extinction again. Therefore, training must commence.

The track the crew of trainees and I use for exercising is one of the few left behind in the wake of the destruction. Most buildings, man-made materials, and organics like the forests were not destroyed because the idea behind the Dust was to only destroy "beings of flesh," leaving behind only the strongest.

This piece of pavement is hot as hell in the summer. The

sun blasts directly overhead, and the heat seeps up from the asphalt, baking our bodies. Don't get me wrong; I am grateful for the fresh air because I loathe running on a belt that is solely powered by my feet in a gym, seeming more like a dungeon. With power being so scarce, we only use it when necessary, and gym equipment isn't deemed necessary.

There are several solar and wind fields currently active, with more in the works. Still, with so few of us trained to build the panels and turbines required, it will take years to complete everything and get our settlement up and running at full capacity. These resources need to be utilized for making food, weapons, and testing. Hackers destroyed most computers, electronics, and any sliver of history before the Dust attack. Consequently, conserving any books and compiling alternative ways to learn to the best of our ability have been developed.

I stretch near the edge of the track as part of my warm-up. While pulling one arm up and behind my head to lengthen my triceps on my right arm, I overhear the guys talking about *her*. In my curiosity, I swivel to look toward the sound of drumming feet.

Damn, my heart literally skips a beat as my eyes behold her beautiful silhouette. Hammering down the asphalt, she is exquisite. Determined and focused as sweat drips down her alluring face and neck. Nearing the lane closest to me, she's only a few feet away now, and I feel a strong pull to her like a physical force. Holding my stare, I'm dazed and captivated by her blue eyes. Continuing to check her out, I'm mesmerized by her dirty blonde hair swishing back and forth in her ponytail. Her wet hair clings to the side of her face. She's sexy as hell and isn't even trying to be.

As she runs past me, I envision her underneath a waterfall

in a swimsuit with water rushing over her body. Shaking my head back to reality, I wonder how long she's been here exercising to work up that much sweat. She's at least gotten a few miles down because her cheeks are flushed, and her entire body is glistening in the early morning sun. For the life of me, I can't break my freaking stare.

A sudden grasp of my shoulders startles me, and I twist my head to see it's my brother Kage. He's a few years older than me and a Superior Protector, meaning he's extremely experienced in this field and is now one of the highest-ranked Protectors in charge of training.

He squeezes my traps as he lets out an exasperated huff, "Let it go, man. See that left hand? Besides, she's turned down most of my men already."

Noticing her finger, I cringe. "Ouch. No, I didn't notice her left hand. Only those stunning eyes tying my stomach in knots." I shrug him off dismissively. "I don't really care about that twine because it's only a gesture, not a permanent 'off the market' symbol."

Now, I am not a guy that doesn't respect when another male avows a female. But the way she held my gaze as she passed tells me that that's not her entire story. There's something more to her, and I need to find out what it is. I'm not entirely convinced that she is under contract. One way or another, I will find out.

3

TOVA

The shadow I notice in the corner of my room moves swiftly to my side. As I lay petrified, the figure presses the blade to my neck.

Again, I awaken in terror. Grasping at my neck, I struggle for air. My hair clings to my wet face as I lay here in sheets that are drenched with my sweat. Forcing myself to push back the bile that creeps up my throat, I slowly roll over and turn on the lamp beside my bed. Searching every corner of my room, I find no one there. So, I coach myself into taking deep breaths in and out. Once my breathing is under control, I cautiously get ready to go for my morning run.

Now, this is better. Hallelujah, a completely testosterone free track all to myself. The sun is just barely breaking over the horizon, and I hum to myself a soft song as I loosen my rigid muscles before I get lost in a trance on the track. The beat of my feet frees my mind of the decisions I'm obligated to make in the next couple of weeks and of *him,* as I focus on my inner peace.

The only sounds are those of crickets, frogs, katydids, and other early morning critters. A shiver progresses up my spine as the cold air briskly kisses my exposed arms in my black, form-fitting, dri-fit tank top. Cotton tops are the worst. If I ever make the mistake to wear one when I run, it always absorbs my sweat and clings to all the worst bits, and leaves me feeling disgusting.

My mom, Shenandoah, but everyone calls her Shenan, is a seamstress, and I'm forever grateful for that fact. She's developed some truly ingenious breathable fabrics used in clothing and some incredibly flexible running shoes. I can't imagine running ten plus miles in stiff leather shoes. I understand they are functional for the farmers, but they would cause severe blisters and pain for training. On top of the desolate conditions we live in, a group of decision-makers determines what attire is practical. The Supreme Seniors only approve clothing that is deemed essential.

Breathing in the fresh mountain air, I scan the tree line just beyond the fence around the track and let out an audible sigh when I notice a herd of deer. There's a precious fawn only barely able to walk; it still has white dots on its hide and remains close to its mom. Standing nearby, a hefty buck with about ten points on his antlers is surveying their surroundings. He's a protector, that's for sure.

I wish all dads were. Mine certainly was not. He should have been my most fierce defender, yet he was anything but. I refer to him as my biological sperm donor or by his name, Cladec. He could best be described as a monster. Sure, he had a rough childhood, but who hasn't lived through some hell in their lifetime. When he was thirteen, he and his dad were outside the Protection Wall hunting, and he witnessed his dad die from a brutal animal attack. The beast responsible for his death, a Sunclouded Leopard. Its brownish-black fur has uneven oval-shaped markings with dark edges, like a cloud's shape, hence the name. Even if the creature is picturesque, it's perilous.

After the attack, his mom became his everything. At eighteen, as is customary, he had to choose a profession. He decided to be a rancher. My mom's family were also farmers, and the land he tended butted up to theirs. My mom was only fourteen years old when they met, but as time passed, they became friends, and he fell in love with her. They were avowed when he was twenty-four, and she was twenty. They were given one thousand acres and a gorgeous white farmhouse with a wraparound porch after the ceremony. The house was centered in various fields growing cotton, corn, hay, tea leaves, and various other crops. A few hundred acres were designated for the horses, the barn, and farm equipment.

When his mom got sick and perished from an illness that was not curable by the clinic, he became bitter toward the world. He sought out Moonshiners, people who make illegal alcohol, trying to drown out his sorrows. He became a violent drunk, physically, mentally, and molesting ensued.

When I was three years old, he put my mom in a coma by beating her so badly we didn't know if she would live or die. She woke up from the coma three days later but wasn't released from the clinic for another week. He appeared to be remorseful, so she didn't separate from him. He was a master manipulator, but I think she was more afraid if she tried to leave him, he'd kill her, and I'd be left alone to his torment.

He abused me physically for as long as I can remember, but the sexual abuse held off until I was eight. That cruelty only happened when he was drunk. After beatings I cried myself to sleep, only to be awakened in the middle of the night by fondling sandpaper fingers on my private areas. Some nights I pretended I was asleep until the torture stopped to avoid a beating in addition to the assault. Other nights I'd wake up kicking and screaming, only to be met with a fist to my mouth and violent shakes by forceful hands to stop my screams. I'd choke on the coppery taste of blood pooling in my mouth from split lips as I silently cried. I'd beg to the heavens above that my tormentor would die and leave my mom and me alone forever. I never told my mom about any of the abuse, doing my best to hide my battered body.

When I was twelve, one of the Supreme Seniors noticed my bruised arms and a swollen black eye when I was at an educational facility. He said he'd been monitoring the suspected abuse for about six months, and when he saw it was getting worse, he intervened. He took me and my mom's situation to the other Supreme Seniors. All seven unanimously voted to have him banished to the unprotected forests with the Savages and wild beasts. Knowing that he'd be living with the same creatures that claimed his father's life made the fury blaze in his unforgiving eyes. I remember the heat of his rage in his gaze as he glared at me, yet I did not waver. I straightened my spine and stood tall, not letting him know that I was terrified to death of him. I'm sure if he could have gotten his hands on me at that moment, I'd be six feet under, pushing up daisies.

Now that he's banished, I've pushed those skeletons way down deep in my proverbial closet, but those demons taunt me still at night. The vision of his sadistic face haunts my dreams almost every night, stealing my rest. When I started running a year ago, I realized that if I got to the brink of exhaustion, I could sleep a handful of hours a night without dreaming.

In my efforts to chase that exhaustion, I run, or when the weather allows, I swim. There are several lakes in the foothills nearby that make for excellent swimming in the summer months. Once the freezing cold of the mountains melts away in the summer heat, I shift some of my effort toward swimming, always staying close to the roped-off beach areas that have been deemed suitable for lake activities. The Dust did away with most of the dangerous aquatic life, so the lake doesn't pose much of a threat to swimmers, thankfully. However, I prefer the gym's lap pool since it's enclosed, cleaner, and usually warmer by a few degrees.

But running has become my passion. Once I found that it released a lot of my stress and could do it most days, I stuck to it even in light rain. I'm always pushing myself to go just a little bit longer, a little bit further.

Rumbling up ahead catches my attention as the group of Protectors approach the track and make no secret of their arrival.

Fan-flipping-tastic!

Man, there *he* is too. Well, I guess it's a good thing I have just two more laps, and my ten miles are done. As I approach the entrance of the track, I recite my mantra to myself.

Just stay fixated on these next two laps. Don't look at them. Or him. You can do this.

I feel him stride up behind me, and I immediately tense in irritation.

Um, did he really just start jogging directly behind me? What the crap?

Okay, drive harder, sprint faster, only two more laps to go.

Run, don't stop, don't think.

Okay, half a lap down.

Now he is getting closer to being beside me. *Toadstool!*

Clearly, he's not driven away by the ring I have on my left hand. I only peek over my shoulder in his direction to see if it is, in fact, him, knowing good and well it is.

Fart!

I make eye contact, and his eyes make my lungs fail me. Now it's even harder to breathe.

Lengthening his stride, he's now promptly running right beside me as I hear him say, "Hey."

Glancing in his direction, barely audible, I mutter, "Hey to you too."

Cheese and rice!

Looking at him causes my feet to tangle together, almost taking me down to the tarmac. Correcting my stride and doing my best to maintain my balance with flailing arms, I barely keep myself from face planting on the pavement. My cheeks heat, getting even redder while I'm still holding my breath. I see him out of the corner of my eye, reaching out to catch me or help me, he still asks, "Are you ok?"

Unable to look at him, I nod my head yes.

Shaking my head, I think, *Well, that just happened.*

Now, if I can manage to stay upright, maybe my dignity will remain somewhat intact.

I'm almost complete with my ten miles, and breath is my

utmost necessity right now. Yelling to myself, I try to coach myself back from the brink of passing out.

You can't faint. Get it together—Force air into your lungs.

Air slowly fills my lungs as I gently count to three on each inhale and exhale.

Alright, that's better. Focusing on my burning lungs, I hear him snicker, and I find myself glaring at him.

What a freak. Is he laughing at me, because I almost fell running, that I can't seem to catch any air? What's his aim?

All I know is that I need to be done running like yesterday. Thank goodness for no more interruptions as I finish my last lap.

Finally, I'm finished for the day. Now I'll just take my humiliated self and exit. There's no way I'm stretching here. I'll head to the gym and stretch there... away from prying eyes.

4

PIERCE

W alking toward the track with the rest of the
Protectors, I look up and grin as I see that girl is here
and appears to, again, be taking out some frustration on the

track. I can't help imagining how she'd look running to me in one of my shirts, the fabric hanging off of her shoulder. Damn, she's hot as hell.

Caught staring at her, I snap out of my daze and look down, around, anywhere but at her. She must have heard us approaching because she's now glaring up at us.

There goes my heart pounding in my chest again.

Okay, after I stretch, I'm going to do this. I'll just jog slightly behind her after she passes. Then I'll catch up to her, not frighten her, and see if I can muster up the courage to actually speak this time.

Bending my left knee, I pull my foot back toward my rear, stretching my quadriceps. I hear jogging feet approaching. I wait for her to pass before I trot after her, attempting not to make my interest too obvious.

Psyching myself up, I repeat silently, *Just do it, Pierce! Go for it! What are you waiting for?*

It takes half a lap before I'm running in cadence alongside her. She peeks at me for a brief second, then turns her head back toward the pavement, never speaking to me, only breathing heavily. I examine her multiple times through my peripheral vision as we're sprinting side by side, but she doesn't break her concentration. She's laser-focused.

I can't help but wonder if she's turned off by my arms, littered with scars. Pushing that thought down, I open my mouth and muster up the courage to say, "Hey!"

Glancing at me, she smiles and replies, "Hey to you, too."

Damn, her eyes keep making my heart thump harder inside my chest. I know it's not the run because I've only just begun.

Oh shit, she just tripped. I'm ready to catch her when she corrects her crossed feet. Watching as she rights herself, I peer at her face from the corner of my eye, noticing her cheeks redden even further. Damn, I don't want her to be embarrassed, but I still have to ask if she's ok. She doesn't look at me, only nods in affirmation that she's alright.

Kage is in the center of the track shouting at us, "You only know one hundred percent! Give all you've got unless you're giving blood!" I chuckle under my breath at his idioms.

Shit, She's scowling at me. I hope she doesn't think I'm laughing at her.

Oh, hell, no. Her eyes are shooting daggers at me now. If looks could kill, I'd be a goner. Yeah, I'm going to scamper toward the middle lane, just in case. I probably don't need to be within kicking distance; for all I know, she'll trip me so I'll crash and burn.

What the hell?

We're nearing the exit on this second lap, and instead of continuing with me, she jets out the gate.

Great! So much for striking up a conversation.

Shit! Shit! Shit! Excellent job, Pierce. Can't even run alongside her without making her glare at you. And now she can't wait to get as far away from you as possible.

Well, at least she didn't trip me because being banged up wouldn't feel so great inside the arena as I train today. Mastering my ax throwing at various targets while avoiding being captured by the Superior Protectors, mostly dodging being apprehended by Kage, is what's on the docket today.

Kage's stealth is uncanny and unmatched by any of the other Superior Protectors. He lives for the cat and mouse games. Once he has you in his sights, he unleashes his wrath by pelting you with rubber bullets until you're on the ground writhing in pain.

He learned from the best, our dad. I can only hope to become as good as he is at his role as Protector. Our father, Elon, is one of the seven Supreme Seniors. During his time as a

Protector, he strengthened the program by expanding intelligence, strength, and stealth training.

The arena we practice in is positioned on an open, somewhat flattened field at the highest altitude atop our mountain, forcing our lungs to max capacity. I must admit Kage's efforts are successful in allowing us to obtain immaculate physical condition. After several months of training up here, it becomes effortless to gain more mileage while running on our only outdoor track every morning, building our endurance.

By the end of the two-year training required to become a Protector, we will be able to demonstrate mastery of our four chosen weapons, run at least thirteen miles in under two hours, stabilize and treat patients with moderate injuries, and ace written tests on history, paramedicine, and combat.

The seven Supreme Seniors evaluate all the tests and let each individual know whether they passed and will work in their designated field or if they will require another year of study. If it's the latter, they're allowed to continue to train for as many years as they wish or until picking another vocation.

Supreme Seniors are voted into place by the community. We hold elections every five years unless a senior passes away, then one is held immediately to fill the vacancy. Seniors do not have term limits on their service, but typically only serve ten to fifteen years. To be eligible to run for a Supreme Senior position, one must be a Superior in their field of expertise, be over the age of fifty, be honored and respected for their decisions and opinions, and voted into place by the people of Iron Mountain.

The typical life expectancy is eighty years in our society. Suppose they only serve ten years. In that case, they can retire and enjoy simple living, knowing that they gave their best in service to their community. However, not everyone who runs for Supreme Seniorship is voted in. That can make for some very disgruntled individuals, like my uncle Morton. My dad's brother has always been jealous of him. Morton signed up to be a Protector, but he came up short on his scores and skills when testing time came.

When he didn't make the cut the first year he tested, and my dad did, he became very frustrated and started volunteering in one of the few mines on our mountain. They mine for Iron, gold, and different metals.

Morton finally tested out of training to become a Protector, shifting his focus to mining. When voting came up ten years ago, he and my dad were aiming for the same position. When dad won the vote, Morton became a recluse; no longer joining in on family gatherings or celebrating holidays with us. He's always scowling from afar. He gives me the creeps.

Finally, after an hour of running and six miles down, we can cool down and head toward the arena to work on our weapons skills. Who knows, maybe I'll see the mysterious *girl* at lunch today in the common area.

5

TOVA

My mouth waters as I inhale the aroma of what can only be lasagna. I'm so flipping hungry. Skipping breakfast so I can run at the crack of dawn has my stomach growling so loudly that it sounds like the mating calls of beluga whales. I'm sure everyone in the cafeteria is staring at me right now.

Lining up, I grab my tray and slide it over the metal slate in front of the buffet. I plop a massive helping of lasagna, garlic bread, mashed potatoes, green beans, and corn on my tray as I make my way down the line. Settling into a seat at the far end of one of the long cafeteria tables, I take in my array of delicious goodness. Right before I take a bite, I hear, "Hungry, are we?" I tilt my head to my accuser only to find my best friends, Adelaide, Dani-Jo, and Cora, grinning from ear to ear down at me.

"Well, it's good to see you too, trouble," I sneer at Adelaide.

Adelaide, but we all call her Adi, only snickers as she positions herself to my right, her wavy brown hair bouncing as she walks over to me. As the miners say, dynamite comes in small packages. But what do you expect from a girl who was raised with four brothers? My firecracker of a best friend is petite in stature, loyal to the core, and has the most beautiful brown eyes. Cora and Dani-Jo sit directly across from us.

Adelaide proceeds, unphased by my snark, "Whatcha so hungry for? I only see you eat like this when it's a holiday."

"I skipped breakfast so I could run before the meatheads got to the track," I admit.

"Hmm, so you're running earlier and further. That can only mean those nightmares are still plaguing you," she frowns.

"Yeah, they never really go away. I just keep pushing myself to the verge of collapse to get at least a few hours of shut-eye," I drop my eyes and explain with a melancholy voice.

Answering Adi, I shift my body toward the entrance of the cafeteria, and to my surprise, *he* walks in. The scrunching of my brows must be less subtle than I hoped because they all, in unison, turn to look in the same direction.

Cora pipes up, "Looks like someone has captured Tova's attention."

I argue, "No, I mean, yes. Whatever. Do y'all know who he is? What's his story? I mean, I've been wearing the twine ring when I run, but he doesn't seem to care or notice every time he's there. He's been running at the track and today he manages to run right beside me. We glance at each other occasionally but as of today have only said, 'Hey.' And my God, when our eyes meet, it's like a fire ignites my bones."

"Um yeah, he's kinda Elon's son, one of the Supreme Seniors," Cora laughs, "They live on the east side, on a farm near the protection wall several miles from here. I'm not surprised you've not seen him before since you live on the south side, quite a few miles in the opposite direction." Pausing for a minute, she crosses her arms. "I noticed him a couple of weeks ago when he was talking to his brother, Kage. I overheard Kage tell him that their dad would be proud of him choosing to be a Protector and that he's glad he got farming out of his system."

I tap my finger to my mouth, one of my many unconscious mannerisms while deep in thought; *Alright, that makes sense.*

"What's his name?" I ask.

"Pierce," Cora replies.

I scoff, "Of course, it's Pierce. Why wouldn't it be? Sexy as all get out. His eyes *pierce* my soul each time I look into them. His name is only fitting."

"Well, you seem to have captured his attention, too. By the way he hasn't been able to tear his eyes away from you, it's pretty clear you're the only thing he's interested in," Dani-Jo acknowledges.

Adi chuckles, "Ha! He must be completely smitten if even the option of eating isn't enough to steal his inquisitiveness. I know I could never coax Larson from his food after morning training, much less for a pretty girl."

Larson is a couple of years older than Adi, but they've been connected at the hip since she was sixteen. He's only ever had eyes for her. He's a ferocious Protector, and no one in his age group has beaten him in the arena. His strength is superlative,

31

and I can't help but wonder if it's a lingering effect of the Dust. We all knew he'd be fantastic at this profession, and he hasn't proven us wrong yet.

"What are you thinking?" Andi asks, pulling me back from my wandering thoughts.

Squirming in my seat, I admit, "When he looks at me, I get...uncomfortable. Butterflies swarm in the pit of my stomach. I unquestionably feel fire, a burning deep inside almost consuming my every fiber. There's an instant connection I've never felt before."

"Well, well, well. I guess Miss 'I'm going to be independent and live a solitary life' might contribute to our increasing population after all," Adi chides.

"Contrary to the opinion that we have a sparse existence, I feel like we have plenty of people," I refute. "I admit, census numbers suggest we don't. Compared to the population before the Extinction Event, we aren't anywhere close to repopulating the world like it was. Even if it is only like eight hundred people, I don't like crowds, jam-packed places, or the likes thereof. I like my peace and quiet, nature, animals, and simple living. I get it, I do. To make sure we aren't near the brink of extinction is essential, but I really do love the simple way of living."

Adi teases, "Ultimately, in the next fifty years, the goal is to have our population in this territory up to twelve-hundred-fifty. So, get that single-minded determination out of your head."

Showing half-eaten food in my mouth and waving an empty fork at my friends, I mumble, "Humph, don't hold your breath." Continuing to chew the bite in my mouth, I point out, "I have no idea who this guy is, what his intentions are, and most importantly...if he even likes me. Anddddd, he has no idea what kind of baggage I carry."

Cora cackles, "Real attractive, Tova. How about swallowing that mouth full before reprimanding us?"

"You have to let the notion go that you're not worthy of love, Tova. None of the crap you've lived through is your fault. No one will judge you for your creep of a father or what he did to you," Adi whispers so no one else can hear, but I don't miss her stern look. I appreciate her honesty. She may be right, she may be wrong, but right now, I'm not trying to prove anything. But that comment still stings either way. These girls right here know me, know my entire story. Cladec made sure of that.

The girls were spending the night at our farmhouse on my tenth birthday, and surprise, surprise, he became violent in yet another drunken stupor. He went to swing his fist at my mama, and I screamed for him to stop. Deciding to turn his sadistic concentration to me, he gifted me with a swift back-hand across the face that sent me flying back against the wall. Dazed from the blow, I slid to the floor, already feeling the split lip and growing black eye, and looked toward my room. All three of them cowered in a corner, whimpering and shaking in terror as they watched the scene in horror. Happy flippin' birthday to me!

Shaking my head, I try to block that memory. In an attempt to change the subject, I ask my friends what tasks they will choose. All four of us are in the current batch of Deciders. I know my mom wants me to pick being a seamstress so she can spend more time with me. However, I'm leaning more toward Protector, but have contemplated Naturopath and farmer as well. The desire to learn self-defense, use different weapons, and protect those who can't defend themselves has become more and more overwhelming, though.

Adi is the first to answer, "Protector! I've always known that was my calling."

"Good choice. Growing up with four brothers, you've

already got the 'kick-butt' skill down pat. I'm going to choose Protector too. Not that the other professions aren't worth looking into, I just know deep down that I can make more of a difference doing this," Dani-Jo claims.

"I'm pretty sure I'm choosing Naturopath, but I'm considering Protector as well," Cora affirms. "What about you?"

"Protector. No doubt." I exclaim, slamming my fist down on the table. "Whew, and just like that, my mind is made up. I mean, I'm already fit. Now, I just need to develop my skills at weapons, learn self-defense, brush up on history, learn more about medicines, and how to tend injuries, and I'm set. I mean, how hard can all that be, right?"

"Oh no, I hope those aren't your famous last words," Cora teases.

We finish up our lunch and head to empty our trays in the trash. And wouldn't you know it, my feet fumble over each other, causing me to trip right into the trash can. No, I don't fall in, but I still stumble into it so hard the sound of my crashing causes everyone to stare at me. I'm pretty sure my face is redder than a ripe tomato.

"Are you hurt?" Adi rushes to my side.

Straightening my spine, I lower my head. "Not physically, just my pride. Can we get out of here? Y'all know I'm gravitationally challenged, but now so does everyone else in here."

"Yeah, we know," Dani-Jo smirks.

6

PIERCE

"Well, looky there." My brother nods in the girl's direction, slapping me on the back as we walk into the cafeteria. Both of us notice she's looking our way, and I swallow hard, holding her stare. Good God, did my heart just get the hiccups?! This girl has me under some sort of spell or something because I can't look away. Maybe I don't want to.

I've never been one to be this intrigued by a female. Have I approached, pursued, and dated other girls? Absolutely. But not one of them has captivated me the way she does, and I don't even know her name.

After she breaks our stare, I stuff my hands in the pockets of my jeans and meander toward the buffet, doing my best to redirect my attention to our lunch choices. Once I've made my half-hearted selections, not really paying attention to what I grab. I take my tray over to the table Kage and the other Protectors and trainees usually sit at. There will be six of us at this table: Jace, my lifelong friend, the twins, Kole and Kaden—our resident heartthrobs—, and Larson, a brute I met a couple of weeks ago. Larson is about to test out of Protector training, and Kage will be here once he fixes his tray. I'm pretty sure Larson is smitten with one of the girls in the mystery girl's group because he keeps eyeing one of them.

Following his gaze, I notice the girls chatting about what I can only assume to be us because they keep glancing in our direction. Hopefully, that's a good sign. The less than discrete actions between the girls and me doesn't slip past Jace's notice. Honestly, I would be disappointed if he didn't catch on; it's not like any of us are even attempting to be subtle in our little exchange. He's a cool guy. With any luck, he won't give me too much of a hard time. Disappointingly, the girls get up to leave shortly after we arrive. I guess we were too late getting to lunch, but we had to clean up. I mean, good God, we were sweaty, and I'm sure a skunk would have smelled better than us when we finished our training.

A loud crash makes me pause for a moment, and my first thought is, *Shit, did she just tumble into the trash can?* As soon as I heard the noise—How, I'll never know—I just knew it was my little klutz. Before I am even fully aware of the movement, I jump up to head in her direction. Her friend is too swift though and helps escort her out of the cafeteria without a backward glance. Surprisingly, it appears she isn't injured.

"Well, it looks like your new friend may have two left feet," Kole teases.

"Ha! Not everyone can be as graceful as you, Kole," Kaden chimes in.

Larson just shakes his head in silence.

"Okay, okay, pretty boys. We get it. Not all twins can be as cool as y'all," Jace smirks. "Pierce, I think her girls have her covered. You can sit down now and eat. We can't have you wasting away now, can we? Practice and training are kicking all our asses."

"Fine," I blurt, reluctantly sitting down to eat my hefty portion of lasagna, corn, green beans, and toast. I must have been hungrier than I thought because I devour my food in less than five minutes.

"Did you even taste your food? I'm pretty sure you just inhaled it." Kaden points out as I finish.

"Growing boys gotta eat," Kole chuckles.

"You two always have a comment, don't ya?" I smirk, staring at the exit the girls just left out of. "Do any of y'all know who she is? What her name is? Is she really off the market? How old is she?" I glance at Larson because it's hard not to notice his interest in someone from her group, hoping he has some answers for me. The guy only remains silent, staring down at what remains of his food.

Kage sits down in front of me, placing his tray on the table. "Man of a million questions, aren't you? I'm pretty sure she and her friends are Deciders. I think they are up for their pick in the next week or so since I've only noticed them the past few weeks eating in here with us," Kage explains. Pointing his spoon at me, he continues, "Now, *your* girl...I've seen her for the past year or so at the track. None of the guys have caught her name, as far as I know, because she always blows them off. However, she only started wearing that twine ring a few weeks ago. I've never seen her with anyone other than her girlfriends. She's usually at the track alone. If I had to guess, the ring is just a deterrent for guys, but I could be wrong."

It didn't go unnoticed that Kage referred to her as *my* girl. It sounds damn good to hear her referred to as mine. I've got to find out who she is, either that or get her off my mind until I can introduce myself and ask her personally. Getting up to leave, I announce, "As soon as you all are done eating, you can find me at the instructional facility."

I swing open one of the exit doors and travel up the hill toward the instructional facility, the building where we receive all of our book and practical training. I make my way to the library at the back of the complex, needing to find something, anything, to keep my mind off her for a little while. Walking down the science section's aisle, I overhear my name whispered by a group of girls in the next row over. Curiosity gets the best of me, and I peer through the books and see that it's her friends. She's not with them, but that doesn't matter because I want to hear what they're saying about me.

"You know, she thinks he's cute, or she wouldn't have been so fixated on him the entire time at lunch," the blonde explains, exasperation clear in her tone.

"Let's not get ahead of ourselves. We all know she's been through some crap, and she's not going to just let herself 'like' someone. He's going to have to build her trust, and you know that will not be easy. If he likes her, he's definitely got his work cut out for him. And Lord knows he'd better be patient," the girl with the tiny frame bites.

"Tova is a strong-willed, tough cookie, but she has a soft side. If he can get her walls to come down, he just might have a chance to see it. God willing, he may actually have a shot, and

7

TOVA

Each step is careful, deliberate, matching the first shadow footstep for footstep. The second silhouette mirrors the first. In the silence, I only hear the pounding of my heart and the blood rushing in my ears. The two figures are now hovering above me in my bed, one holding a rope and the other holding a machete. As the first one reaches for me with the rope, the second one with the blade rears back, aiming for my chest.

"Tova! Tova, wake up! You're thrashing in your bed." Adi shakes me until I'm awake.

I'm barely able to open my lids that feel like they're weighted down with lead. Finally, when I'm able to peek at Adi she crawls in the bed behind me and wraps me in a gentle hug as I tremble against her slight frame. My eyes are burning as I try to keep my tears at bay.

"I'm here, Tova. No need to be afraid," Adi soothes as she strokes my shaking arm.

"Thank you, Adi. I'm sorry I couldn't shake this nightmare." Popping up out of her embrace, I throw my legs over the side of the bed and cover my mouth. I muffle, "Sorry, Adi, but I think I'm going to be sick."

Rushing to the bathroom, I empty the contents of my belly into the toilet. Eventually, when I'm able to stand, I grip the rim of the porcelain sink as I try to steady my shaky hands so I can wash up. Looking in the mirror, all I see are blood-shot, droopy eyes staring back at me.

This getting to the track early with no breakfast thing is getting old. I'm so hungry. Oh well, if I must make sacrifices to maintain my inner peace, then so be it. At least that family of deer is here again to greet me and keep me company.

Seven miles down, only three more to go. This run is different; it feels so good to lose myself to it, knowing I already solidified my decision and no longer need to worry over it. My mind is made up. I'm choosing Protector next Friday. The crisp mountain air, fresh smell of dew on the pines, is simply breathtaking. I close my eyes to inhale, only to have my peaceful thoughts drowned out by the sounds of raucous men.

"Seriously, why are they here so early?" I snarl under my breath.

They jog for a few minutes after stretching, and wouldn't you know it, Pierce ends up sprinting right behind me. At least this time, I know his name; I grin outwardly. He doesn't pace up beside me; I guess he likes the view.

Try not to think about him; just keep trotting along.

Glancing up the hill that leads from town down to the track, I see Adi, Dani-Jo, and Cora finally making their way here. I throw them a quick wave, eager for them to join me like they promised yesterday, and they return it with mild enthusiasm. Then I notice Adi cover her mouth, trying to hide a smile or laugh. Confused for a second, I scrunch my eyebrows together. My neck and face heat as I realize they notice Pierce is running several paces behind me.

Good grief!

I shake my head. These girls are going to give me one hell of a time. Refusing to think about that, I reminisce about our conversation last night, and a smirk forms at the corners of my mouth as I remember Cora's bantering.

Her initial response was to refuse with as much snark as possible. "Run spelled backward is NUR, so it's a nur from me." I can't help the giggle that slips out. Thankfully, after much deliberation, I convinced them to join me anyway.

Adi and Dani-Jo want to get a head start on training, hoping to make it a little less brutal when we officially begin. True to their words, they are here today, and even if I end up having to do more than the planned ten miles, I don't mind. These girls are my everything. I'll do anything for them, even bust my butt till I drop, and I'll do it with a giant smile on my face.

For the past year, I've run alone, and now they'll keep me company, all except Cora, that is. She's only begrudgingly agreed to run, claiming it'll help her stay fit. We all know it's because I threatened to throw icy water on her to wake her up this morning if she disagreed, though. She ultimately told us yesterday she is going to choose Naturopath. Being a Naturopath doesn't require her to do physical training, but I care about her health and well-being.

Last night before it was lights out at the cabins, she finally gave in, saying, "Fine, I'll agree to run, but I'm complaining the whole time." So here she is, pouting all the way to the track.

They make it down to the pavement and stretch. I keep running, giving them time to warm up a little. They know, and I know they won't be up to my speed, but just having their company around does my soul good.

As I'm running along the straight away opposite them, I close my eyes. I frequently do so to absorb the sun's rays kissing my skin. Suddenly, my eyes pop open when I hear the most ferocious snarl, unlike anything I've heard before. As I glance in that direction, I notice something large flying toward me out of the corner of my eye. I tumble to the ground in a flash, and everything goes dark.

8

PIERCE

"What the hell? Everybody get down!" I hear Kage shout as I run straight for Tova.

Damn it! Tova's body is sprawled across the pavement, seemingly lifeless, when I reach her side. Her friends' panicked cries and questions fill the air as they rush toward us. Fighting to control the rush of adrenaline coursing through my system,

I drop down next to Tova and immediately begin checking her over. Taking deep breaths to slow my racing heart and cool my heated body, I reach for her neck to check for a pulse.

Her pulse is faint but steady, thank God. I assess her face, cupping her head in my hands. "She has a contusion and laceration on her right eye, a deep gash on her right shoulder blade, bumps, bruises, and road rash all over. I'm pretty sure she has a concussion as well. She's unresponsive," I yell toward Kage. Pausing for a moment, I continue to examine her. "I need bandages and some water to clean up the blood and assess how deep the wounds are."

As her friends and medical assistants surround us, my focus is solely on Tova. "Come on, Tova, I know you're in there. Open those beautiful blue eyes. It's okay. Your friends are here; we're all here." Lowering her head gently back down, I continue explaining, hoping my voice will bring her back. "If you can hear me, my name is Pierce. I'm going to put a pressure bandage on your back and place you on the backboard, then take you to the clinic."

Kage approaches me, holding an arrow. "Where did that come from?" I ask him.

"Your guess is as good as mine, but it appears to have come from outside the protection wall. It sounded as if that Lynxwolf gave a warning growl while a hawk crashed into her, getting her out of the way of the arrow. If I didn't know any better, I'd think these animals were working together trying to save her, but the bigger question is, why is someone after her?"

Her friends share a look between them like they may know something we don't, and it sets my hackles rising. "Do you girls know who would want to hurt Tova?" I ask them directly, calling them out.

Larson, standing with his arm around the petite girl, counters, "I don't think it's them you should ask."

"What are you talking about? We need to know who did this so we can bring the asshole to justice," I bark, sneering in the arrow's direction.

"Look, man, I know you want to know, we all do, but she's the only one who would know that," he says, nodding toward Tova.

"Fine," I glower. Still kneeling beside Tova, I roll her on her side to slide the backboard under her. As we get her settled on the board, she lets out a pitiful groan. I immediately stop what I'm doing to see if she can respond to me. "Tova, answer me. If you can hear me, say something."

She blinks rapidly and mumbles, "Wha… What just happened? How…how in the world do you know my name?" Blood trickles down the right side of her swollen face as she slowly scans the crowd now surrounding her, finally landing a scowl on Larson.

"Hey, it wasn't me," he defends, throwing his hands up in submission.

"Okay, then who?" she gripes.

"It's not important how I learned your name. I just need to know you're okay," I interject. "Can you tell me how many fingers I'm holding up?"

"Three," she sneers, pushing my hand away. "Ouch. What in the flyingflitterflotter happened to my shoulder?"

"An arrow slashed you open." I point out.

"An arrow?" she questions, mostly to herself. Taking her right index finger, she rubs the gaping wound in her brow. "And my eye…is this gash from the pavement?"

"No, I think one of the talons from the hawk accidentally sliced you when it flew into you," I explain.

"A freaking bird took me out?" she asks, jerking her head in my direction.

"Umm, it seems it was trying to save you, and maybe the

47

Lynxwolf was too," Kage interrupts from his position, standing close by.

"What!" Tova exclaims, clearly still in shock.

I reflect, "The Lynxwolf gave a warning growl so intense it vibrated my chest, then a hawk appeared out of nowhere and dove into you. The arrow narrowly missed your head, thanks to the damn hawk, but the arrow still sliced open your shoulder blade as you fell. If you hadn't fallen, I'm certain we wouldn't be here having a conversation right now," I state, attempting to keep to the facts as much as possible. "You've been out cold for at least five minutes. We need to get you to the clinic to be checked over and stitched up. If that's alright with you?" I say, making it sound like a question, at least.

"Do I have a choice?" she snaps, rolling her eyes and smearing blood into her right eye in the process.

"You always have a choice, but I recommend getting it tended to before infection sets in," Kage encourages, crouching down beside us.

Squinting in his directions, Tova asks, "Alright, fine, but can't I walk?"

"You shouldn't right now, at least until we fully examine you and make sure your cervical spine is okay," I answer.

"Great. Just great. Okay then, let's get on with it," she huffs, raising her good arm to shield her eyes from the bright sunlight.

Glancing at her friends, I reassure them, "She'll be taken care of, I promise. We'll make sure Larson is there, so she has a familiar face around while we tend to her injuries." They all nod and back out of the way. Kage, Larson, Jace, and I strap her to the backboard, leaving her arms free. As she puts pressure on the wound above her eye, I instruct her to keep her arms against her chest as we lift the board and start carrying her to the clinic.

"It's about a two-mile hike, and it'll take some time assessing and tending to her injuries. She should be able to leave around lunchtime, if I had to guess, we should be wrapping things up by then," I inform her friends. They all nod their understanding and wave weakly as we pass.

It's eerily quiet as we trudge up to the clinic, none of us saying a word as we focus on our surroundings. I don't know about the other guys, but if they are like me, I can only assume we are all keeping a keen eye for any further threats. Tova presses a section of gauze to her brow, attempting to staunch the flow, all while trying to shield herself from the blaring sun. She's going to have one hell of a headache when this is all said and done.

Finally, arriving at the clinic, a Naturopath is holding the door open for us. Crossing over the threshold, we're instructed to take her straight to the treatment room down the hall. Inside the treatment room, there's a lone x-ray machine we managed to keep up and running along with other various items. My eye catches the lidocaine and stitching materials that we'll definitely be needing.

My heart races, palms start to sweat, and hands begin to shake because I know the Expert Naturopath, Mr. Hughes, will ask me to suture Tova's wounds. He helped train me to recognize and treat injuries from my first two years of study and enjoys giving his students hands-on experience whenever he can. I need to; I know I do. It's only a matter of time before I'm required to stitch someone without an expert guiding me, but I'd rather my first time not be on the most beautiful woman alive. What if I scar her? I can't do it. I have to bow out and let one of the others handle it.

The Expert Naturopath barrels into the room and immediately looks over at me, gives a small smile, and nods. He then shines a light in Tova's eyes, causing her to wince and grumble in protest.

"I'm Mr. Hughes, Expert Naturopath. Sorry to blind you, but I needed to inspect your pupils to make sure they are the same size and react to light equally. Your pupils give no indication that you have a potential brain bleed, but I need to ask you some more questions to assess you further. Then we can tend to your other injuries. Can you tell me your full name and date of birth?" he asks with calm, professional efficiency.

"Um, yeah. Tova Jensen Campbell. November twenty-first."

"Ms. Campbell, do you know what happened to you?" he inquires.

"Not really. I remember the hair on the back of my neck standing up and hearing a loud growl. I think I remember seeing a large object coming toward me out of my periphery. Then everything went blank from there," she explains.

"She was shot at by an arrow; it grazed her right shoulder blade. A hawk flew into her, lacerating her right eye. She did roughly two somersaults as she hit the ground and rolled a few more feet. She was unresponsive for about five minutes, but she never stopped breathing nor lost a pulse," I inform.

Mr. Hughes's eyebrows raise in minor surprise. "Sounds like you took quite a tumble." Tracing his finger over Tova's forehead, he notices the blood has stopped trickling down her face from the pressure she's holding on it. "The bleeding seems to have blunted. We need to x-ray your neck to make sure your spine is okay, but first I'm going to do a few more neuro. Follow my finger with your eyes."

She does as he requests, and he continues his examination.

"Okay, good. Close your eyes for me. I'm going to rub a soft cotton ball on each arm and each leg. Let me know if you can't feel anything or if one side feels any different."

As he wipes the cotton on her in various places, she replies, "I feel everything the same."

"Can you tell me how many fingers I'm holding up?" he asks, moving to the next test.

"Two," she answers, squinting up at him.

With a nod, he clasps his hands behind his back and informs her, "Before I do the rest of my examination, we're going to get you x-rayed. You won't need to move. We'll bring the machine to you. Just lay as still as you can."

"Okay," she replies with a raspy voice.

"Gentlemen," Mr. Hughes says, turning to address the rest of us, "I'm going to ask you to step out for safety reasons."

We all turn to leave, shuffling toward the door reluctantly. I'm almost to the door when I barely catch Tova murmur, "Um, Mr. Hughes, can someone stay with me? I don't want to be alone in here." I don't turn around, as I'm sure she wants Larson to stay. They seem to know each other already.

"Sure, who would you like to have stay?" Mr. Hughes obliges, "I need to get them a lead apron."

I stop in my tracks when I hear in the faintest voice, "Pierce...do you mind?"

I answer without a second thought, "Of course I'll stay."

Turning back around, I walk over to Tova, and the x-ray operator gives me a lead apron just as Mr. Hughes instructed. As I don the heavy apron and stand at her side, I ask, "Tova, would you like me to search for your special someone and let them know about your incident?"

Looking confused, she replies, "Huh?"

I silently gesture to her left hand.

She glances over and sighs, "Uh, well about that...there isn't really a 'someone.' I just started wearing this to keep from being pestered while I ran. It worked...for the most part." She slides the ring off, tossing it into the trash can beside the exam table.

"For the most part?" I ask, my brows furrowing in confusion.

Eyeing me up and down the best she can through a bloody, almost-swollen-shut right eye, "Well, you didn't seem to care one way or another that the ring was on my finger," she explains.

Holding up my hands in surrender, I admit, "I'm not one to dishonor any man's wishes. But when you looked at me, my heart skipped, and it felt like someone knocked the breath out of me. I knew then that I needed to know if you were seriously involved with someone else. I've never had someone look into my soul the way you look into mine."

She carefully turns her head to look at me, full-on. "That's deep for a first conversation, but I'm not going to lie. You intrigue me too."

Folding my arms across my chest, I retort, "Intrigue you, huh?"

Closing her eyes, she turns her face toward the ceiling. "What? I may not be as forthcoming as you are, but yes, you 'intrigue me.' So, what's your story?"

A voice sounds through the room, interrupting our exchange. "Ma'am, take a deep breath in and hold until I say breathe," the x-ray specialist announces.

She does as he says, then exhales deeply. Opening her beautiful blue-green eyes, she squints them as they wander to my face, trying to read it like a map. I see the questions cross her mind, wondering who I am and what my intentions are as she waits for my reply.

Clearing my throat, I bite the bullet and give her an answer, unwilling to let this moment pass. "Well, my story is simple.

I'm twenty years old. My full name is Pierce Leo Stetson. Farming was my first choice when I made my Decision at eighteen. My family has a large farm on the east side, near the protection wall. I wanted to make sure I knew how to tend to it and appreciate every aspect of all the hard work that goes into taking care of it before moving on. Now that my two years have been completed, I can redirect my attention to another task. I chose Protector, if you haven't already guessed. My dad is Supreme Senior Elon, my brother is Superior Protector Kage, and my mom is Brecklyn, a homemaker." Coughing out a little laugh, I add, "Dad would describe her as a blonde-haired beauty. She has crystal blue eyes that you can see through, like the ocean on a bright sunny day. She's the best cook in Iron Mountain. She makes the finest tea in the south and wears her heart on her sleeve. She taught us boys to love and respect just as fiercely as she does. But most importantly, to always stand for what is right and don't let love go without a fight."

Interrupting us again, the x-ray tech cuts in. "Once the films develop, Mr. Hughes will be back to discuss the findings," he explains before slipping from the room.

"Thank you." We both acknowledge as he exits.

Turning my attention back to her, I remove my lead apron. "So, tell me a little bit about you. What's your story?"

Biting her bottom lip, she hesitates, "Let's see, you already know my full name and birthday. Hmm, my favorite color is purple, like sunset purple. Those girls at the track are my best friends. Adi is the petite one. Dani-Jo is the other brunette, and Cora is the blonde." Pausing for a moment as if trying to decide what to give away next, she resumes scrunching up her nose, "I loathe tea. It's absolutely disgusting. I love my horse Lightning with all my heart. I'm an only child. My mom has the most delightful name, Shenandoah, but she goes by

Shenan." She falls silent, and I guess she's told me all she's going to for the moment.

Placing the apron on the hanging rack, I walk back to her side. "Wait, did I hear you right? You detest tea? Are you sure you're even from here?" I tease.

A little smile forms at the corner of her mouth. "Born and raised. And yes, I abhor tea. It tastes like the earth!"

Chuckling, I pester, "The earth? Ate one too many mud pies growing up?"

"Ha, maybe." Changing the subject, she closes her eyes and sighs, "Thank you, Pierce."

"Thank you?" I ask, confused.

"Yes. For rushing to help me, for making sure I was okay, stabilizing me, assisting with my transport. And most of all, for staying with me and telling me about your family to keep my mind occupied. I'm a little freaked out right now, and having you with me has helped me stay calm. I have no idea why this happened." Lingering on the thought, she eventually looks over at me. "Do you think it could just have been a hunter's arrow gone awry?"

"First off, no need to thank me. I needed to know that you were okay. Second, I'll tell you anything you want to know about my family and me. Anytime you need company, I'll be right there. Third, I guess anything's possible, but the way the animals seemed to want to warn you has me questioning the hunter theory. I know that the Dust has altered some of us. Do you know if it has affected you? Do you have the ability to communicate with animals or something?"

"Communicate? No. I do sense them around when they're near, but I can't 'talk' to them if that's what you mean," she explains.

"Hmm, that's interesting. You can tell when they're near?" I ask, attempting to put all the pieces together.

"Yes, I guess. I've never really thought about it, though." Grabbing her head, she lets out a pained cry.

"Shit, you're hurting. Let me get Mr. Hughes." I rush for the door.

"Don't, please!" she exclaims, fear evident in her voice.

Stopping myself from exiting the door, I search, "Why not, you're hurting?"

Hesitantly, she admits, "I really don't want to be alone. If you think someone is out to get me, I just...I'll be okay."

Clenching and unclenching my fists, I feel the heat simmer from my palms because I hate the fact that she's in pain. Looking for a chair, I pull the closest one up beside the bed and sit down. I lay my hand on the bed next to hers, and I can't help but notice she's trembling. Ever so gently, I spread my warm hand over the top of hers. Miraculously, the quivering ceases. Not sure if she's cold and the heat is helping, or if the soothing touch is what she needs; either way, I'm glad she stopped trembling.

Unable to shake the thought that someone may be out to hurt her, I press, "Is there anyone you can think of that may have it out for you? We can search for them and bring them to justice."

Doing her best to shrug her shoulders and avoiding eye contact, she answers, "No, no one off the top of my head. I'll just have to be more focused when I'm near the protection wall. I'll keep my eyes peeled for anything and keep my body in-tune with the animals, if that's even possible."

"Well, I'd really like to know why this happened, but if we can't seem to find out, then I swear I'll protect you. You won't be on the lookout alone, I promise. The guys and I will be watching as well," I assure her.

Seeming to not care at all about my battered and scarred arms, she remains hushed but intertwines my fingers in hers, taking my hand and squeezing gently. Thankfully, sparks don't fly from my palms at the contact. My stomach, however, does freaking somersaults. That's the only reinforcement I need. I'll do everything in my power to protect her.

9

TOVA

Mr. Hughes, the Expert Naturopath, walks in with radiographs of my neck. What was once considered 'modern' medicine may be a thing of the past, but I'm grateful that devices like this are still around.

"Ms. Campbell, it looks like your spine is intact. I'll let Pierce and the other guys unstrap you from the backboard, and I'll finish my exam. We'll get an IV started and get some pain meds in you. I don't want you sleeping for the next four hours, though. I'm going to move you to an exam room and keep you here in the clinic with some IV fluids going," Hughes explains. "Is there someone you'd like to keep you company and keep you from dozing off? These medicines can make you very drowsy, so I would rather have someone here with you."

"I'll stay," Pierce volunteers quickly. I offer him a small smile of thanks as the men work to get me released from the backboard, and the Naturopath finishes his exam.

"These two lacerations need to be sutured," Mr. Hughes stresses. Looking at Pierce, he instructs, "Young fellow, looks like you get to do the honors."

"Sir, I mean no disrespect, but I can't. I can't inflict more pain on her. Can't one of these other Protectors do it?" Pierce explains, holding his hands up in surrender.

"Pierce, we've worked side by side for a couple of years now, and I have confidence in you." Turning to the other guys he dismisses them and continues, "Now's the best time to do it. If you conquer your fear of hurting someone you care about and successfully stitch her up, you'll be able to do it any other time without hesitation. It's the most uncomfortable situations we must overcome that enable us to better ourselves and our skills," Hughes states.

Pierce, as pale as a ghost, looks as if he's about to faint. Shaking his head no, he contests, "I can't."

"Can't or won't?" Mr. Hughes tilts his head a little to one side, analyzing Pierce.

Pierce visibly swallows and refuses to look at me. Reaching my hand out for him, I soothe, "Pierce, it's okay. Someone has to do it. It might as well be you."

Taking my hand in his, he confesses, "I don't know if I can.

Lidocaine burns like hell. And I don't want to be the reason you have a nasty scar."

"I'm going to have an ugly scar anyway, and not from you. Not to mention, Mr. Hughes will be right here, guiding you. I trust you. I'm not scared. You can do it. I know you can."

Pierce squeezes my hand and wipes his brows with the index finger and thumb of his other hand. He mutters, "Shit! Fine, okay then."

"Excellent! Let's get started." Mr. Hughes eyes the suture material, rubbing his hands together eagerly.

"Humph," Pierce complains.

Closing my eyes, I feel Pierce clean the dried blood from my wounds. I wince and hiss when the combination of heat from his hands and the sting of the alcohol-soaked cotton ball sends a shooting pain through the laceration above my eye.

"Fuck! I'm sorry. I can't do this, Mr. Hughes, you have to."

"Now, now, it's okay, Pierce. We all know it's going to sting. Come on. You've got this," Mr. Hughes calmly nudges.

Sneaking a peek up at Pierce with my good eye, I see his eyes are scrunched shut in consternation. Needing to at least attempt to offer some comfort, I reach for his arm closest to me. Dragging my fingertips lightly across his bicep, I notice the heat radiating from his skin and the slight goosebumps rising down his arm. "You can do this. Trust yourself as much as I trust you. You have steady hands and a determined heart. The quicker you do it, the quicker you'll be done, and I'll be all fixed up," I encourage.

Slowly opening his eyes, his hand returns to my face. The heat of his palm scorches my skin, but I refuse to show any discomfort or alarm him any further. Inhaling deeply through my nose, I hold back a grimace at the fire spreading across my cheek. He injects the lidocaine, and I have to bite my tongue to keep from wincing or showing any sign of pain.

Crap noogies that stings like the worst bug bite ever.

Holding my breath, I'm pretty sure Pierce knows I'm seconds away from passing out.

"Breathe, Tova. Just breathe," he coaxes me soothingly.

I feel the first tugs at my brow and know he's sewing me up. Surprisingly, it doesn't hurt, and I can focus on breathing through it. As I'm taking my deep breaths in and out, I have a flashback of seeing that large bird heading toward me. Goodness, this scar will be a permanent reminder of the bird that saved my life.

"Alright. The laceration on your forehead is closed. Now, we need to fix up your shoulder blade. I need you to flip over onto your stomach. We have to expose your back, okay?" Mr. Hughes requests.

"I understand, do what you've got to do," I slur.

"The pain meds are taking effect. She shouldn't feel the lidocaine or you suturing up her back as much as she felt her head," I overhear Mr. Hughes telling Pierce.

Trying not to nod off, I feel Pierce clean the sticky blood off my back with his warm hands. For the love of God, why does alcohol sting so flipping bad? I accidentally let a groan slip, and I hear Pierce mutter another curse, but he doesn't stop.

"Gracious alive," I mutter, my back muscles tightening involuntarily as he injects me with another dose of lidocaine. "I thought you said this wouldn't hurt as bad?" I snarl at Mr. Hughes.

He simply reminds me to breathe. More tugging, and I know that the torture is about to end. Thank God, because I don't know how much more I can handle without letting a few curses slip.

"You're one tough gal," Mr. Hughes proclaims. "And you, fine sir, fixed her up good as new. Well done! You're going to make an exceptional Protector. Only three and a half more hours, and you two are free to go."

Fear overrides my drowsiness, and I plead, "What about running, showering, and maybe swimming?" Needing to see him as he answers, I flip over to my back on shaky limbs. The fact I can't sleep without exhausting myself is now at the forefront of my mind.

"No running or swimming for the next ten days until the stitches come out. I'll let Pierce do that, so you won't have to come back here for it. Showering is okay, but limit yourself to no more than five minutes and dry those sutures straightaway. Make sure to monitor for infection. If you have fever, chills, or pus draining from the injury sites, let us know immediately so we can put you on antibiotics. You're going to have a pretty severe headache for several days. I'll send you home with pain pills you need to take for the next five to seven days. Take them with food, or you could become nauseous. I'll make sure the caregiver gives you these written instructions. Your memory over the next few days may seem hazy as well. That's normal and will improve with time. If you have any questions or concerns, don't hesitate to stop by and ask," Mr. Hughes explains with cool, practiced efficiency.

"What about training? I have my Decision next Friday," I press.

"Do you know what you'll choose?"

"Protector," I declare with no hesitation.

Rubbing his chin, Hughes responds, "That'll be the day your stitches come out, and you'll start training the following Monday. You'll be okay to proceed, just take it easy and listen to your body. If you feel any ripping or notice any bleeding from your wounds, back off the intensity." Pausing for a moment, he surveys Pierce and me before continuing, "Any other questions or concerns?" Both of us shake our heads no. Mr. Hughes nods his head once and steps out, leaving us alone.

Heavens to Betsy! We're going to be alone for three and a half hours. What am I going to do? More notably, why are these drugs drawing out my innermost slang?

Pierce interjects, "I see those wheels turning. Penny for your thoughts?"

10

PIERCE

Tova's eyebrows are pinched together as she stares at the door to the exam room. She's deep in thought, so I ask what she's thinking.

She tucks a strand of her hair behind her ear. "Oh, uh, thank you. For, you know, sewing me up."

Smirking, I tease, "The first three are free, then I'll have to charge you."

"Ha, Ha, Pierce has jokes."

"No, really, what were you so deep in thought about?" I press, not letting her deflect the conversation.

"I dunno. Just about why this happened. Is there really a threat? Or was it just a stray arrow? Is there anyone from another territory possibly, that just so happened to be hunting in this area unaware the track is close enough to the wall's opening that an arrow could easily fly near it? Have I pissed off anyone without knowing?" Biting her lower lip and looking up at the ceiling contemplating, she whispers, "Could it be... No, never mind. My mind won't stop whirling, trying to figure out what might be going on."

Leaning back into the chair, I affirm, "Given your current circumstances, I think Protector is the perfect decision for you. You'll learn self-defense, master weapons, and learn to treat the injured. I'll personally see to it you're well equipped to defend yourself in the event that I'm not around."

Shifting her body onto her side, she tucks her arm under her head and pillow, repeating my words back to me, "In the event you're not around? Pierce, I really do appreciate everything you've done. I have no doubt you'll help me every way you can, but I can't expect you to be my own personal bodyguard."

I raise up off the back of the chair. "Like hell you can't! When I say I'll protect you, I mean it with every ounce of my being."

Her left hand lifts, as if to stop me. "I don't doubt that you would, but you hardly know anything about me, and you're just willing to be at my beck and call? I won't have that; I *can't* have that. I'll do my best to learn to protect myself and all that being a Protector entails. You need to focus on your own training and be free to do whatever you want to do with whoever you want."

Knowing Tova needs a protector, whether or not she admits it, I fight back my agitation as I emphasize, "I *am* free to do what I want, and what I want is to be there for you."

I lean forward placing my elbows on my knees and resting my chin on my fists. "Whether you like it or not, I'm not going anywhere. I'll learn all I need to know by being around you more. I already know you're a determined little spitfire with looks that can kill. Sure, I wish I already knew everything about you, but that will come in time."

Closing her eyes, she breathes deeply. "Pierce, I really don't think you want to get to know me. I'm not good for you."

"Why do you think that?" I ask, scooting my chair closer to her bed.

Refusing to open her eyes, she continues, "I'm not going to elaborate because who hasn't made it through some sort of hell? For that matter, who doesn't have a story to tell? All I'm saying is that there are plenty of gorgeous girls here that don't carry around as much baggage as I do. Look at you! You're lascivious as a God. I don't want you wasting your time protecting me when you could be pursuing a future partner."

"First of all, lascivious? And second, what?" I am trying hard to hold back a laugh.

"You know, lascivious…arousing sexual desire? And other girls already drool when you walk by, I've seen them check you out in the cafeteria. You'll have your pick of the mill." She waves her arms in my general direction.

"Damn, girl! I'm grateful these drugs are hindering your ability to filter your thoughts. Obviously, you've been through some tough shit, but let me determine what or who is good for me, yeah? If you haven't already noticed, I don't scare off easily." My laughter is now replaced with a soft smile.

"Ha! I guess we'll see."

She becomes tight-lipped after that, clearly done with our conversation. After nearly five minutes of quiet, I notice her eyes start to droop closed.

Gripping her hand, I give it a gentle squeeze and whisper, "Hey, wake up. You can't go to sleep for at least another hour."

She moans softly, pinching the bridge of her nose. "But I'm so tired, and it's so bright in here. My head feels like it's going to break off."

"I'll turn off the overhead lights; maybe that'll ease some of the headache."

Loosening my grip on her hand, I head toward the door and turn off the bright lights, leaving only dim lights on. I sit back down beside her and tangle our fingers together, careful to keep the fire from erupting from my palms.

Taking her other hand, she rests it on top of our twisted grip. She opens her good eye slightly, the right one is now almost black and blue and completely swollen shut. "If I'm going to stay awake, tell me something, anything."

"Let's talk about weapons. What four do you want to choose?" I ask, stroking our joined fingers with my thumb.

She shrugs her left shoulder. "Oh, uh, I'm not sure. What weapons will I have to choose from, or which do you suggest?"

"There are several. You look like you'd handle an M48 Hatchet ax well. It's an ax with a large blade on one side and a curved smaller blade on the other that can hook around a throat and slice it right open. Then there's switchblades, just smaller knives, excellent for throwing. Firearms are my personal favorite, and there is a variety to choose from, like long-range AK-47's, AR-15's, M 4's, etc. and short-range hand-guns/pistols/Glocks. Crossbows are an excellent choice as well if you want to go a bit more traditional and hunting bows if you like more of a challenge. The list goes on and on. To be honest, I'm glad some territories we trade with still make ammunition and firearms. I'm also very grateful for the metalsmiths' ability to craft such fine weapons like the axes and knives," I explain, getting a little lost in my thoughts as I roll through the catalog of weapons in the armory.

"What are your top four?"

"Firearms, knives, crossbows, and axes."

"Do you think I can choose those as well?" She follows up, sounding genuinely curious.

"I don't see why not? Plus, I'd like nothing better than for you to be by my side as we kick some ass," I say with a grin.

"Can't wait." She squeezes my hand, throwing me a wink despite the groggy droop of her good eye.

We continue to chat idly as we wait out the rest of her required stay in the clinic. Promptly on the four-hour mark, a caregiver comes in with the discharge orders, giving reminders on wound care, medicine, and when the stitches need to be removed. I'm not entirely sure Tova registers everything that was said, but that's why I'm here.

Leaving the clinic, I have to keep my heat in check, a lovely alteration I have from that damn dust. I grasp a hold of her left hand and lead the way toward her cabin. She doesn't buck me on it, though I'm not sure if that's the medicine or if she's actually okay with it. Either way, I'm not letting go. It's a good thing she is in shape because the two-mile trudge ahead of us will be brutal with her wounds. We make our way slowly through the woods, navigating the steep hills and valleys in silence. I continually scan the surrounding woods, keeping a sharp eye out for anything unusual. The last thing I am expecting to see wandering around is my uncle, Morton.

Why the hell is he out here?

As Tova and I draw closer to my uncle, he notices us and calls out, "Say, she gonna be okay?"

"Not sure what it is to you, but yeah, she's gonna be okay," I retort, drawing my eyebrows together in a scowl.

Morton slows his pace, seemingly cautious of getting too close to us. "Just heard some rumbling about a girl getting shot with an arrow. Didn't know I'd actually see the injured girl, or better yet, see her with *you.*"

"If you rubberneck around the clinic long enough, you're bound to see the person in question, are you not?" I snipe, not entirely believing his concern.

"I guess you have a point there, Pierce." He tips his hat toward me.

Before I let my anger bubble up at the fact that he's gawking and seemingly stalking my girl, I snap, "You take care now, Morton." Perhaps he's genuinely concerned, but I doubt it. Shrugging off his impertinence, we continue toward her cabin.

We're no less than twenty feet from the door when it bursts open, and Tova's friends all come charging toward her. I fill them in on her injuries, how she'll have a headache, when her next dose of meds are due, and how to recognize an infection.

As the others continue to fawn over Tova, I pull Adi aside and let her know I'll be posted outside their cabin tonight, keeping watch. She tells me she'll have Larson switch off watch shifts with me so I can get some sleep as well. I attempt to beg her off, assuring her I will be fine, but she insists and informs me she will have Larson here by ten o'clock tonight.

True to her word, at ten PM on the dot, Larson strolls up to the cabin, dumping a pile of stuff at my feet in a small clearing. I'm leaning against a large oak tree with my arms folded across my chest. From this vantage, I have an unobstructed view of three sides of the cabin and perform regular perimeter checks.

"Ready for a catnap, Pierce?" Larson teases as he nods at the pile he's placed at my feet.

"No! I told your girl I'd be fine. If you want to sleep first, be my guest," I bite out, aggravated they think I can't protect Tova on my own.

"Just to let you know, 'My girl' has a name. Adelaide." He props himself up against the tree opposite mine. I notice a shadow of something he's holding. "She means well. I can assure you she's not trying to offend you. And just to let you know, I'm not taking the first sleep shift. I know if I sleep first, you'll never wake me up. You can't stay awake on watch all night and think you're going to be alert enough for training tomorrow. Now let me take first watch; Jace is coming next, then Kage is taking a turn, and last, we'll get you."

"What do you mean, Jace and Kage, are taking shifts?" I ask, kicking off the tree and uncrossing my arms. I walk to the center of our little clearing, the moon shining through the break in the canopy above.

"They'll be here shortly. I let them in on what you were planning, and they offered to help. We'll take two-hour shifts. You've had a rough day, and we're helping, like it or not." Tossing me the object in his hand, I reach up and grasp it, it's a pillow. He directs, "Stop being pig-headed and sleep for a while. I brought a tent and a few sleeping bags." He points to where he deposited the load of camping supplies.

Punching the cushion, I vent, "I don't know if I'll be able to sleep. My adrenaline has been on overdrive all day. I have no idea if someone is after her. How am I supposed to sleep?"

Moving from his tree, he approaches me and places a hand on my shoulder. "Listen, man, I know that you're concerned for Tova's safety, but you'll be in no shape to protect anyone without getting some rest. You'll have an adrenaline crash as soon as your head hits that pillow. Trust me," he says, giving my shoulder a slight squeeze.

Begrudgingly, I shuffle over to the mound of supplies and set up the tent without further argument before stumbling inside. I guess Larson knows what he's talking about because I don't remember anything after my head hits the cushion. It was lights out.

11

TOVA

In the four weeks since the attack, there hasn't been a single sighting of a possible rogue hunter. I've successfully convinced the guys they don't have to stand guard at the cabin every night.

Rolling my right shoulder, there's only a slight twinge of sharp pain, indicating that it's healing up nicely. The stitches have been removed, but my scars are still fresh and an angry beefy red, which is a good thing because that indicates there's no infection. The Decision has been made. Now, Adi, Dani-Jo, and I are in the arena for the second week getting ready for our mock battle between the Superiors and trainees. This week I'll be practicing with an M48 ax. This one has a rubber ax head, not a real one, so any hits won't do too much damage but will still hurt.

A sly smile creeps up the sides of my mouth, and I rub my hands mischievously together as I think, *This should be fun.*

We're about to be set loose in the arena, which is nothing more than a ring of cement walls with two gates on opposite sides. Various targets are placed within the arena, some in the shape of animals and wild beasts. Some are actual bullseye marks, and the other targets are the Superior Protectors. There are two teams, the Superiors, and the trainees; whichever team takes out the most targets at the end of this two-hour cat-and-mouse game are deemed the winners. At the end of each week, the team with the most losses will be forced to wear pajamas to the Friday night campfire while the winners get the luxury of indulging in steak dinners while the loosers get hot dogs.

Shaking my head at that thought, I study the forest around the arena as a distraction, taking in the gigantic oaks with their thick, dark green leaves. Looking up, I squint at the exceptionally tall pines and the less than perfect shade they offer. The dense foliage is going to make it difficult to sneak around quietly. I notice a few downed trees, old rusty vehicles scattered in the underbrush, and some random debris on the ground. We're all decked out in camouflage from head to toe, war paint all over our skin; only the whites of our eyes are visible. My adrenaline is pumping through my veins, and I can feel my heart pounding against my chest.

The buzzer sounds, and we're off.

Tiptoeing from the exit, I move away from my group. Making my way toward the river that runs right through the arena, I hope the sound of the flowing water will muffle any noise from my movements. Squatting behind a large oak, I analyze my surroundings. There's a fake Sunclouded Leopard just to the left of an old pickup truck.

Making a break for the truck, I'm sought out and pelted with rubber bullets to my right shoulder blade. The bullet rips open my newly closed wound, knocking the breath out of me. Tumbling to the ground, I use the momentum to roll to the nearest downed log I can find for cover. Trying to catch my breath, sucking in air rapidly, I reach for my back with my left hand to assess where there's a fiery burning sensation. Sure enough, touching my shirt, there's sticky liquid staining it. I bring my fingertips in front of my face and spot fresh, bright red blood.

"Son of a biscuit eater," I puff, realizing the wound is oozing. Screw that. I won't let them take me down. I'll destroy this Sunclouded Leopard *and* the jerk that shot me. Finally able to catch my breath, I look over the log to my surroundings and plan my next move. I have to get to the truck for shelter, take out the leopard, and demolish my attacker.

Ten feet away, I can do this. I'm fast. It's only a small amount of blood.

Scrambling to the door of the pickup, I dive inside the driver's side window. Peeking out the passenger side window, I realize my ax is within throwing distance of the leopard. I look to my left, then to my right, and let my weapon fly. My aim is thankfully true, despite my injury, and the artificial leopard goes down. I crawl out of the truck to retrieve my ax. Fully equipped once again, my next mission is to find the idiot who ripped open my damn wound. Crawling on my belly, I'm finally able to crouch behind the rusted remains of an airplane wing. I sit as still as possible to watch and listen. I'm not sure how long I sit there, but eventually, I notice a bush rustling.

Yes! This prick is going down.

I sneak around to the end of the wing, and right before I advance on my new target, I catch out of my periphery, a large form barreling straight at me. Scrambling to my knees and gripping my ax, I'm grabbed from behind with sweltering hands covering my mouth. I'm about to bite the person's fingers when I feel lips near my ear, sending chills up my entire body.

"Don't move a muscle; he'll see you and shoot again," a voice whispers. Tilting my head in the direction of the low tone, Pierce winks at me. My stomach flip-flops and my heart pounds even harder as fire courses through my veins.

I huff, "How do you know he'll shoot me again and that I won't take him out first?"

"I know his tricks; he's not in the bush. He's about twenty feet away behind an Oak. He's tied a fishing line to that bush and tugs on it, making you think that's where he's hiding. Once you reveal your position, he'll unload on you. He's been watching your every move since you left the group. Word to the wise, never leave your group and go solo. That's the fastest way to die out there on a hunt or outside the wall for any reason."

Shrugging Pierce off, I demand, "Who is this 'He' you're referring to?"

"Kage," he grunts.

Scooting back up against the wing, I grumble, "What the hell is his problem? Is Kage trying to kill me? Why does he hate me? He's always seeking me out in the arena. Last week, he got me in the left shoulder before I could lose the bolt from my crossbow. I had a wicked bruise for days after that one. Today,

I was about to take down the leopard with my ax, and he shoots me in my bad shoulder, splitting it back open." I pull at my wet shirt. "I won't let him win! I'll press on toward every target in front of me until I can't move if that's what it takes."

Inching up next to me, Pierce explains, "He doesn't hate you. He notices your fierce determination, and it's his goal to make you better, stronger, and stealthier. If he didn't see potential in you, he wouldn't be so hard on you." He leans in and breathes, sending goosebumps up my arms. "Putting yourself in harm's way just to prove a point will only hurt you in the end. He knows whoever shot that arrow at you is still out there. He wants you to be able to protect yourself."

I nudge my left shoulder into his chin. "Well, what do you suggest I do?"

Scanning the area, Pierce devises a plan to climb one of the trees behind the wing. "We need to get to higher ground. Once you have a clear shot, aim your ax for his shoulder. I'll cover you," he instructs, motioning with his gun.

Thank God my legs are strong because my upper body is pretty much worthless right now. I grab a branch and shimmy up by pushing off with my legs. Thankfully, the blood from my wound isn't leaving a trail, so I'm not overly worried about anyone else tracking me at the moment. I'm focused solely on taking out Kage. Pierce has to give me a little push a couple of times, but I manage well enough independently.

Once we've scaled at least seven limbs into the canopy of the tree, Kage is in clear view. Nodding my head in his direction, I check that Pierce is ready for our attack. He gestures once again with his Glock, giving me the go-ahead. I pull back my arm as far as my injury will let me and release the ax in Kage's direction with as much power as I can muster; simultaneously, Pierce fires his pistol.

"Stop! Stop! I surrender," Kage commands, diving for cover.

The buzzer sounds, indicating the two-hour challenge is over. Thank God. My arm is now throbbing in pain, and I desperately need to get my shoulder bandaged, not to mention I smell like manure and need a shower.

"Let me give you a hand," Pierce offers, reaching out for me from his perch.

We successfully scale back down the tree limb by limb, Pierce landing on the ground first while I'm sitting on the lowest branch facing him. Reaching up for me, he places his warm hands under my arms and lifts me from the branch. Sliding along his body, every part of me grazes against his. I quickly realize just how close we are when I feel a rigid length press against my belly. My face flushes. My breath is coming in fast and hard. Good God, I want to kiss him, but I'm not sure. Our foreheads are touching softly. I tilt my chin and meet Pierce's intense gaze as he presses further into me, leaning in so close I can feel his hot breath on my cheek. Frozen in uncertainty, my body stiffens. Apparently, reading my unspoken language, Pierce takes a couple of steps back.

"Do you mind if I look at your wound?" he asks quietly, gesturing toward my back.

"Ew, it's going to be gross. I'm sweaty, stinky, and sticky with a mixture of blood and dirt. Can't I shower first?" I scrunch my nose and crease my brows.

"I just want to see how bad it is and make sure you're not going to need stitches again," he presses.

"Ugh, fine." I turn my back to face him. He lifts my shirt, peeling it away from my scar.

Pierce shouts a curse.

Startled at his response, I peek over my shoulder. "What? How bad is it?"

"I'm going to pound his cocksucking face in." Pierce rubs

his sizzling finger along the entire length of my scar. "The whole thing is open. There's flesh just hanging by threads, and a gaping hole at the top of the scar. The entire laceration is probably going to need stitches. Your shirt did a good job of sealing off most of the bleeding, but now that I've removed it from the wound, blood is trickling pretty good. I'll apply a pressure bandage at the first aid tent outside the arena, but we need to get you to the clinic quickly. The last thing you need is an infection on top of everything else," he rants.

"Just Jim Dandy. Mr. Hughes is going to write me out for at least a week. I can't stay cooped up in that cabin any longer. Why did your sorry excuse for a brother have to do this?"

Tears are welling up in the bottom of my eyes. Pierce traces my scarred eyebrow with the pad of his thumb, and it's sweltering. I'm not sure if I'm super sensitive or if Pierce just has really warm hands.

I look up into his eyes as he consoles, "Hey, it's going to be okay. Rest is the best thing for you at the moment."

Fighting the urge to lean into his warm palm, I whimper, "Pierce, you have no idea. You think rest is the 'best' thing for me...I don't rest. I don't sleep. I can't. Keeping me confined is the worst possible thing for me right now."

He pulls me snuggly into a tight embrace, careful not to cause more pain in my back. I can't help but release the unshed tears. They stream down my face, soaking his shirt in a matter of minutes. He strokes my back with the tenderest touch as I sob, letting out all of my frustration.

Once my trembling and sniffling subside, he gingerly kisses the top of my head.

He exhales deeply. "Want to talk about it?"

"No, not really," I rasp with a shaky voice.

Sighing, with his cheek pressed to my hair, he doesn't push

me on it. "Okay, we need to dress your wound. Are you okay to walk?"

Pulling slightly back from his embrace, knowing I must look like death warmed over, I simply wobble my head up and down in a 'yes' motion. He slips his fingers in-between mine, and we proceed to the exit.

12

PIERCE

H and in hand, I do my best not to singe her. I've gotten my fire to simmer down, and now our fingers are locked. We're finally leaving the clinic only to be bombarded by her friends Adi, Dani-Jo, and Cora.

Adi charges us. "Do you want me to kill Kage? I can bury the body where no one will find it!" I'm pretty sure she's only half kidding; the sparkle in her eyes tells me she'll do whatever it takes to defend Tova.

Tova giggles then yelps, "Oowwww!" Grimacing, she hisses, "Don't make me laugh, and no need to threaten anyone's life. I'll be fine. He's just hard on me to make me a better Protector, but thanks, Adi. I know you've always got my back."

"Pierce, I can take her from here," Adi declares.

"She needs to lie down and take it easy, like Mr. Hughes advised," I instruct.

"You think I don't know that? She also needs to shower, and I can help her with that," she sasses, placing a hand on each hip. "She'll be fine. I'll make sure she's taken care of. Always have. Always will." Stealing Tova's left arm, Adi slings it around her neck to help her hobble up to their cabin.

"Hint taken. I know when I'm not wanted." I throw my arms up in surrender, and I'm pretty sure a spark emanates from my palms, but it thankfully goes unnoticed.

"I'm not saying you're not wanted, Pierce. You're a good guy. I'm just saying I've got it from here," Adi reaffirms, looking over her shoulder back at me.

Tova stops them in their tracks and turns to face me. "Thank you, Pierce, for everything. I'll get cleaned up and do my best to rest. Mr. Hughes has written me out of training for an entire week, so I'll catch up on reading. Don't worry about me. I'll be fine."

"He said you couldn't practice and need to rest, but he also said you could go out and about if you take it easy. I'll come by later and check on you and see if you're up for a walk," I say, with more than a little hope in my voice.

"I appreciate it, Pierce, more than you know, but I promise I'll be fine," she says, slipping a small smile.

A fter dinner, I head to Tova's cabin to check in on her. When I arrive, the girls tell me she went to her mom's house several miles from here. Dani-Jo gives me detailed directions. Clutching my fists, I shove my hands in my pants pockets and then begin my trek to her farm.

What is she thinking? Did she not think I'd really come back to check on her? Is she avoiding me?

Remembering the conversation I overheard her friends discussing in the library; I know she may, in fact, be trying to distance herself from me. I kick a rock as I walk and shake my head. I'm still going to show up and check on her. As I continue my hike, my mind keeps re-envisioning her injury that's just been sewn freshly back together.

She can't be around all that dirt, dust, and hay. Her injury could get infected.

An hour later, I approach the most detailed metal gate I've ever seen, with horses etched inside each panel. Peering ahead, I notice a white farmhouse with a wraparound porch, and to the right is a white barn with brown sliding barn doors and brown accent shutters on the top window of the loft. Unlocking the gate, I make my way down the gravel driveway. The rocks stop crunching under my feet when I halt at the barn's sliding doors, they're open slightly, and I squint inside. I notice Tova on the ground near a stall at the end of the barn. A horse is lying beside her with its head in her lap. Stroking the delightful animal, she hums a soft song. Utterly oblivious to me being here, I take a moment to admire her. She's so damn beautiful, compassionate, gentle, and I'm pretty sure I'm jealous of a horse right now because I sure wish that was my head in her lap.

Unable to resist any longer, I clear my throat, letting her know that she has company. Startled, she jerks her head in my direction but doesn't move to get up. When she notices it's me, she lifts her right arm and waves me over, patting the ground next to her for me to come to sit. Creeping inside, I do as she signals. When I reach her, I slide along the stall door to settle down right beside her. The horse, with its head still in her lap, lifts its nose to my side, sniffing me. I raise my left hand, the whiskers from its nose tickle, and I fight back the blaze trying to erupt from my palm. There may be a hint of smoke that seethes up because the horse sneezes. It's kind of cute and funny at the same time.

Tova snickers under her breath as she resumes petting the gelding. "His name is Lightning," she explains, tracing the lightning streak down his muzzle. "He was born in the stall behind you when I was four. He's fourteen, almost fifteen now. His stall is the last one on this side. He and I grew up together. He's never liked men, well anyone really for that matter. He never let any of the farmhands near him. I'm the only one he'd let feed, clean, and ride. When I was younger, he actually let me do handstands on his back for as long as I could keep my balance, which wasn't very long." She chuckles at the memory. "I've taught him everything he knows. He must sense you're not a threat because he rarely takes kindly to other people."

Placing my hands in my lap, I ask, "What exactly does that mean?"

"Well, he bucked my father off once, breaking his back. It took him a solid six months to recover. Then, my dad tried to exert his dominance on him another time, and Lightning kicked him in the chest, breaking so many ribs he couldn't farm for six weeks. After my father recuperated, he was going to shoot Lightning. So, I snuck out that night. I led Lightning to the edge of the woods near our farm and released him outside the fence. He was still inside the protection wall but laid low, so my father never found him," she explains quietly.

"I'm guessing since Lightning is back that your father doesn't hate him as much anymore?" I ask, stretching my legs out in front of me, crossing my ankles.

"Something like that." She shrugs.

Not understanding what she means, I probe, "Care to elaborate?"

"It means that Lightning is here to stay," she states, not fully answering the question.

Probably pushing my luck, I'm not completely satisfied with her answer. "And your father?"

"He's no father, merely a sperm donor. His name is Cladec, and he's gone for good." Her tone is cold and distant, almost unaffected.

"Did he get sick and die?" I ask, treading carefully on the topic.

"Ha! Nope!" she laughs bitterly.

"Did something kill him?"

"No, but a girl can always hope, right?" She tilts her head, slanting her eyes, examining me.

"Damn, that's brutal!" I chuckle, shifting back so I can see her better.

"You have no idea!"

"You keep saying I have no idea, so tell me." She's silent. I press further, perhaps pushing my luck, "Is he the reason you can't sleep?"

"Honestly, I've already told you too much. I just want to love on Lightning and forget about Cladec. Can we just do that?" Answering my question without actually answering it, I now understand that he is, in fact, a large part of her sleepless nights.

Not pushing the situation any further, I give in. "I guess. How's your back?"

"The bandage is airtight and thick, no dust or dirt will get to it, and it's not throbbing too badly. I took the pain medicine Mr. Hughes gave me," she declares with a grin.

I smile back, placing my hands on my knees to stand up. "It's getting late. Are you staying with your mom?"

Eyeing the stairs that lead up to the upper floor of the barn, she responds, "I'll sleep up in the loft tonight. There's no way I'll fall asleep in that house, let alone in my old bedroom." She's now standing in front of me with Lightning upright beside her.

"It's the middle of Summer, won't you melt? Does your mom even know you're here?" I ask, dusting off my pants.

"No, at night it cools off. I listen to the songs of the crickets, frogs, and cicadas." She points to the window. "You can see the stars glowing through that window; it's calming and peaceful. I simply count them when sleep evades me. And yes, my mom knows I'm here. We ate supper together. She's known for a while that this place is my escape and is aware that I'll be sleeping up there."

Closing the space between us, I wrap my arms around her waist. "Obviously, this isn't your first time sleeping out here, but I hate the thought of you being alone. Want some company?"

Placing her hands on my biceps, she delicately tips her head up to meet my eyes, penetrating me with those ocean blue eyes. "If you spend the night, how will you make it to the track on time?"

"I'm an early riser; as soon as the sun rises, I'll head out."

At least she didn't immediately shut down the idea of me staying.

"I promise I'm a big girl and will be fine on my own, but if you really want…you can stay. The company might actually keep my mind off everything," she concedes.

As she wraps her horse's reins around her left hand, I

remove my arms from her waist. After she puts her horse up in his stall, she strolls to me, taking my hand in hers as we head up the steps to the loft.

Taking in the view of her bedding options, I gape. "Wow, you've already got blankets and pillows thrown about. You're really prepared."

"Yeah, I did this before I got Lightning out of his stall. I really and truly hope I can get even a few hours of sleep."

Sitting down on the pile of blankets, we lean against the wall next to the window and gaze out.

"Well, I'm here now, and I'm not going anywhere. I have my pistol holstered in my jeans and my knife in my back pocket. You'll be safe with me." Removing the items from my jeans, I fill her in, "My dad had Kage and me shooting at targets since we were five and throwing knives since we were eight. He took us on every hunting trip he could. He's a great father, taught me most of everything I know. I can only hope to be half as good a man as he is."

"That's great that you and your family have such a close bond and that you don't take that for granted." Her face looks solemn, and I see that glow in her eyes fade.

"Why don't we lay down and try to get some shut-eye," I nudge, sensing the need for a topic shift.

We both get pillows adjusted under our heads, and Tova lays facing the window while I spoon behind her, draping my arm across her torso.

As she traces the mutilations on my arm, she asks, "Where did your scars come from?"

"Well, you know how some people have alterations from the Dust?" I ask quietly.

Nodding a yes, she affirms, "Mm-hm."

Appreciating her delicate touch, I resume, "Kage has the ability to emit water from his hands, specifically his palms. At first, we thought he just sweat a lot. But there was this trip we went on that showed otherwise. My dad, Kage, and I went on a hunting trip when I was ten. We were climbing up a tree stand when Kage's nerves got the best of him. He was either really excited to drop a deer or terrified. All I know is that dad made it to the blind first. Kage was above me, almost to the top, when it suddenly felt like there was a waterfall above my head. As I was climbing, I reached up with my left hand and left leg when I lost my grip because everything was tremendously wet. I plummeted to the ground about twenty feet, and I swear I landed in the biggest thorn bush in the entire forest. By the time dad and Kage got me out, I was nothing but a bloody mess."

"Why do you only have scars on your arms and nowhere else?" she presses.

"It was the end of Autumn, much cooler outside. I had a backpack on with a blanket fastened above the bag, or else my back and head would have been torn up by the thorns as well. Thankfully, only my arms were tattered."

"Wow, y'all must have been terrified."

Tracing circles on her stomach with the pad of my finger, I snort, "Kage wouldn't stop apologizing for weeks. He finally realized I was going to be okay and stopped being so hard on himself."

Gripping my arm, Tova squeals suddenly, "Look! A shooting star! All the stars are twinkling so bright tonight."

Pressing my chest against her back, careful not to press too firmly on her bandage, I lean over her to look further outside. The night sky is the darkest ebony overspread with specks of light. However, in my attempt to see the shooting star as I hover above her, I can't help but become entranced looking into her eyes. I now notice they are soft blue-green and gold-flecked with a dark blue rim. They are breathtaking, but there's deep anguish behind them. "The only star I see is right in front of me." I breathe, barely above a whisper.

She tips her head to look at me and then adjusts in my hold to face me. Holding my stare, she licks then bites her bottom lip. That's all the invitation I need. Capturing her mouth, she presses her lips hard against mine, parting them with her tongue. Swiftly moving our tongues against each other's, I pull her into my chest. She digs her fingers into my back, the intensity of the kiss sweeping both of us away. She throws her right leg over my lower half and draws my body even closer to hers. Breaking the kiss just enough to catch our breath, we continue our passionate exploration of one another; the kisses turning tender and less frantic. I trail my hands over her back, and her leg hiked above mine when she lets out a moan. My pants bulge in the middle, and my hands are heating quickly. Withdrawing my kiss breathlessly, I pant, "I have to stop."

"Ugh," she huffs. Cautiously, she leans back slightly, taking in my expression. Closing my hand around the back of her head, I tangle my fingers in her hair, tugging her forehead to mine, and I simply breathe.

"You okay?" she exhales.

"Yeah, I don't want to hurt you," I explain. Releasing my hold on her, I roll onto my back. The warmth subsides in my palms as she lays her head on my chest. I wrap my right arm around her body, keeping her close.

"Mm, k," she groans, not pushing the subject further as she closes her eyes.

It doesn't take her long to go to sleep. I, on the other hand, can't keep my eyes off her. Not wanting this moment to end, I struggle to sleep, though eventually, I doze off a couple of times. As soon as I finally slip into a deeper sleep, I'm awoken and aroused by a perfect little rear wiggling against my damn waist.

13

TOVA

The sun peeks through the window, waking me from the best sleep I have had in my entire life. No demons taunted me, no memories of Cladec haunted me. For once, I was sleeping so soundly. I'm sure if it weren't for the sun shining in my face, I would still be asleep. The warmth of Pierce's body is still pressed tightly against my back, and I know he will be late for training if I don't wake him up.

This ought to be fun.

Our bodies are perfectly aligned, with his knees tucked up behind mine and his arm draped protectively around my middle. After that kiss we shared last night, I can't resist torturing him just a little. Pressing back into him a little more fully, I wiggle my rear against his groin. With a slight groan, he squeezes the arm around my middle to keep me still.

Not a chance of that, buddy.

"I've been pressed against you all night, fighting the urge to devour you. You'd better stop that before I can't control myself any longer, and I pounce," he growls between kisses to the nape of my neck.

"What if I don't want to stop?" I challenge.

"This isn't the right time," he mumbles, rising on one elbow to loom over me.

Turning over to face him, I nudge his chest, eyeing him suspiciously. "Yeah, um, okay." Sitting up to face him, I drone, not meeting his eyes, "You'd better hurry and get to the track. Thank you for staying with me." Picking up a piece of straw, I tear it as I quietly reveal, "I slept like a rock."

I really am grateful for a good night's rest. It's been years since I've slept without being awakened by nightmares or night terrors.

Gently kissing me on the forehead, he gets up to leave. As he gathers his shoes, weapons, and shirt, he says, "Thank you for letting me stay. I'll grab my stuff and head out. Are you staying here all week?"

Inhaling his scent, I close my eyes. Gosh, he smells so good, like bitter bark and lemon leaves, just like the Hophornbeam or Ironwood tree. Opening my eyes, I respond, "I plan to. I'll go crazy staying inside that cabin. At least here I can groom the horses, help mama out around the house, and keep myself busy without tearing my stitches."

"I'll come to check on you at the end of the day." He pecks my lips and turns to leave the barn.

Following him down the stairs, I watch him walk down the gravel drive and out the gate. My God, he's so freaking gorgeous. Right before he leaves the gate, he turns back to see me standing in the barn, I wave goodbye, and he does the same.

Crossing my arms across my chest, I lean against the barn door and ponder what he could mean about it not being the right time. Does he think I'm repulsive? I mean, in my opinion, I am. I'm trash that the dog brought in. *Just forget about him. Let him go, Tova. You're no good for him!* I slap my palm to my forehead, attempting to get out of my head. *Ah, I can't think like this, or I'll go insane.*

M ama and I finish up our lunch and are washing the dishes when I see Adi, Dani-Jo, and Cora filing up the stairs of our front porch. I rush to the door, flinging it open, and hug them all together.

"You doing okay?" Adi asks, patting my lower back, making sure not to touch my mutilated shoulder.

"Kinda." Closing the door behind me, I ask softly, "Can we sit on the porch swing y'all? I have a ton to tell you."

We scramble to the swing, sitting side by side. I fill them in on the events of last night, and all that went down between Pierce and me...and all that *didn't* go down between us.

"You know this has nothing to do with your past right, Tova?" Adi presses.

"Well, what other reason would he have?" I ask, unwilling to believe her.

"Um, the fact that your back is battered probably has everything to do with it," Dani-Jo chides.

Dropping my head in shame, I sigh. "I mean, I guess, but still, I felt like we had such a connection. I mean, a fire lit up inside me, and when he pulled back, it was like a physical blow to my gut."

"It's normal to feel like that if you think he's rejecting you. I promise no guy is going to walk all the way out here to check on you, make sure you're safe by staying the night with you, and make out with you if he's not totally into you. Now get a hold of yourself and DO NOT, I repeat, DO NOT run this guy off. I see the way he looks at you. He's got it bad," Adi nags while elbowing me in the side.

"Not to mention he's a gentleman, and he *is* a couple of years older than you. He wants to respect you and not force you to move too fast. He's coming back tonight; that says a lot of his character. Cut the guy some slack," Cora advocates, placing her arm across the back of the swing and around my shoulders.

I lift my chin. "That's one of the many reasons I love you girls, talking me off the ledge all the time." Stopping the swing with my feet, I question, "Do y'all have to go back for class or training, or can y'all ride horses?"

"Girl, we've already skipped the first hour. We're not going to march all that way just to get there when it's over," Dani-Jo teases. "Let's go riding. I mean, if you can with your back and all."

All saddled up, the girls and I head out not too long after they arrive. "Let's go to the creek bed that leads to that small lake. The horses can drink, we can cool off, and just horse around. Pun intended."

"Ha, Ha. You think you're funny, don't ya?" Cora chides.

"Think? I *know* I am," I giggle in response.

Trotting in silence toward our destination, Adi, riding

Sundance, a palomino paint horse, and Lightning's mother, is the first to break the silence. "Tova, you're the bravest human being I've ever met. You walk through storms like they're a field of daisies. You're fierce yet kind, strong yet gentle, firm yet compassionate, not to mention drop-dead gorgeous. But when it comes to finding the love of your life, you shut down and refuse to let anyone close to you."

She glances back in my direction. "I don't want you to do that with Pierce. Eventually, he's going to find out what that piece of crap father did to you. And don't think I haven't noticed that when things start to get even remotely serious between you and a guy, you shy away. I want to challenge you." Riding on my right side, she cross-examines me, smirking, then continues, "I know you never back down from a good challenge. Be brave enough to listen to your heart and strong enough to live the life you deserve. Conquer your nightmares and chase down your dreams. Never let fear hold you back. And stop thinking you're damaged goods."

"I second that challenge," Dani-Jo pipes up.

"Me too," Cora agrees.

I try to contradict their arguments, concentrating on the trail ahead. "Listen, girls, it'll be a cold day in Hell before I let Pierce know what Cladec did to me. Once he finds out, he's just going to see me as damaged goods, and that's going to hurt like hell. Sure, I can tell that there's something between us, and of course, y'all would see right through me." Taking a deep breath in, I lament, "I'll accept your challenge, but understand that it's hard for me to let someone in, knowing good and well that my heart will most likely be shattered."

"Look, Tova. Last night, he showed restraint, revealing self-control; that's pretty amazing for a guy," Adi emphasizes. "No doubt, he sees the hurt behind your eyes. He has already started tearing down the freaking fortress you've built around your heart. He will eventually demolish your walls. You need to let down your guard. I'm holding on to the hope that when he understands all the muck and mess you've crawled through, when you lay awake crying at three AM, when you're fighting your demons in your nightmares…that he'll truly see YOU and that he cares. That he isn't surprised by the obstacles you're overcoming, and that he'll walk with you, holding your hand, and helping you climb every mountain and trudge through every valley while loving every part of you."

"When I grow up, I want to be just like you," Dani-Jo laughs, breaking the sentimental moment.

I appreciate Adi's insight and confess, "Adi, you're wise beyond your years. I want to find a love like you and Larson have. But first, I have to see if Pierce even sees me in his future, and it's way too soon for that. Sure, we have a fiery connection, but what if that's all it is? Not everyone finds love. I will promise you this, though, if things start to get serious, I'll do my best not to push him away. I'll tread those waters lightly and see where it leads. Okay?"

"That's all I ask." Adi beams.

After we let the horses lap up a drink in the stream, we trail back to the barn.

Cora chimes in while untacking the horses, "Will we see you at the campfire Friday evening?"

Considering it's still a few days away, I deliberate, "I think so. Hopefully, I'll be healed up well enough. I'll look for you girls there."

We hug out our goodbyes, and they head down the driveway toward the path to their cabins.

Standing in the barn entrance, I notice a figure walk past them and beam when I recognize Pierce. An inferno seemingly consumes my every fiber, and I tingle all over at the mere sight of him.

14

PIERCE

Waving to her friends as they pass, they are all smiles, and I can't fight my responding grin. Turning toward the barn, I notice Tova standing in the doorway in all her glory, like a goddess. Immediately my hands begin to simmer. God, she ignites my soul. If she only knew the spell she has on me.

"Hey, Spitfire!" I greet as I approach her.

"Spitfire?" she asks, eyeing me quizzically.

Attempting to joke that she's resilient, I jog her memory, "Hell yeah, you take a licking and keep on ticking."

"I try not to be a wimp. So, if that's what a spitfire is, then I guess I am," she retorts, her hands landing purposefully on her hips. I know she's attempting to sound sassy, but there is no hiding the smile tugging at her lips.

"Want to help put away some tack?" she asks over her shoulder as I finally reach the barn. She makes her way toward four saddles set out on racks in front of the stalls without looking back at me.

"Certainly! Go on a horse ride without me?" I tease, following her inside.

"The girls came to chat around lunch. We had some time to kill, so we went on a trail ride to the 'watering hole' as I call it. There's a stream that leads to a lake at the edge of the property. We can go there if you'd like," she explains, nervous excitement in her smile.

"Maybe another time. Seeing as how you just got back, I don't want you to overdo it. How's your back holding up?"

She stops in her tracks, holding a saddle, and turns to face me. "I know my limits, Pierce. I can handle another ride. There are other horses here that need the exercise. My back is unquestionably superb."

Sensing a hint of sarcasm, I know she'll go without complaint. "Let me change your bandage and examine the damage. If it's not too terrible, we can ride to the lake," I concede.

"Yay! The wound care kit is by the back door." Clapping her hands briskly while bouncing on the balls of her feet, she leads me to the supplies.

As I open the kit, she lifts the back of her shirt, holding it up on top of her shoulders with each hand on either side. Damn, her form is perfect. Her back muscles flex, causing the curves of her spine to be more pronounced, and my heart thrashes inside my rib cage.

Focus Pierce.

I redirect my concentration. Careful not to pull at the healthy skin surrounding her wound, I remove the old bandage now covered in dried blood. Assessing the damage, I find the stitches are intact. No puss is oozing from the injury. The angry red granulation tissue indicates healing flesh.

Painting on some Mercurochrome, a reddish antiseptic, I let it dry before applying a clean bandage on the wound. "Surprisingly, your shoulder looks great. I think exercising the other horses will be fun."

"Told you." She sticks out her tongue at me.

Biting my lips together, I can't hold in a chuckle.

We tack up two horses named Aspen and Denali. Both Appaloosa horses are white, with colorful brown spots along their coats. Their physical characteristics are linked to the leopard complex mutation or Dalmatian-like spots, another one of the mutations from the Dust. Hefting our legs over the saddles, we settle in and travel toward the lake.

"So, tell me about your time farming for the past two years," she queries.

"It's hard work, that's for sure. Rising before dawn just to tend the fields, and then to the pastures to manage the livestock, will certainly build stamina and humble you all at the same time. After I finished my daily duties, I'd go to the learning commons to study naturopathy and brush up on history. Did you know that this mountain was named Iron Mountain because we mine the most iron anywhere in the world? I mean, mountains in this territory also contain gold, manganese, and copper. Still, ninety percent of all metals refined nowadays are iron. I read that people have been using iron for over five thousand years, and some of the oldest iron literally dropped from the sky. Meteorites made up of iron crash-landed on the planet after penetrating the atmosphere," I explain, unable to hide my excitement at getting to share some of the knowledge I've accumulated through my studies.

"Well, aren't you just a wealth of knowledge! And no, I didn't know that we mine the most Iron in the world. I mean, I kinda figured we were one of the few who mine anything since there are so few territories." She shrugs.

Arriving at our destination, we dismount our horses and let them graze around us as we plop down at the edge of the lake. It's now dusk and has cooled off several degrees, and as Tova leans into my side, I notice her trembling.

I place my arm around her shoulders. "Want me to build a fire?"

Nuzzling into the crook of my neck, she points out. "We didn't bring a fire starter."

I boast, rising to stand. "Not a problem, now promise not to freak out and don't be afraid."

"Um, freak out or be scared about what?" she asks, raising her left eyebrow eyeing me curiously.

"Just promise," I say as I get up to gather some firewood.

"Umm, okay." She slants her eyes.

I find some large stones along the shore, and construct a makeshift fire pit, piling logs and branches I've gathered together inside it. While I work, I watch Tova through the corner of my eye as she ties the horses to a nearby tree.

She sits and watches me intently, positioning herself near the fire pit.

Channeling my inner inferno, flames erupt from my hands, and within a matter of seconds, the firewood is blazing to life. Back peddling across the ground, Tova scoots her body away from the fire with wide, panicked eyes.

"Please, don't be afraid," I plead, reaching out for her to stop her retreat.

"Will you burn me?" She eyes my outstretched hand skeptically.

"No, I've pretty much mastered the on and off switch. My palms still get heated when I'm next to you, though. I admit I've never had to fight the flames with anyone else before," I confess.

Curiosity gets the best of her as she takes my hand and yanks me down beside her. I wasn't expecting that, so I land with a not so graceful, "Oomph."

"Oh crap, I'm so sorry. I didn't know I tugged so hard," Tova exclaims, hiding a giggle behind her hand.

"Don't know your own strength, do ya Spitfire?" I laugh, rolling onto my back.

"I think your center of gravity was off and that heave I gave you took full advantage of it, that's all," she explains, inferring that it wasn't her strength. "Now, back to the subject at hand. When did you realize you could harness fire?"

Propping up on my elbows, I divulge, "I guess I was twelve or so. Kage fell from the rafters of our barn and broke his collarbone along with a few ribs. It terrified me. The only thing I knew I should do was stabilize his injured side. Looking around for any bit of clean cloth I could find, there was a thin sheet covering some feed, so I grabbed for it. As soon as I did, I seared it in two. Not understanding what happened, I tossed it down and stared at my hands. They were completely engulfed in flames. For whatever reason, I didn't get scared. I just focused until the flames were merely sparks, then picked the sheet back up and burned a strip away to make a sling. Once the sling was in place, Kage asked if I had ever started a fire with my hands before, and I told him no, that was the first time. He chuckled, 'What are the odds...you make fire, and I make water.' We still joke about it."

"You two undeniably had an interesting childhood," she says quietly. Gazing out at the tranquil water reflecting the thousands of twinkling stars above, she tangles our fingers together.

"I guess so. We knew no different growing up. What about you, though? You were able to grow up here on this picturesque farm. We had to dig wells for our livestock, and you have streams, lakes, and waterfalls, I'm sure."

"I suppose. We indeed have a few waterfalls; they're a decent hike, but worth it. I swim in the ponds at the bottom of the falls every so often and let me tell you, they're frigid, even in the summer. There's a couple of jumping rocks that will steal your breath away at that height. It's a total adrenaline high," she ends with a bright smile.

"Adrenaline junkie, huh?" Damn, I knew I liked this girl.

"Maybe. Not scared of heights, are you?" She elbows me in the side, and smirks up at me.

I return her smile, lifting one eyebrow and tease, "I've never jumped off a perfectly good rock into the depths of the unknown, but I wouldn't say I was afraid of heights. I scale mountains just for fun, you know?"

Tilting her head back, she laughs. "Ha! Good to know. Next week, when I'm cleared to go swimming, bring your 'A' game, hiking boots, swimwear, and dry clothes."

"Throwin' down the gauntlet, huh? I like good friendly competition. And who knows, maybe I can make the waters a bit more tolerable," I joke with a wink.

"We'll see," she snickers.

She watches me watching her as she stands to put out the flames that have almost completely burned out at this point. Once the fire is entirely doused, we mount up our mares and make our way back to the barn.

Sliding the stalls shut once we have both horses settled for the night, I announce, "You know I'm staying tonight, right?"

"I wouldn't expect anything less." She curve up at each end. We climb to the loft, the blankets and pillows just as we left them this morning.

Yawning, Tova relaxes down first on the covers next to the window. I follow right behind her after stripping out of my shirt, pistol, knife, and boots. Snuggling into my chest, she tells me through yawns about how last night was the best sleep she's gotten in years and how she's forever grateful I offered her even a little peace in her never-ending struggle to find rest. With just that one declaration, I'm on cloud nine.

Propping up on my side, I lean over her to offer a good-night kiss, careful not to let my emotions run away with me again like the night prior. We kiss tenderly before she pulls back all too soon and turns to face me.

"Can I ask you a question?"

I'm caught off guard and lean back to observe her facial expression. "Anything you want."

"Will you always promise to be honest with me?" She tucks her chin, refusing to meet my gaze.

Not knowing where this conversation is going, I narrow my eyes. "Of course! I don't make a habit of lying, and I promise I'll never lie to you."

Still refusing to look at me, she picks at the fuzz of the quilt for a moment before finally continuing, "Last night when you said you didn't want to hurt me and we stopped kissing, what did you mean? That you didn't want to get me emotionally attached only to let me down? That you thought you'd burn me because you harness fire? Or that you'd re-injure my back from my wound if we went any further? And then this morning, you said it wasn't the right timing. Please, just let me know, are you disgusted by the thought of being with me that way?" she asks, her voice barely audible.

I rub my hand down my face; I can't believe what I'm hearing.

"What the hell, Tova? Why would you ever think you'd repulse me? You're the most breathtaking woman I've seen in my entire life. Honestly, I didn't want to literally burn you, and I definitely didn't want to add insult to injury to your back by taking things further. As for the timing, truthfully, I'm not sure you're ready for things to progress."

I feel her body tense up in my hold, so I press on, needing her to understand, "Don't get mad. I see a shit load of hurt you're hiding behind those gorgeous eyes, and more than anything, I want you to be at peace. I'm not entirely sure where all of this hurt is coming from, but let me mend your broken heart before we take it any further. The last thing I want is for you to regret being with me."

Her muscles relax as she leans against me. I place two fingers under her chin, tilting her face up, forcing her eyes to meet mine. I need to see she understands what I'm telling her.

"I appreciate your honesty and honorable intentions. But most of all, I'm glad to know that I'm not repulsive. And for what it's worth, I've never experienced peace like I do when I'm with you," she whispers, finally meeting my gaze.

After planting a soft kiss on her soft lips, I lay back onto my back, scooping my arms around her as she rests her head on my chest. "The thought of being with you could never disgust me," I assure, breathing into her hair.

This time it's easier for me to drift off to sleep, unlike last night. But God, the look on her face has my stomach twisting into a hard knot. I can't believe she would ever think I wouldn't want to be intimate with her. Nothing could be farther from the truth.

15

TOVA

Moaning, I stretch my arm forward and attempt to block out some of the sun's rays currently assaulting my eyelids. It's morning already, and I slept through the night for the second time in a row. I could get used to this. Getting a full night's sleep with no interruptions is incredible.

I rub my face into Pierce's warm chest, attempting to fight

off waking fully just yet, and notice a strange dampness on my cheek and the pec I was just nuzzling.

What the heck? Was I drooling?! No! No! No!

I scramble to grab a free blanket to wipe it off him before he awakes, but as soon as my cheek leaves his chest, he opens his bleary eyes.

Fungus! I reach for a smaller blanket and watch in horror as his left hand moves toward his chest. *Crap!* In a last-ditch effort to hide my mortifying faux pax, I fling the blanket on top of his chest and catch his left hand with mine, tangling our fingers together.

His eyes flicker to mine, the question I'm dreading burning clearly in his eyes. "Umm, why is my chest wet and your cheek glistening?" Looking down at the blanket I threw on him; he jokes, "Did you drool on me?"

Fartknocker!

I didn't even think about my appearance.

Red-faced in humiliation, I stammer, "Oh, good morning, Captain Obvious. Now, if you'll lie still, I'll remove my saliva from your chest, then my face, thank you very much."

"I think it's safe to say you had another good night's rest." He grins.

Wiping his chest clean then my face, "Mm-huh, I guess you could say that."

"You can drool on my chest anytime you want," he chuckles, pulling me onto him, attempting to kiss me.

I throw the blanket over his face. "Un-uh, morning breath!"

He removes the cover and cups his hand around the back of my neck as he growls, "I don't give a damn about morning breath. Waking up next to you takes my breath away."

I give in and collapse against him, kissing him passionately with a groan. In the blink of an eye, he flips me on my back and hovers over me.

My God, I want him here and now.

I wrap my legs around his waist, pulling him closer to me. His arms begin to shake, and he retreats, panting.

"Dang it, woman, you're going to make me forget all my good intentions."

"I'm okay with that." I dare him a sultry look.

"God, I want you. In due time, I promise," he says, his voice rough with restraint. With that, he collapses on top of me.

I let out a frustrating sigh. "Okay, you big brute, you're crushing me."

He quickly moves to a sitting position and runs his fingers through his tousled hair, then reaches to gather his belongings. "I guess I'd better get going."

"Yeah, wouldn't want to be late on a count of me. Kage will never let you live it down."

Cupping my face, his eyes widen, and a smile takes over his features as he corrects, "I don't give a shit what Kage thinks. I'll stay here all day if I want, and there's not a damn thing he can do about it."

I smack his rear. "Oh Pierce. I was just teasing. But in all seriousness, I don't want you to be late."

Once he's fully dressed, I escort him, hand in hand, down the driveway to the gate. He brushes his lips against mine softly, then struts down the dirt road heading toward the track. After he's out of sight, I head to the house to shower and clean up.

As it gets closer to the lunch hour, I decide to head down to the common area to eat with everyone. It will be good for me to make an appearance with the rest of the trainees and see my friends for a bit.

Arriving at the cafeteria, I open the doors and scan the large room. I catch Adi, and the girls sitting at the table all the Protectors dine at, though the guys haven't made it to the table yet. Adi reaches up and waves at me when she sees me, and I nod before continuing to scan the crowd for Pierce.

I finally catch sight of him and am about to take a step towards him when...

What the hell?

His back is facing me as he side-hugs a girl with long brown hair and then proceeds to kiss her on the top of her head. My facial expression must have given away my fury because Adi follows where I'm staring and beholds the entire nightmare. I turn immediately and storm out of the cafeteria, taking off at a dead run toward my mom's house. I hear Adi yell my name, but I don't stop, don't look back, just keep running.

When I finally reach my mom's house, I stomp up the porch steps, my fury still burning red even after my long run. My mom must hear me coming because she flings open the door and takes in my scowl. "Sweetie, what happened? Why are you back so soon?"

"Mama, I... I... I saw him kiss another girl in the cafeteria. He didn't even try to hide it," I stutter, my anger quickly melting into sobs.

"I'm so sorry you witnessed that. You saw Pierce kiss another girl? Maybe it's not what it seems. You need to talk to him about it," she soothes, pulling me into a warm hug.

"Yes, he kissed her on the head. And what is there to talk about?" I ask, weeping into her shoulder. "We've never said we were seeing each other exclusively. I told him he needed to pursue other girls because of all the garbage I carry. I just never thought he'd actually take me up on it. He's supposed to come tonight, like he has for the past two nights, but mama, promise me you won't tell him I'm here. I can't see him right now."

"Anything for you, baby girl," she coos, stroking my back.

J ust like clockwork, I watch Pierce enter the gate and head toward the barn once dinner is done. Noticing I'm not there, he comes up to the house and knocks.

Mama opens the front door, leaving the screen door closed. Pierce asks, "Hi ma'am, is Tova around?"

"No, son, she's not here," she answers politely.

"I'm sorry. I'm Pierce. Do you know where she went?"

Mama steps onto the porch, closing the screen door behind her. "I know who you are dear. But no, she didn't tell me where she was going."

"Oh, ok. Do you know when she'll be back?" He replies despondently, dropping his head and shoving his fingers in his hair.

"She's an adult now. Unfortunately, that means she can come and go as she pleases without letting me know her whereabouts." Crossing her arms over her chest, mama finally gets the point across that he's not getting any answers out of her.

Dropping his head in defeat, he walks down the gravel drive and out of sight. My chest hurts as I watch him leave from mama's kitchen window. Running to the couch, I pull a throw pillow to my chest and bury my head in it as I and bellow tears into it. Mama comes in, pulling me into her and rocking me as she strokes my hair while humming a soft tune attempting to calm me down. Once my tears dry up, she searches my face.

"You need to talk to him about this. I don't like seeing you hurting."

I wipe the wetness from my tear stained cheeks. "Mama, that's just it. I have no reason to be hurting. He can do as he pleases."

"You're right. Pierce can do as he pleases, but if you establish boundaries, he'll know where you stand."

"I'm standing on my own two feet. I don't need a guy."

"No, you don't, but you're not fooling me, sweetheart. I've seen a spark in your eyes that I haven't seen since Lightning was born, and I don't want that spark to fade. You're the master at sweeping things under the rug, never letting certain issues see the light of day. Now, please promise me you'll talk to Pierce."

"Okay, Mama, when the time is right, I'll talk to him. Now can we eat ice cream and play cards?"

"Of course, sweetie, what kind of ice cream, or do I even have to ask?"

"You know what I like, chocolate all the way." I muster a soft smile.

16

PIERCE

I approach Adi and Dani-Jo on the track the next morning.

"Hey ladies, how are you doing?"

"Fine, you?" Adi snaps with a glare.

"Uh, well, I was hoping you could tell me why I can't seem to find Tova. Is she avoiding me? Is she back at the cabin with y'all?" I ask.

Adi scowls. "No, she's not back at the cabin! Have you *given* her a reason to avoid you?"

"Not that I know of," I say with a shrug.

"Well, I've known Tova for a long time, and if she is, in fact, avoiding you, you won't hear from her until she's ready. She's as stubborn as a mule. Once her mind's made up, it's a done deal," Dani-Jo interjects, eyeing me apologetically.

Both the girls jog away from me, Adi looking like she could kill me, and Dani-Jo like she feels sorry for me.

What on God's green earth is going on?

I have to figure this out. I'll keep going back to her mom's farm until she agrees to meet with me. She's not staying at the cabin. I know she's staying at the farm because the fire in my veins surges when I feel her around.

God, I hate that she's alone there, probably beinging inundated with nightmares.

Tearing my fingers through my hair, my brother comes up behind me and pounds on my shoulders. "What's the matter, Pierce. You look like your dog just died."

"We don't have a dog, asshole. Though it may as well be like it died, my soul feels like it's being torn into a million pieces. I have no idea why Tova won't talk to me. We were getting to know each other, establishing trust, developing a relation-ship...at least I thought we were. And just like that, now she's avoiding me like the plague," I gripe, shaking off his hold.

"Seems like you need to do some soul searching."

I'm baffled as all get out, eyeballing him. "I'm as confused as a chameleon on a rainbow."

"I mean, look deeper. What do you think could be the cause? Is she afraid she's falling for you and of being hurt? Were you two moving too fast, and she simply needs time to figure things out? Have you done, said, or not done some-thing that would cause her to push you away? When a girl does something like this, it's more than superficial issues causing it. The withdrawal goes deeper, and you have to figure out what's really happening. What has mom always taught us?"

We impersonate mom in unison, "Always stand for what's right and don't let love go without a fight."

"I've seen the way you look at her, Pierce, and knowing she's never given another guy the time of day, but has allowed you into her life, speaks volumes."

"It all means nothing if I can't get her to talk to me," I sulk, my shoulders slumping in defeat.

"The brother I know never backs down without a fight. Show her you're not going anywhere. Just keep showing up. Eventually, she'll come around and let you know what's up, even if it's not something you want to hear." When the hell did my brother get so smart?

Nodding to him, I hit the pavement, pounding out my frustrations just like Tova was doing the first time I saw her.

Two evenings in a row, it's the same song, different tune from Tova's mama. I know she's in there. The fire in my bones ignite when I'm near her. I don't call her bluff, though; I simply keep showing up, like Kage advised.

It's now Friday, and all the trainees and Protectors are at the track running when my bones begin to burn. I look up the hill and notice Tova strutting to the track, proceeding to talk with Kage. They don't say much. He nods, and she exits the track.

Oh shit, did she just tell him she didn't want to be a Protector anymore?

I ramp up my pace to get to him as quickly as I can. Barely

able to breathe, bending over placing my hands on my knees, I gasp, "Wha... what did she say?"

"Good God, Pierce, get a hold of yourself. She said that Mr. Huges has released her for light training, and asked if she could do laps around the pool instead of run. I said yes. What did you think she said? Have you two still not talked?" he asks incredulously.

"No," I huff, "she's still avoiding me. I thought she was telling you she didn't want to be a Protector anymore, so she wouldn't have to be around me." Finally able to stand upright, I breathe heavily and pant, "It's Friday, not Monday, and Mr. Hughes has already said she could train again?"

"I have his note right here. I guess she's a fast healer. Why don't you do a couple of cool-down laps and catch your breath." He motions for me to walk it off.

After dinner, all the Protectors and trainees head to the bonfire. Of course, we trainees have to wear our damn pj's because we've lost all of our mock battles. Probably because my mind is stuck on Tova avoiding me. In my house shoes, flannel bottoms, and t-shirt, I sit on a log nearest the forest, away from everyone else. As I observe Adi making a s'more, she catches me watching and makes her way toward me. She lowers herself onto the log next to me.

Marshmallow seeps out of her graham cracker and chocolate drips onto the ground, as she disappointingly shakes her head.

"I was rooting for you and went to bat for you. I told her to open up, but then you go and do something so stupid. Now, she won't even talk to me. Thanks, Pierce. Thanks a lot for making me lose my best friend."

I place my palms up in surrender. "What do you mean? What did I do?"

Adi moves the s'more closer to her mouth. "If you don't know, then I'm certainly not going to tell you."

"Do you know where she is so I can at least try to get her to talk to me?" I rest my forehead in my palms, shoving my fingers into my hair.

"Yeah, but good luck with that," she scoffs, wiping chocolate from the side of her mouth.

I turn my head in her direction and plead, "Will you please tell me where she is?"

Wrapping some dripping marshmallow around the graham cracker, Adi eyes me cautiously. "She's swimming laps at the pool."

"In the dark?" I snap.

Adi glares over at me. "She took a lantern. Don't you dare tell Tova I told you. The only reason I know is because her mama told me when I went to check on her and she wasn't there."

I jump to my feet, clasping my hands together and lengthen my arms in her direction. I quickly back away toward the gym. "Thank you, Adi. I'll fix this if it's the last thing I do."

Shaking her half-eaten s'more at me, she does her best to threaten, "You'd better, or else…"

17

TOVA

The hair raises on the back of my neck, and that oh too familiar burn floods my veins as I approach the shallow end of the lap pool. I glance up and see a spectator. I place my feet on the bottom of the pool and draw nearer to the stairs, letting the water drain from my face as I wipe my eyes. The figure doesn't budge, merely watches me as I get closer.

Reaching for my towel beside the lantern, I hear Pierce ask, "Are you tired yet?"

"What the hell does that mean?" I bark, drying off and wringing out my hair as I step out of the shallows.

His hands rise up in the air, and he shouts, "Oh, I dunno, tired of swimming. More importantly, tired of avoiding me, tired of living the lie that you're just fine alone."

"Oh, don't sit there and act like you know anything about what I'm tired of. Some people need to be high-fived in the face with a chair!" My blood's on the verge of boiling, and I can feel my face redden.

"Easy killer, I surrender," Pierce acquiesces, holding his hands above his head.

"I never threatened you, but don't tempt me," I growl, pacing back and forth.

Standing up, he places his hands on his hips. "Damn it, what did I do? Why are you pushing me away and shutting me out?"

I scowl, stopping in my tracks. "I shut everyone out. Don't take it personally. It's just easier, and why do you care anyway?"

"Because I do. If I didn't care about you, I wouldn't come to check on you every single day. I wouldn't have stayed every night that I could just to make sure you're safe and could get some sleep."

Mirroring his stance, I place my hands on my hips and snarl, "Is that what you tell all the girls? I'm not letting you pull wool over my eyes, slick talker!"

Pierce retorts, "What?"

I pick my pace back up and fearlessly walk toward my bag of things. "Oh, don't play stupid! I came to the cafeteria the other day for lunch. Adi and I both saw you hug and kiss some brunette." Gathering my bag, I continue, "I get it, I do. I told you to find someone else. I just didn't think it'd hurt this bad watching you do it. And to think, Adi told me to give you a shot. It was more like a shot to the heart. Now, if you'll excuse me, I'll be on my way." I grip the lantern and go to side-step him to exit the gym.

Pierce shoves his fingers roughly through his tousled hair. "Fuck me! I wished I'd known you saw that."

"Well, I did see it, whether or not you wanted me to. So good night and have a nice life." I storm toward the door.

Running to get in front of me, Pierce cuts me off, "Oh no, you're not leaving that quickly."

I scowl and shove him. "Like hell I'm not."

He grabs my wrist. "I want to talk to you, Tova."

Twisting out of his grip, I bark, "And people in Hell want a drink of water, Pierce."

He's not taking no for an answer, continuing to talk while maintaining his distance, inches away from me. "You remember my uncle Morton?"

Stepping back, I fold my arms across my chest and glare. "What the hell does *he* have to do with anything?"

"In this instance, he has *everything* to do with it. He has a daughter; her name is Emerys. She's my first cousin. She's about the same height as you and the same age. We only see each other around the holidays. This past Wednesday, she was in the cafeteria at the same time we were. When she spotted me, she snuck up behind me and hugged me. Realizing it was her, I got excited, kissed her on top of her head while hugging her back, telling her it was good to see her. I asked what vocation she chose. We're affectionate, but not in a gross way like kissing cousins or anything like that. She's in training to be a caregiver; she has the kindest spirit and means no harm."

"Humph," is all I can muster.

"See, if you'd only talked with me, you'd know I only have eyes for you, Tova." Pierce reaches his hand out for mine.

Retreating further from him, I shake my head. "From where I was standing and what I witnessed, it sure didn't tell me you only have eyes for me. Again, Pierce, I'm sorry to have inconvenienced you in any way. You're free to pursue anyone you want. I apologize for not explaining myself fully. You're not tied down to me, nor do you need to be."

Once more, I try to get around him. I exclaim while gesturing to the pool, "I'll let you have the pool all to yourself." He catches me around the waist as I pass, but I demand, "Let me go, now."

He backs away but keeps his hand on my waist. "Tova, I swear, she's my cousin. I don't want to pursue anyone else. I want you! Since the first day I laid eyes on you, I've wanted only you. Maybe I wasn't clear when I said I wanted to mend your heart. I never in a million years meant to break your heart or for you to question my intentions. I would betroth you right now if you'd have me. I'll never stop caring for you, never stop pursuing you, and never stop loving you. Maybe you don't believe in love at first sight, but after seeing you…I'm a believer."

Removing his hand from my waist, Pierce holds his hand out to me once more, searching my eyes. I glance down, knowing there are crocodile tears in them just waiting to spill over, but I refuse to blink. I can't move. I can't speak. My bottom lip is quivering, and I can feel my entire body start to tremble. And just like that, with his words and actions he walks into my heart like he's always belonged there and destroys the walls I've built up and sustained for so long leaving a clear path to my heart lighting my soul on fire.

He steps into me, embracing me. Noticing my tremoring, he rubs my damp skin, drying me quickly with his warmth, but

I'm shaking for all kinds of reasons now. Yes, I'm a little chilly, but I'm more shocked and elated that he practically just said he loved me. I love him too, but there's a massive lump in my throat, and I don't have the courage to say it back; so, I just lean into him, hoping he knows I love him too.

His palms caress my back as he says, "Can I walk you home?"

"Uh, sure. I just need to put on my shoes." I bend over and slide into my shoes, using his shoulder to balance myself. Once I have them on, we begin our way back to mama's farm.

Pierce and I are walking the footpath and we're about halfway there when, abruptly a flying object zooms past mine and Pierce's heads. Yanking me back, Pierce yells, "What on God's green earth was that?"

The hair stands up on the back of my neck as I try to look around to see what whizzed past us but it's so dark, I can't find anything.

Pierce tugs me in closely and urgency overtakes his voice, "Let's get a move on it. I'm not sure what that was, and I don't like the thoughts of us being out here in the dark with a potential threat."

We pick up our pace and make it to the barn in record time.

Without discussing the plan, we climb up to the loft as soon as we reach the barn.

I pace back and forth as Pierce and I try to figure out what could be going on. We come up empty handed as we exhaust all the possibilities each of us think of.

"Uh, I need to get out of my bathing suit and into some dry clothes," I blush shyly.

Searching the pile of blankets for clothes, Pierce asks, "Do you have pajamas out here or any clothes for that matter? All I see are blankets."

"I can just wrap a blanket around me tonight, and after mama goes to the stitchery in the morning, I'll change at the house."

"I'm not so sure I can sleep next to you, knowing you're completely naked," he admits as he tugs off his shirt. "Here, wear this." He offers me the garment with a grin.

Pierce holds up a blanket so I can take my swimsuit off with a modicum of privacy. Slipping on the cotton t-shirt, I bunch the material in my hands and close my eyes, rubbing it against my face. "Mmmmm, this well-worn baby soft t-shirt is now mine, you know that, right?"

"Babe, anything I have is yours…even if it is falling off of one of your shoulders."

Babe, hmmm? I love the way he just let that roll off of his tongue without even thinking about it. I can get used to that.

A small blanket is wrapped around my middle, and I collapse down at Pierce's side, facing the window again. Knowing I only have on this shirt, my face reddens a little as we assume our usual positions.

Pierce spoons behind me, hovering over my neck and sending goosebumps all over me. He whispers into my ear, "How did you sleep the past two nights?"

Reversing to face him, I squint my eyes. "Umm, is that a trick question? I stayed at the house both nights and attempted to sleep on the couch. Mama woke to my terrifying screams in the middle of the night. All she could do to soothe me was to get me to drink water and hum softly to get me to escape the hell I was reliving in my night terrors."

"Oh babe, I knew you suffered, but not to that extent. If I

had known, I would have slept on your front porch just to be there for you."

I close my eyes, and sigh, "There's no way you could've known. I've hidden so much from you. I'm sorry, I promise to do better and fill you in on my past. But you have to let me do it on my own time."

His lips graze mine as he vows, "I promise."

Not hesitating a second longer, he wraps his hand around the nape of my neck then slides his fingers into my hair as he slowly devours my lips with a fierce hunger. He nips my bottom lip, and we breathe into each other's mouths, tasting and craving one another, breaking away only a few times to come up for air. Our ignited passion seems to simmer after a time as our kisses morph from aggressive to passionate, slow, and tender.

After that last hungry kiss, I'm unable to open my eyes for a few moments. I feel Pierce relax, and as he lies on his back, he tugs me close. I rest my head on his chest, praying to God that I don't drool on him again. Recognizing that we don't have to wake up early to train, I know I'll sleep better with Pierce beside me. Before long, sleep consumes me.

18

PIERCE

B *lasted sun! There has to be a way to close these shutters and keep the light from brutally waking us up at the crack of dawn.* Moving my left arm to shield the rays from blinding me, I'm comforted as I look down. Tova is still asleep on my chest with her face tucked against me, protecting her vision from the bright light. Her blonde hair is glistening in the soft morning light. She's so beautiful. I can't keep myself from running my fingers through the silky strands. God, how did I get so lucky?

Groggy eyed, she lifts her head to look at me.

"Morning, glory. Seeing as how you didn't move a muscle at all last night, I'd say you slept pretty well."

"Uh, huh. I'm glad to see I didn't drool on you this time. God, that was mortifying." She yawns, mumbling against my skin, her cheek still pressed into my chest.

I squeeze her ever so snuggly. "So, Mr. Hughes cleared you for training?"

"He gave the okay for swimming, light jogging, and hiking. So long as it's not a terrible climb, requiring me to use my shoulder excessively. He removed the sutures and said that I was healing up nicely."

"That's impressive. I didn't think the stitches would come out until Wednesday. I'm not second-guessing him, but do you mind if I look at your back?"

Keeping the blanket wrapped around her bottom half, she lifts the shirt—the one she's now claimed—over her back and onto her shoulders, attempting to keep her front half covered and consents. "Sure."

I whistle an astonished catcall and trace her scar with the pad of my thumb."Your laceration…it's entirely closed up."

She hums "Mm-hm," dragging the top back down over her torso.

Tova shifts to face me and crosses her legs. She adjusts the blanket over her lap, so she doesn't reveal anything. "Mama is probably out of the house now. The Hands aren't supposed to be here at the barn for at least an hour or so. So, no one should see me scamper off to the house. I'll shower and get dressed. Are you up for a hike today?" she asks, avoiding the topic of her scar.

"Absolutely, but Mr. Hughes said not to overexert yourself. I'm cool with just hanging out here if you'd rather," I emphasize, not wanting her to re-injure herself.

Placing her hand on my thigh, she continues, "No, I want to show you the waterfall. Do you want to go grab some swim trunks from your cabin and meet me back here?"

"I mean, I guess, if you're sure." I reach for her hand.

Squeezing my fingers, she assures, "I'm positive."

As I stand, I pull her up with me. Poised in front of her, I give the tip of her nose a peck. "Okay, Spitfire. I'll meet you back here in a bit."

Back at my cabin, Jace greets me at the door with a knowing grin. "Hey man, all is forgiven?"

I clap him on the shoulder, not making eye contact as I walk past him and head inside. "More than you know."

"Woah now, cat got your tongue? You've never held anything back from me." He follows me to our shared room.

I grab my duffel bag and start shoving my few belongings inside.

Jace, unsure why I'm packing every single thing I own, asks, "Care to tell me why you're packing up all your stuff?"

I plop down on my bed and sigh. "Jace, take a seat."

Curiously surveying my body language, he cautiously sits on his bed. "Pierce, you're starting to worry me."

I wave him off, reassuring him, "Awe, don't worry about me. I'm better than I have ever been before. I have a serious question to ask you."

"Don't egg me on. What is it?" he grumbles, stern-faced.

Without dilly dallying any longer, I ask, "Care to be my best man? I'm going to ask Tova to be mine and only mine for all eternity today. We're hiking up to some falls she's been raving about, and I know it's the perfect time to ask her. She's the only one for me, Jace. I don't expect there will be a long courtship because, God...I can't hold out any longer." I laugh.

Jace wrinkles his forehead. "Bro, you sure about this? You've only known her for what, like six weeks. Here you are packing up all your shit like she's done gone and said yes. You got balls of steel, man. I'll give you that."

"Never been more sure of anything in my entire life, I've known since the first day I saw her that she was the one. There's no doubt I'm going to build a life with her, share a home, have a family, and love her with all that I am for the rest of our lives."

He props himself up with his arms and leans back on his bed. "I'm happy for you, man, really I am. You know I'll be right by your side. So, why are you packing all your stuff right now?"

"We may not be hitched just yet, but I can't live another day without her. I'll be staying in their loft in the barn. Tonight, at suppertime, I'm going to ask her mom if I can make it into a living quarter for Tova and me. I want it to be a surprise, so don't mention it to Tova."

His eyes widen and his mouth gapes open at that thought. "I'm not planning on staying there forever. There's a lake at the edge of her mom's farm. I want to purchase some of that property from her mom and build a quaint little lake house for us there."

Shifting from his relaxed position, he leans forward, placing his elbows on his knees. "I can only hope that one day I'll be as happy as you are, buddy. When are you going to tell Kage, the rest of your family, and the guys?"

"After she says yes, of course," I chuckle. "So, maybe Sunday, we'll have supper with my family. I'll introduce her to my family. I know Kage has definitely told them about me being lovesick. I'm not about to walk into the lion's den on

Monday with Tova wearing a promise ring and Kage not knowing anything about it. He'll have my head on a platter and embarrass the shit out of both of us. You know that."

He stands up and smiles. "Sounds like you've thought it all out. Just tell me where and when to show up, and I'm there."

"Thanks, man, that means a lot. As soon as we iron out the details, I'll fill you in."

Grabbing my bag, I pounce out the door of the cabin toward my new home. I guess I am overly confident, but I'm not taking no for an answer.

I wander on my path, picking up some twine and attempt to make it into a promise ring. *Dang it.* My hands are dripping sweat; that's supposed to be Kage's area of alteration, not mine. *Crap.* Wiping my hands nervously on my jeans, I finally finish the braid, placing it into my right pocket.

Completely oblivious that I've made it to the gate at her house, Tova jumps up on it, causing it to rattle, and I jump out of my skin as it startles me.

"Ahh! Woman, are you trying to give me a heart attack?"

She's laughing hysterically. "You should have seen your face." Bending over and gripping her stomach, she continues to bellow.

Finally, wiping tears from her eyes and trying her best to stand tall, she asks, "What were you so deep in thought about that you didn't even hear my feet crunching on the rocks as I was approaching you?"

I throw my duffle to the side, closing the gate behind me as I enter.

"Humph, you think I'm going to tell you, after I just about shit my britches."

"Oh come on now, don't be a sour puss. I'm sure some of my undies will fit you until we wash yours." She giggles and slaps me on the rump.

I grab her by the waist. "You think you're funny, don't you?" I lean into her, kissing her softly on her smiling lips.

"Ha, it's pretty obvious that I'm hilarious," she laughs. "You don't pack lightly, do you? How many swimming shorts do you think you'll need," she asks, gesturing to the sack.

"A man can never be too certain which set of trunks to wear."

"K, let's take your bag to the loft. Grab whatever set of shorts you want. Judgment-free zone right here, buddy. I've got a picnic packed. I'll grab it and meet you outside the barn."

We hike up a cleared path for about a mile and a half. Tova veers us off the beaten pathway onto a smaller trail and within another mile, we finally reach our destination. Roaring waters deafen my train of thought. When we stop near the edge of a cliff on a jagged rock, I'm in awe of the breathtaking view.

Tova clutches my hand. "Magnificent, isn't it?"

It's definitely spectacular. Rapid gray and blue water whooshes from overhead, cascading into a dark abyss below, spraying us lightly as it passes. Taking the satchel of goodies from my other hand, Tova sits it on the ground.

Shucking her clothes, she reveals a slinky bikini and an already gleaming wet body from the hike up here.

"You mean to tell me that you just jump into depths of the unknown, and I'm supposed to be okay with that?"

"Not getting cold feet, are you? I've done it my whole life, and I've not died yet."

"Never, I just want to make sure that..." Before I can complete my sentence, she swan dives into the ravine below.

Holy Hell! Where is she?

I search for what seems an eternity when she finally surfaces. Good God, this woman is fearless. She's yelling something, but the thundering falls drown out her voice.

Discarding my jeans and shirt, I leave my swim trunks on, figuring, *Why the hell not.* I leap out as far as I can when suddenly gravity consumes me, plummeting me into the void below. Heat immediately surges from my hands. Holding my breath, I swiftly swim to the top. I finally emerge, taking in a gulp of air and search for Tova. She swims to me, taking my hand, and the heat simmers as my adrenaline calms down.

"Such an adrenaline rush, right?" she shouts.

"Yes, Spitfire. You could say that," I retort loudly.

Approaching the edge of the riverbed, we climb out onto dry land.

"Now that I've made you pee yourself, I've worked up an appetite; wanna eat?"

"You really know how to keep a man on his toes, don't ya?" I leer at her.

"You wouldn't have it any other way," she responds with a bright smile and a quick peck to my cheek.

Locking our fingers together, we trail back toward the food. My eyes wander to her sleek legs; they're lean, toned, and perfectly etched out, defining her muscles with every step she takes. Tracing her body, my eyes appreciate the view even more, watching the drops of water dance off of her toned abs that, unfortunately, I wasn't able to view when she got out of the pool the other night in the gloom of the gym. Oh, but not now... She's stealing my breath away, in broad daylight, all over again.

As we reach our destination, Tova releases my hand, leans down, and grabs our towels. Turning to hand me one, her front grazes my chest revealing that she's either cold or is as attracted to me as I am to her. I wrap my towel around her, using the excuse of the cold to my advantage, and pull her even tighter against me, her breath hiccupping at the sudden move.

"Cold?" I ask, beginning to dry her off. Warming my hands and rubbing them against the towel, I dry her back. She wraps her arms around my waist and throws her towel over my back and shoulders as well, mimicking my movements. She's so damn considerate. I'm not cold, but she doesn't know that.

Continuing to dry her, I notice chill bumps all along her arms, so I bring the towel to them, wiping away the rogue drops.

In the heat of the moment, the fire rages in my bones as she throws our towels to the ground and her lips meet mine. We taste each other feverishly, caressing and exploring each other's bodies.

19

TOVA

We recover from our heated make-out session, Pierce stopping us before going any further saying, once again, "The timing isn't right." I lay out a red and white gingham blanket and spread the food out, placing our canteens of water beside each plate. Sitting crisscrossed facing each other, we make our sandwiches, then heap potato salad, cowboy caviar, and some cut-up fruit onto our plates.

"When exactly is the 'timing' going to be right?" I ask. I sure flipping know that I'm ready now.

"Well, I already see a little sparkle in your eyes. When all the darkness and doubt go away, your eyes will let me know."

"I'm so glad that my eyes get to determine what my heart wants." I toss a strawberry at him.

"Now that you mention it, what does your heart want, Tova?" he asks, biting into his sandwich.

"I want you, Pierce. I love you. I'm pretty sure I've loved you from day one," I admit, blushing timidly as I tuck my chin, peeking up at him through my lashes.

Leaning over our plates, he skims his lips over mine. "You have no idea how happy that makes me to hear you say it."

He sits back down, reaching for his pants. Sliding his hands into one pocket, he extracts a piece of braided twine—a promise ring. My heart stutters inside my chest, and my breath comes in fast and shallow.

Fartnocker, is this really happening?

My eyes go blurry as my heart races.

No. No. No. What in the world is happening?

Shaking my head, I close my eyes, trying to focus. When I open them again, everything is freakishly sharp. I can see the individual hairs on Pierce's face. I glance at his arms, and I swear I can see blood cells coursing through his veins, leaving behind a trail of flames. Redirecting my gaze to the twine, I can see each fiber of the respective threads. When I gaze at the landscape ahead, my focus is on particular things instead of the full view.

I can see a single mouse sniffing a flower, but it blurs the rest of the countryside out. My vision is acute when things are two to three feet from my face. Still, my peripheral vision seems to have increased in diameter as I'm keenly aware of smaller things moving, like the birds stirring in the trees. Not only that, things are not very colorful. My vision is restricted to two, maybe three colors. Not understanding what the hell is happening to me, I smack a palm to my head. When I open my eyes, I can see color again and things as they're supposed to be.

"Ummm, Tova. You ok?" Pierce asks, stroking my arm.

Stunned, I stammer, "Uh, honestly? I have no clue."

"Come here, baby." He tugs me into his lap. "Has anything like that ever happened before?"

"Anything like what exactly? What did you see? What did I do?" I ask, not understanding what he witnessed.

Tucking a small strand of hair behind my ear, he exposes my face. "I was getting the promise ring out of my pants pocket when I saw your eyes go from their normal bluish-green flecked with gold to a solid blue cat-eyes."

Snapping my head, I survey his face. "Hold your horses! Did you just tell me that my pupils went from round to slits and changed color?"

"It was hard to miss, Tova. You were searching all around like you were trying to figure out what was going on. After knocking the shit out of yourself, you snapped out of your trance, and your eyes turned back to normal." He brushes his knuckles delicately down my cheek.

"I'm sorry you had to watch that. I've never had that happen before." I bashfully tuck my chin.

Pierce tips my jaw up with his fingers, forcing me to meet his gaze. "Don't be embarrassed by it, Tova. A lot of us have differences from that damn Dust. That's totally beyond our control. Now, you just have to learn how to connect with it, utilize it when necessary. It's nothing to be afraid of. You're still the most beautiful woman in the world. Okay?"

"If you say so." Pausing for a minute, I reflect, "You know, come to think of it… I've always felt like I've had this sixth sense, so to speak. Like when I saw you on the track for the first time. I somehow knew that you were good, and that I didn't need to be afraid of you."

Pierce squeezes me in a tight hug as I continue, "But I'm kinda freaked out by the whole 'new vision' thing. I mean, how will I know when it's coming again? How do I make it go away? Will I be able to just manipulate it on my own when I need to? I have a million questions, and I'm worried. What if it happens when I least expect it, like just now? You know how clumsy I am. I do frequent gravity checks against my will, all the time."

I laugh heartily. "Yes, I'm aware of you frequently attacking the ground. But think about it this way, if your eyes revert to feline vision, then you shouldn't trip as much. Cats are able to judge distance accurately, are better at detecting motion, have a wider periphery, and have excellent night vision. When we go on hunts, you can tune into your inner sense and detect prey faster. Our hunt time could be cut in half, lessening exposure in the woods with all the wild beasts." He sounds excited as he rattles all that off.

"Always looking through rose-colored glasses, aren't you?" I smirk.

"When I'm with you, that's all I do." With exaggeratedly puckered lips, he leans in and gives me a smacking peck on the cheek.

"So, what's with the ring?" I change the subject and bounce on his lap.

Twirling the twine in his fingers, he laughs, "Yeah, killjoy, about that… This was supposed to be romantic, you know?"

Arching my left eyebrow, I cup his cheeks in my palms. "It is romantic. We're at the most picturesque waterfall ever. Yeah, I freaked out, going all 'cat eyes' seeing the ring, but now I'm back to normal, so…"

He takes my left hand, and I begin to quiver. I feel intense warmth emit from his palms

"Tova, I love you with every part of my being. I know beyond the shadow of a doubt that I want to spend the rest of my life with you. Yes, shit is gonna happen. Things will get complicated. We'll be weak at times, and we'll be strong at times. We're gonna lose our shit and yell. We'll break down and cry. We'll be on cloud nine some days, and some days we'll feel nothing at all. We'll get on each other's nerves. One day we'll know for sure exactly what we want, and other days we'll have no fucking clue. Love isn't always a bed of rose petals. Roses have thorns, sometimes we'll get stabbed by them and be wounded, but we'll mend those wounds, and no matter how hard life gets, we won't leave. We'll be there for each other, striving for the same purposes and goals."

I pause for a moment, then continue, "When you fall, I'll be right there to pick you up. And I hope you'll do the same for me because nobody's perfect and we all fall sometimes. I can't spend another day without you, Tova. I'm not going anywhere. I don't want you to be only in my dreams. I want to wake up next to you every day for the rest of my life. I want to go to bed with you every night, whispering I love you and sweet nothings in your ear. I promise you I'm yours forever, but I need to know, will you be mine?"

Water pools in the bottom of my eyelids, and I'm rendered speechless. I've never felt so loved in my entire life, nor did I ever think I was worthy of such love. I'm afraid if I speak I'll burst into sobs; so, I bobble my head up and down in a nod, careful not to blink.

"I need to hear the words, Tova." Pierce looks deeply into my eyes.

Unable to force the burning tears back, they escape down

the sides of my face. "Yes, Pierce. I love you more than words can say. I promise to be yours forever."

He places the twine on my left ring finger, and I spring from his lap and into his arms, devouring his mouth enthusiastically. Enfolding his arms around me, he clenches me ever so tightly, reminding me, "You're mine."

I repeat, "And you're mine."

20

PIERCE

Dinner with Tova and her mama was delicious. There's nothing like a good ol' home-cooked meal. It's a heck of a lot better than the dehydrated, prepackaged food we take on our hunting trips and barter excursions. The food in the cafeteria is okay but often lacks seasoning...or any flavor, really. Supper tonight was anything but bland.

"Ms. Campbell, I can't tell you how long it's been since I've had a meal that scrumptious," I praise, resting back in my chair.

"Thank you for the compliment, but Pierce, please call me Shenan," she demurs, wiping her mouth with the cloth napkin. "I chalk all the savory tastes up to homegrown spices. The chicken was basted in butter and marinated in rosemary, cloves, and sage." Pointing outside to a small herb garden, she explains, "I grew them myself."

Tova pushes away from the table, her chair skidding across the hardwood floor. "Mama, you sure know how to show off your culinary skills. I can only pray that one day I can cook half as good as you." Pecking Shenan on the top of the head she says, "If you two don't mind, I'm going to shower and get cleaned up."

Shenan pats her on the cheek. "We don't mind at all, darlin'."

"I'm not going anywhere," I say with a slight smile and a wink.

As she waltzes out of the kitchen toward the bathroom, I turn my attention to her mom. "Actually, I'm glad to have you alone, Shenan. Can I speak to you about a few things?"

"Why certainly, Pierce. Want to help me clear the table, and you can tell me what's on your mind while we wash the dishes?" she asks, placing her napkin on the table.

I place my fork on my empty plate as I stand. "Yes, ma'am."

Having cleared the table and now washing the dishes, I can't seem to find the words I need to say.

"Just spit it out, Pierce, no need to be anxious around me," Shenan urges.

"Oh... ahh... of course. I just don't want to come across the wrong way. It's not a secret that I'm head over heels for Tova. No denying, this is soon, but I know beyond the shadow of a doubt that I want to spend the rest of my life loving and cherishing her. I declared my intentions at the falls today and asked her if she'd promise to be mine forever, and she accepted. I hope to God you're okay with it. I know I should have asked your permission first, but you were gone this morning, and I wanted to ask her at the waterfalls, hoping for a romantic setting. Please forgive my impulsiveness." The words tumble from my mouth in a jumbled string, but at least they are out.

"Son, it didn't escape my attention that Tova had that ring on her left finger. I might not have said anything, but don't mistake my silence for stupidity."

Almost dropping the plate in my hand that I'm rinsing off, I clarify, "Oh God; no. I would never in a million years think that."

Cackling, Shenan says, "Good to know." Contemplating the gravity of my confession, she lingers in silence for a few seconds, then professes, "You know, you have made her smile more than I think she's smiled her entire life." She points at me while lifting a butter knife out of the soapy water. "But I also know that you hurt her, deliberate or not."

I focus on the silver, and explain, "Yes, I know, but I never intended to. The girl I kissed in the cafeteria was my cousin I hadn't seen in a while; it was on the top of the head. I swear, I don't have a habit of kissing girls, nor do I ever want to kiss another girl the way I kiss Tova."

Taking a rag to the silverware, she admits, "Okay, okay. Too much information. You make her happy, and that's all I've ever wanted for her. But let me tell you she's endured more than any person should ever have to in a lifetime."

"She's not opened up to me about what's happened in her past, but I can see the hurt she's hiding behind her eyes clearly." I glance at her from the corner of my eye.

"But the fact that she's agreeing to spend the rest of her life with you should tell you everything you need to know. She doesn't trust easily. She's got a lot of inner healing to do, so be patient with her."

"Yes, ma'am, I promise I will." I place a plate in the drying rack.

"She's a closed book, Pierce. She tends to sweep things under the rug and not address the elephant in the room. She was raised to act tough and have thick skin."

I slouch my shoulders. "Please don't feel obligated, but I think if I understand a little of her past, I may be able to help with the healing process."

Resuming washing the other dishes, she warns, "I'll tell you a little of what she went through, so you're not too alarmed when she opens up. But be forewarned, it's not going to be easy to hear."

Resolving the fact that this information is going to be a hard pill to swallow, I ultimately determine, "I can handle it."

"Her father was an extremely abusive man. He wasn't always like that. He lost his own father on a hunting trip, help-lessly witnessing as a Sunclouded Leopard ripped the man apart. He finally snapped, when his mom developed an an acute illness and passed away from it. Cladec changed into another person altogether after that.

"He began drinking, and turned into a brutal monster. When Tova was just an infant, her dad beat me so badly, I ended up in a coma. I came out of it thankfully, but it took months for me to recover. The more he drank, the worse he became. He turned his beatings onto Tova at a young age. I think she was trying to protect me by not telling me.

"When I'd ask where she got a bruise, she'd say she tripped and fell, which was easy to believe because that girl could trip on air. Other times, she'd blame it on the horses or bumping into random things in the barn. She had every excuse under the sun, but deep down, I knew better. I hate myself for not doing anything about it sooner, but I'll die trying to make it up to her. Unfortunately, the older she got, the worse the beatings got, and she couldn't hide the injuries well enough any longer.

"When she was twelve years old, a Senior noticed her bruises and reported it. It was decided that he would be banished to the outskirts of our protection wall. But Pierce, I feel like there's more that happened than she's let on."

I'm sure my face is blood-red because my hands are on fire, not visibly, but if I touched anything right now, I would singe it. For now, I just hold them under the cold running water for a minute as I process all I've been told. "Shenan, I'm not going to lie. I'd like to get my hands on him right now."

"He's away from her, and she has you now. So, I have peace knowing that you'll do everything in your power to keep her from harm. But please promise me you'll not go searching for trouble. She needs to do the best she can to get beyond the hurt he's caused. If you're bound and determined to hunt him down and torture him, then you'll only bring back terrible memories for her. She'll continue to question whether every man is the Devil. Remember, an eye for an eye only leads to blindness."

"Alright, I'll simmer down, but that doesn't mean that I don't want to hunt him down and tear him apart. I won't seek him out, but if he ever reappears, then all bets are off, and I can't be held accountable for my actions." Seething anger seeps from my voice.

"Fair enough."

Placing the last plate in the drying rack, I continue, "I have another question if that's okay."

"Ask away." Shenan nods toward the living room and I follow before continuing.

We settle onto the couch, and I resume my questions. "The

loft in the barn: do you mind if I stay with Tova there until we make our vows official? I can transform it into a dwelling if you allow me. I'll build a woodshed near the barn for hay storage, so you won't lose anything. I don't want this to be a long-term situation. Tova took me to the lake on the edge of your property. I wondered if I could purchase a few acres from you on one side and build us a lake house. Eventually, I'd like to have a barn, horses, and a small farm."

She smiles from ear to ear. "Oh, that sounds divine, Pierce. Does she know?"

"No, ma'am, I'd like it to be a surprise." I glance toward the bathroom door.

"Your secret is safe with me." Shenan winks.

The sound of running water in the bathroom subsides, indicating that Tova is done showering. "When she's finished, do you mind if I get cleaned up, too?"

"Not at all. There are towels in the closet, shampoo and soap in the shower. Help yourself."

Tova emerges with fresh clean clothes on and a towel wrapped on top of her head. Standing from my spot on the couch, I stroll in the direction of the bathroom. Giving her a quick kiss as I pass, I say, "I'm going to shower. I'll only be a few minutes."

She pats my backside with an affirming smile, giving me the go-ahead.

21

TOVA

Rushing to mama's side, I plop down on the couch, eager to know if Pierce spilled the beans, "Soooo?"

"Yes, dear?" she laughs.

"Ah, mama staaaaap! Did he tell you or not?"

"Young'un, you know I saw that ring as soon as you came through the door, right?"

Tucking one leg underneath me, I fold my hands and slide

them in between my legs. "I figured as much. Mama, I know it's soon, but…" Before I can finish, mama interrupts me.

"No need to try to convince me. I've known since the first day you came home, yammering on and on about him. I just hoped you'd realize it and not push him away like you have all of your other boyfriends."

"Mama, all those other guys were just guys. I never felt for any of them the way I feel about Pierce."

"I know, love. I can see it in your eyes. That twinkle is coming back. You're smiling more than I've seen you smile your entire life. I'm so glad you've opened yourself up to love."

"It kinda whacked me right in the face. I didn't have an option to open up to it or not. Mama, I was so excited to see the ring that my vision went all weird. I thought I was going crazy."

Slack-jawed and bug-eyed, she leans in closer to me. "Tell me more."

"Well, we'd just jumped off the cliff into the pool below the waterfall. It was around lunchtime, and we worked up an appetite hiking to the falls. So, we were getting ready to eat. When I saw him pull out the promise ring, I guess my emotions got the best of me and made my vision go wild. It was like everything was near-sighted. Pierce, having witnessed the entire spectacle, said my eyes turned cat-like. After I got myself together, my vision went back to normal. I wasn't scared, but it felt bizarre."

"That's some experience. I'm glad you're not afraid of it. I always knew you had something special about you. You have always been drawn to animals, but little did I know how close the connection lay." Chagrined, I frisk over the couch fabric to pick at some nonexistent loose thread as mama drawls, "Learn to channel that gift and never be ashamed of who you are."

"I'll do my best, mama," I assure her quietly.

"That's my girl." She massages my hand. "Now, tell me, when is the vow ceremony going to take place? Have you thought about what you'd like to wear and where you want it to be?"

Sitting up straight, I now fix both legs up underneath me as I turn to face her. "You know me like the back of your hand, don't you? I couldn't stop thinking about it the entire hike home and in the shower," I say with a smile. I place my hand on mama's and continue, "I want to have the ceremony close to the lake, with just a few people. Do you think you can make me a simple off-white lace gown that flows ever so slightly behind me? I don't want anything big or bulky. Also, I want to do it soon, like as soon as you can make the dress."

Mama's eyes sparkle. "Okay, love. If I work non-stop over the next six weeks, I can have it completed for you. That'll be the middle of September and still be warm out. Do you want long sleeves, short sleeves, strapless? And who all do you want to come? If we have it at the lake, then we can just come back here afterward and have refreshments, if you want. I just need to know how much food to prepare."

"I think I want to go with a strapless dress, a heart-shaped neckline, tapered waist flowing out as it goes down to a short train. I'll compile a list of people so we can have a generalized headcount. I know I want it to be relatively small, though. Honestly, I just want it to be a close, intimate setting. Just off the top of my head, I want you, obviously, and Adi, Dani-Jo, Cora, a few of the Protectors, Pierce's family, and that'll be pretty much it. We shouldn't have to prepare too much food then."

Mama beams. "Absolutely, sweetheart. That's a perfect amount of people. We can talk about what foods y'all want when it gets closer to time."

Reaching for my shoulders, she pulls me to her and places a

gentle kiss on my forehead. "I couldn't be happier for you, darlin'."

I hear the creak of the pipes from the bathroom, then the running water subsides. The knob on the door twists, and Pierce stands in the entrance in all his rugged glory. His chest is bare, displaying his chiseled abs. His pants hang low on his hips, dipping to reveal the V carved out of his abdominal muscles causing a faint blush to glow from my cheeks. *Holy cow, he's sexy.*

Trying to keep my mouth from falling wide open, praying that my face isn't red as a beet, I clear my throat. "Ut-um. Do you feel better now that you're all nice and clean?"

"Like a dog with two tails. I have all of my other clothes in the loft. Care if I head over there so I can change out of my dirty ones?" he asks with a broad smile, revealing his pearly whites.

"Sure, I'll go with you. We can bring our dirty things over here tomorrow or another day soon and wash them." Springing up from the couch, I hug mama one more time. Then Pierce and I head over to the barn.

Pierce tangles his fingers with mine as we walk. "What did you and your mom talk about?"

I can't keep from smiling as I answer, "Oh, you know, the ceremony, my dress, where we'd like to have it, who all is invited, and about my wild cat vision escapade."

His lips curl up at the sides. "Well, what did you decide about all of that?"

"I gave mama very detailed descriptions of the dress I want. She said she can have it made in six weeks. I told her I'd love to have the ceremony down by the lake, with just a handful of friends and family. We decided we'd all come back to the house to eat afterward. She didn't freak out about my visions, merely told me to embrace it. God, I love that woman." Startling, I yank his hand, realizing that I had not discussed the timing of it all with him. "Oh God, are you okay with six weeks?"

Laughing, he affirms, "Yeah, she is kinda great. Now I know where you get it from. As for the Vows... absolutely, six weeks sounds perfect."

Beaming with joy, I'm pretty sure I'm crushing his hand from squeezing it so hard. Using his free hand, he slides open the barn doors and we stride inside, locking them behind us.

Ascending the stairs, Pierce struts over to his giant duffel bag. As he bends down to retrieve his sleeping attire, he asks, "Do you mind us going over to my family's house tomorrow? I want to introduce you to them and tell them the wonderful news."

I settle onto one of the comforters, taking in the scene. "Um, not gonna lie, I don't think they'll be as receptive as mama was. I mean, we've only known each other for a few weeks. I've never met them, and we're just going to up and tell them, 'Hey, so, we love each other, and we're exchanging vows in six weeks, you okay with that?' Honestly, I'm not sure they'll even like me."

Dropping his pants and replacing them with shorts, he pads over to me, palming both of my cheeks. "What's not to like? One look at you, and they'll fall in love just like I did."

Unable to reciprocate his joy, I tilt my head down but lift my eyes to his. "They don't know me. They may think this is a horrible idea, that I'm not good enough for you, and change your mind."

Not withdrawing his hands, his eyes pierce mine as he states, "They'll get to know you. They'll never think you're not good enough for me, and they damn sure won't change my mind. Just give them a chance, you'll see."

Breaking his stare, I confess, "Pierce, I...I just don't know. Honestly, if you knew everything about me, even you might think I'm not good enough for you. If you knew everything… I mean everything, you may, in fact, see that I'm right, and realize that you don't love me at all, that you're just in love with the idea of being in love."

"Try me." He sits on the comforter and faces me.

Deciding to say what I need to say before I can chicken out, I close my eyes, take in a deep breath, and bite the bullet. "You know, it's only fair that you know what kind of person you're agreeing to spend the rest of your life with. As painful as it is for me to admit my past, you need to know. If you change your mind and want your ring back, I totally understand."

I peek my eyes open and realize that I have his undivided attention. I push on, refusing to meet his stare, "There's no easy way to say this…so I'm just going to tell you. I'm not sugar-coating it."

I begin to tremble, but I pause, take a deep breath in and close my eyes again because I can't see the rejection I'm preparing myself for. As tears burn in the back of my eyes, I continue, "I'm going to tell you, but I'm afraid my emotions will get the better of me and show my weakness, so please bear with me."

My eyes are still closed tight as tears begin to trickle down my cheeks. Taking another deep breath, I grip my hands in my lap until my knuckles blanch white. I let the past rear its ugly head as I tell Pierce through a shaky voice, "As a child I was viciously abused for many years, physically and sexually, by my father, Cladec." My voice begins to crack but I don't stop talking, "Used and abused, that's what I am. No matter how many showers I take, I can never be clean enough. No matter how many tears I cry, I can never take back what was done to me. No matter how many sleepless nights I fight off, how many demons taunt me at night, or skeletons I bury deep in my closet, nothing will ever undo or change the fact that I'm trash, filthy, and not worthy of you."

Waiting for him to say or do anything, my trembling becomes violent shaking, and tears pour as I sob, covering my face with both hands. I can't look at him. I won't. I can't handle it when he walks away. I take my shaking right fingers to my left hand, feeling for my left ring finger about to slip off the ring when I'm suddenly engulfed in the warmest, tightest embrace. I still can't pry my eyes open. Not yet. I need to know this touch is real.

22

PIERCE

I can't stop myself. I immediately scoop Tova into my lap, careful not to singe her as my palms are searing right now from my raging anger. "Baby, open your eyes. Look at me."

Struggling to make a sound, she rasps, "Pierce. I can't."

"Babe, first of all, you are *not* trash. The furthest thing from it." Taking the pad of my thumb, I stroke her face, wiping away tears from her wet cheek. "And this... these tears... They're not your weakness. They show how strong you are and how strong you've had to be. One day, when you look back, you'll know you have been tough enough to overcome what's been done to you and mark my word, you'll fight off those demons that torment you every night."

Looking up at me with tears filling her already swollen eyes, she asks, "But why? Why would you love me?"

I tighten my grip, pulling her more snugly into my embrace and reaffirm, "I'm not going anywhere. What that piece of shit did you has no reflection on you, your worth, or how I feel about you. I love you for who you are, your kind spirit, your witty ways, your love and devotion to your family and friends, and mostly for how you love me."

Taking my index finger, I graze her trembling bottom lip. "I know that must have been the most difficult conversation you've ever had. I promise you this; if the opportunity presents itself, I'll make sure he pays for what he did to you. Mark my words, come hell or high water, that man *will* pay."

Her sobbing finally ceases, and the violent shaking has now eased to a mild quiver. With a hoarse voice, she admits, "He's banished now. For all I know, he could be dead. Please don't go looking for him on my account. I've made it this far in life; I'll keep trudging on. I just need you to be honest with yourself and me. Can you seriously be with me now, knowing my entire past? Don't feel like you owe me. Don't do me any favors. Don't feel sorry for me. But, be completely honest with me, please? I beg you. I'll be fine. Tell me now so I can start to get over you, if that's even possible."

"Damn it, babe. I said I'm not leaving. When I said I want you forever, I meant every damn word. Stop thinking you're less than anything. You're everything I could ever want. You're compassionate, kind-hearted, considerate, humble, caring, determined, stubborn, and a spitfire full of sass. I can't think of a better companion for me." I pepper her face with soft kisses as I speak, trying everything I know how to make her hear and understand me. To believe me.

Tova glances at me through blood-shot swollen eyes, wiping her nose with her shirt and sniffling. "All of those things may be true, but there are a lot of drawbacks making me a lot to handle. I'm fluent in sarcasm. I tend to shut down, and harbor hurt feelings, not wanting to discuss them. Mama always says if life hands you lemons, just mix them in your tea. I'll have to work on that because I'm far from perfect. But if you're sure that you still want me, then I'm yours forever."

Grinning mischievously at her, I try to lighten the situation. "Considering you hate tea, I'd suggest when life hands you lemons… throw them at people." Pressing my lips to her wet, puffy lips, stroking her back, I continue, "I'm so grateful you haven't pushed me away and out of your life. I hate that you went through hell growing up. But I swear I'll make sure the rest of your life is anything but anguish, suffering, torment or torture."

"Thank you, mama seems to think I suffer from pistan-throphobia."

"Um… piss ant, what?" I ask, holding back a startled chuckle at the strange word.

Managing a small laugh, she corrects, "No, not piss ant silly, pistanthrophobia. The fear of being in a romantic relationship because of past trauma. It can also be an overwhelming fear of trusting others, thinking that eventually, betrayal will surface."

"Babe, you may, in fact, have a bit of piss-ant whatever, but I'll spend the rest of my life proving to you that not every male is a douche," I assure her with a smile.

Resting her scared face on my chest, she breathes, "You're my peace, you know that?"

I give her a tight squeeze, yawning. "Glad to hear it. We've had an exhausting night; want to get some shut-eye?"

Shuffling around to get under the covers, she mutters, "That sounds fantastic. I love you, Pierce, good night."

I kiss her tenderly, then whisper, "I love you more than you'll ever know."

Damn, waking up to her tight ass pressed into my crotch every morning for the next six weeks is going to be atrocious, but I'm not going there until we seal our vows. I have self-control, but her being so eager, not to mention how attractive she is, will make restraint much more difficult. I pray to God when I tell her my intentions; she doesn't see it as rejection. I know in my gut that it's the honorable thing to do.

Holding her closely, in the same position we drifted off to sleep in, I'm careful not to wake her as I turn my head, taking in the surrounding loft. Taking stock, I plan out how to make this a living space while building the lake house. I may ask the boys for help with the house because this space is small and smells ripe at the best of times. I don't know that I want to cook or even eat a meal here in the heat of a hot July day. If those stalls have shit in them, then that's all I'll be picturing as I'm eating. The simmering heat sends the asinine aroma to an entirely new realm of putrid. Okay, I have to stop thinking about that; I can feel the bile rising in my throat.

Tova stirs against me, and I massage her shoulders, pulling a soft moan from her sleepy lips. For the love of God, those moans have me hard in an instant. I shift my hips away from her as I roll to a sitting position.

I tug her feet. "Morning, lovely."

Stretching her arms out and every which way, she yawns, one soft hand flying to her mouth to stifle it. "Morning."

"You ready to get this day started?" I shake her leg.

Raising onto her elbows, she bellyaches, "Um, no, Mr. Over-eager, not really, but I guess I'll comply just for you."

"Well, it's a good little trek. You're on the southernmost side of the territory, and my folks live on the far east end. Want to tack up some horses or just walk?"

Raising to a sitting position, she grins. "I'll use any reason to take my horses on an outing."

"That's what I thought you'd say. After breakfast, we'll tack up and head out. Sound like a plan?" I clap my hands together with a smile.

Tossing the covers aside, she hisses, "Whatever you say, babe."

I swoop over to kiss her soft lips. "Awe, did you just call me babe?"

"Staaap, you do it all the time." Grunting, she elbows me in the chest.

I kiss the top of her head, pulling her in closer to me. "Yeah, but this is the first time you've crossed that proverbial boundary and said it back."

"Get used to it because, with you, there's going to be a lot of 'firsts.'" Tova nuzzles my neck.

Swallowing hard, I breathe heavily. "Yea, about that..."

Lifting her head and quirking an eyebrow upward, she eyes me skeptically. "Um, what do you mean, 'Yea, about that?'"

"I want to have a serious conversation with you without you thinking the worst or getting mad at me. I want you to know that I've been thinking about this for a few days, way before I knew everything you told me last night." I loosen my grip.

Backing out of my embrace, she tilts her head to one side.

"Okay, you're starting to scare me. So, I'm really going to over-think this now."

I scooch up closer to her, wrapping my arms around her middle. "Have you ever wanted something so bad you can taste it, and the thought of you actually devouring it makes your entire body shudder?"

Seeming despondent, she shrugs her shoulders. "Um, I guess. What's this about?"

She meets my gaze, and I thumb her bottom lip. "It's about you and me. Being together...two becoming one."

"What about that?"

Breathing audibly and brushing her baby-soft cheek, I run my nose against hers and say, "You know I want you. I've wanted to consume you, to devour every cell of your being, and bind our souls so completely they can never be separated."

Closing her eyes, she presses her forehead into mine. "Uh-huh, and you keep saying 'when the time is right,' so...?"

"I want to wait until the night of our vows. Will you do that for me?"

Snapping her eyes open, Tova's face abruptly recedes from mine, going from soft to peeved, her eyebrows pull together. "Are you kidding me?"

Great! Just great! She thinks I'm rejecting her; I knew this would happen. "Ahh, is that a rhetorical question?"

Seething, she snaps, "No, are you freaking kidding me?"

"Um, no, I'm serious as a heart attack." I won't back down from my decision.

"You honestly think I would be mad at you for wanting to wait?" she bites cantankerously. Her entire demeanor changes from hard to soft with a sigh, "I admire that about you. All the other guys I went out with couldn't wait to get into my pants; I never let them. You'll definitely be my first. But my God, I would never think any less of you for wanting to wait. Yes, I'm incredibly attracted to you. It's going to take tons of self-control. Still, I want our first time to be the most exquisite intimate experience possible, and what better way for that to happen than on the night of our ceremony."

I exhale in relief and collapse onto my back. "Thank God that piss-ant crap didn't rear its ugly head. I was terrified of how you'd react."

Belly laughing until tears roll down her face, Tova says, "Bwahahahaha. You crack me up." She stands, whacking me on the stomach. "Let's go eat breakfast with mama."

Grasping at my chest, I smile after her, "You know a way to a man's heart is through his stomach. I'm right behind you."

23

TOVA

Trekking over the trail to the east side of Iron Mountain, me on Lightning, Pierce on Sundance, my mind wanders to the worst possible thoughts. What if his family detests me? Will they ever think anyone is good enough for Pierce? Holy crap, what if they find out what Cladec did to me?

Will they go off the deep end when they find out my eyes freaking turn into cat eyes? What will they think of my scarred face and back?

Getting myself worked up, I reflexively grip the reins until my knuckles turn white. *Oh my lord, I'm about to have an anxiety attack.* Breathing rapidly, the sound of blood rushes to my ears and my vision tunnels.

Crap! Crap! CRAP! This cannot be happening right now.

"Tova, babe, you okay?" Pierce asks, quickly recognizing my current predicament. I force myself to glance in his direction for a brief second, then back to the path in front of me. "Breathe, baby, just breathe. Right now, I want you to challenge your thoughts. Don't be afraid of what you're seeing. Nod if you hear me."

It's hard to focus on what he's saying and what I'm looking at. Heaven knows I don't want to fall off Lightning and reinjure my shoulder or break a bone. So, instead of looking at him, I bob my head up and down.

In a soft voice, I hear, "Babe, can you tell me what you see?"

Loosening the grip on my reins, I utter, "Looking at Lightning's mane is like seeing an assemblage of a billion straws of hay."

Hearing Pierce's horse clomp beside me, he replies, "That's impressive. Now what about the path, what can you make out of it?"

"I can see the individual specks of dust right in front of us. I'm pretty sure if I wanted to jump off Lightning's back, I could calculate the distance from his saddle to the ground and land perfectly. And that says a lot coming from my clumsy self."

"Tova, let's try it. Let's see if your vision can assist with your landing. You up for it?" he challenges.

"Um, I guess." Pulling Lightning to a stop, I slowly let go of the reins and toddle up to a crouch in the saddle.

"Now focus on your target where you want to land. Be sure to bend your knees so you won't jolt your spine or hurt your newly healed wounds."

"Got it. I see where I want to land. There are two oak leaves side by side about a foot ahead of Lightning's nose. Oh, and a pair of bluebirds are feeding their babies in the tree to our left, on the ninth branch from the ground, just in case you're curious." I hold my arms out, lifting them from my side and level with my shoulders, then I balance and count myself down.

I leap, not moving my gaze from my anticipated destination. Sticking a perfect landing, I squeal, "I did it!"

Pierce dismounts from Sundance and rushes to my side, kissing me promptly. "Yes! You did it, babe. I knew you could."

Gazing up at him, smiling, I let myself take in the sight for a moment longer. His eyes are impenetrably dark. I usually can't tell where his iris ends, and the color starts, but now I can see a sleek line defining the two. Every strand of his eyebrows is twisted in an elegant cluster, forming the perfect arch.

Startling me out of my trance, he asks, "Amused by what you see?"

"Very much so." A smirk tugs at the corner of my mouth.

Peirce palms my cheek with his immense temperate grasp. "Do you think you can focus on changing your vision back? Or are you going to go the unconventional route and slap yourself silly again?"

"Ha, ha. I'll try to focus and see if I can manage to do it without self-inflicted pain this time."

Closing my eyes, I inhale for a count of three and exhale for another three, attempting to think the most pleasant thoughts possible. I envision Pierce's lips, the gentle way he touches my face, the way he looks at me when he says he loves me...

Just like that, I feel a shift in my eyes, and when I open them, everything is as it was before.

Clapping, Pierce congratulates, "Way to go, babe! You never cease to amaze me. So how did you do it?"

"I just went to my happy place."

"And where, may I ask, is that?" he probes as we make our way back to the horses, hand in hand.

"My happy place is anywhere when I'm with you. You help me find hidden serenity. I just thought of the way you look when you tell me you love me and how it feels when you kiss me." I beam.

Aggravating me, he nuzzles the top of my head, teasing my hair in all different directions. "That's fantastic. To know that my love for you helps you so much it can be your touchstone."

"Well, you may be my peace, but you're also the source of my anxiety," I grumble, slapping his hand away. "So, I wouldn't gloat too much about it."

With a laugh, we straddle our horses and trudge on toward Pierce's family's house.

An hour into our trip our horses start to become restless and goosebumps pepper my skin. I try to coax Lightning down and Pierce does the same to Sundance but they aren't having it. I look to Pierce to see what he suggests, when we both hear the crunching of leaves behind some trees a few feet away.

Pierce glances at me and yells, "Babe let's get out of here." Then we grab the reins and both shout, "Ya!" to get the horses cantering as fast as their hooves will go.

Once we make it to a safe distance past the presumed danger, we slow the horses down to a trot.

Pierce is on edge and says, "Babe, I'm not super convinced you don't have a target on your back."

I try not to let my fear show as I respond, "Well, let's just say I'm glad you've been by my side each time something suspicious happens."

"Yeah, but we need to find out if you really do have a stalker or if someone's out to hurt you."

"Pierce, I'm sure it's nothing. Let's just focus on me meeting your parents. Ok?"

"I'm not sure I'll be able to keep from thinking about this."

"Well, for tonight will you try? I'm nervous enough as it is."

"Alright, Spitfire. You've got it. I'll do my best."

"Thanks, love, that's all I ask."

Another hour into our excursion, I whirl around to my right and see a meadow filled, bursting with the brightest, tallest sunflowers I have ever seen. Gasping, I point in the meadow's direction. Pierce, trotting close to me, leans over, "Sunflowers are mom's favorite. She made dad promise to dedicate a field to them."

"This is your property?" I ask in shock.

Pierce clarifies, "It's my parents. They farm several crops, have land for livestock, and of course, flowers."

"Oh, Pierce, I can't wait to see it all!" I exclaim, unable to contain my excitement.

"You'll love it." One side of his lips curls up in a sweet smile.

"Once I get over the shock of meeting your parents, I'm sure I will. Right now, I just need to keep my nerves in check because the last thing I want to do is frighten your family as soon as they meet me. First impressions are everything; there's no going back, no do-overs. I'd better win them over right away, or I'll throw up and never be able to show my face here again."

"Tova, you have to get out of your head. First of all, they're big ol' lovey-dovey huggers who only see the good in people. Second, there's absolutely nothing they won't love about you. Trust me. They're going to love you just as much as I do. You think I fall in love fast? Well, I've got nothing on Mom. She falls in love in the blink of an eye. Just you wait."

"I pray you're right, Pierce. I couldn't live with myself if they don't think I'm the right choice for you."

We trot past the field of sunflowers and finally arrive at the intricately designed wrought-iron gate guarding the piece of the property where the house sits. The entrance is a massive work of art, featuring an intricate pattern of vines and leaves intertwining through the entire facade.

Descending from our horses, we walk them through the gate and onto Pierce's parent's property. Following the wide path, we take the horses to a pasture that's the perfect size to contain the two. There's a water trough for them to rehydrate and plentiful lush green grass for them to graze on. Releasing them into the paddock, we lock the fence behind us.

I wring my fingers as we walk, trying to soothe my nerves. Pierce must take notice of my anxious movements because he sweeps me up against his side, settling his arm across my shoulders. "Spitfire, no need to be nervous."

"Not everyone has nerves of steel like you, Pierce," I snip.

"Ha, I don't have nerves of steel. I have confidence in who I am; there's a difference," he says with a smug yet reassuring grin.

I crook my head into his neck. "Yeah... well... I don't have that confidence, okay?"

Wandering toward the steps of his parent's house, I admire the charming and welcoming ranch house. A large porch extends to two sides of the home, forming an "L" shape and providing generous amounts of space to entertain guests when the weather is favorable.

"I see no reason for you not to have all the confidence in the world," Pierce preaches.

As we reach the bottom step of the porch, the front door swings open, revealing the most stunning woman, with long blonde hair stopping mid-back and sparkling crystal blue eyes standing in the doorway. She has a strong yet warm ambiance radiating from her smile. "Pierce. I didn't know you were coming over today, and with company!" The woman all but squeals with delight. Not wanting our first encounter to be more dramatic than it needs to be, I cram my left hand into my pants pocket.

"Mom, this is Tova." Pierce presses a quick, indulgent kiss to my temple before continuing his introduction. "We met at the track a couple of months ago in training."

The woman rushes from the doorway and down the steps, sweeping the both of us into a warm hug. I'm forced to retrieve my hand to reciprocate the startling affection. At first, my body is stiff; she catches me entirely off guard, but I quickly melt into her embrace. Her hug is warm and tight and real, a genuine display of a mother's love.

"Ah! Welcome, Tova! I'm Brecklyn, Pierce's mom. It's so pleasant to meet you!" she gushes.

Brecklyn lets the two of us go only long enough to hook her arm through mine and drag me up the stairs, leaving Pierce to follow behind. "Y'all come in, and I'll pour you a glass of tea," she insists as we enter the house.

Pierce glances at me sideways, ensuring the overwhelming gesture of affection hasn't rattled me and, knowing him, to see if he needs to mention my disdain for tea. I smile and shake my head, silently pleading with him to not let the cat out of the bag. Thankfully, he keeps it to himself.

Crossing the threshold, I take in the living room with a view that flows directly to a back porch with floor to ceiling windows displaying a stunning view of a grove of large pecan trees. I notice that one tree has a rope swing hanging from its branches.

I'm definitely swinging from that!

Pierce, whose arm has once again settled around my shoulders, tugs me gently toward the kitchen to the left. We sit at a large farm table with benches on both sides and large dining chairs at each end. His mom bustles to the fridge and fetches a glass pitcher full of tea. Placing glasses on the table, she pours, "So, Tova. What makes you want to be a Protector?"

Trying to remain calm and not let my nerves show, I softly reply, "Mrs. Stetson, I believe it's essential to know how to protect yourself and others. Especially those who can't protect themselves."

She gives me a genuine smile. "That's very noble, Tova, and please call me Brecklyn."

"Yes, ma'am."

"Where's Dad and Kage?" Pierce asks, thankfully taking some attention off me.

"Oh, they're rustling up some food for dinner tonight, quail hunting. They'll be back in a couple of hours. When they get back, they'll have to dress the birds, and we can prepare the veggies. In the meantime, we can catch up on the back porch."

We head to the massive oak backdoor that's already propped open, then out the solid glass storm door that lets in fresh air and light. Glancing to either side of the porch, I notice several groupings of rocking chairs, and we make our way to the ones closest to the backdoor.

Brecklyn's rocking chair creaks on the hardwood as she sways gently back and forth. After a long moment of uncomfortable silence, she looks over at me and urges, "So, tell me a little about yourself, Tova."

My heart rate picks up, and I keep my folded hands tucked between my knees as I answer, "Uh...what would you like to know?" I'm so incredibly nervous I can't even think of a single thing to tell her.

Sensing my uneasiness, she taps her finger on the arm of her rocker, her face and eyes softening in thought. "Hm, let's see... I guess we can start with, what part of Iron Mountain did you grow up in? I mean, if you're alright with discussing that."

I stammer, "Oh um...please forgive me, my nerves some-times get the best of me," I explain, blushing. "I...grew up in the southernmost part of the territory on a farm with my mom. She's a seamstress. Her name is Shenandoah. The farm is much like yours with crops and livestock; we just don't have any land dedicated to beautiful flowers like y'all."

"Yes, flowers are my passion. It brings me a sense of joy to take in their beauty while watching the butterflies flutter about taking in their meal. Not to mention the fragrance they bring to the house. They bring an overwhelming aroma that undu-lates your senses. It's pure nirvana."

"Sounds like heaven," I speculate.

"Oh, it is," she affirms. "One day, you and I can meander through the meadow, and you can experience it yourself."

"I'd love that!" I reply with a smile. We rock for a couple of minutes in silence, taking in the view of the large pecan trees. There's so much I want to know, like how old those trees are. Who hung the swing? Finally, I muster the courage to ask, "How old are those pecan trees?"

She stops her rocking and leans forward, appearing to assess the trees before responding. "I'd say at least one-hundred-fifty to two-hundred years old, maybe older. They were here and fully developed when my great-great-great-grandfather started farming this land. If you're wondering, no, the Dust hasn't altered the pecans."

"It's incredible these trees are so old! And yes, my next question was the Dust. So, I'm guessing you're able to eat them just fine?"

Brecklyn leans back in her rocker. "Just you wait and see. They make the best pecan pies you've ever tasted. We'll make one this evening."

"That'd be wonderful." I lick my lips in anticipation of the treat. But I still don't have the backstory on that swing. "So, what brave soul hung the swing?"

Cackling, she gestures toward Pierce. "That may be a better story for Pierce to tell."

Twisting my attention in his direction, he chuckles as well. "That damn swing was bound and determined to be the death of me. I had wanted a swing for my birthday when I was four or five years old. Dad saw that the wooden seat was strong, the ropes were thick, and none of it would break down from the weather. Once we threaded the rope through the seat, we tied strong knots to lock the seat in place. Those ends have frayed over the years, but I swear it'll still hold a horse. The tricky part was getting the top of the swing tied to that branch," he explains, pointing to a large limb about forty feet off of the ground.

"I was a daredevil, and because I wanted the swing so badly, I begged dad to let me climb it. I hauled ass up the tree with the rope barely fitting between my teeth. Once I got to the limb, I shimmied to the branch's edge and tied the rope. When I got to the spot where I would tie the second rope, the branch swayed, and I almost lost my balance. Dad yelled, 'Son, I've got you if you fall.' I dropped the damn rope out of my mouth in fear as I screamed, 'Promise?' He declared, 'Promise!' I swear I dropped that rope at least five times before I finally tied the knot. Dad, with his unlimited patience, didn't stop me. He simply let me press on, knowing my determination would override any fatigue or fear."

Reflecting a brief second, I pause, then continue, "After a few hours, the damn thing was finally hanging and secure. I was so tired that when I climbed back to the ground, I crumpled in exhaustion. I didn't even think I'd be able to enjoy the swing that day, but Dad insisted. Crawling over to it, I heaved one side of myself up while Dad scooped me up under my arms and positioned me on the seat. I sat there, gripping the ropes while he pushed, swaying me until I almost dozed off. Once my head started bobbling, he knew it was time to stop. He carried me inside while my droopy head rested on his shoulder. I'll tell you one thing, that's a birthday gift I'll never forget."

I'm so engrossed in Pierce's story that when he gets to the part where he almost fell, I don't realize what I'm doing as I grip my knees until my knuckles blanch white. Brecklyn reaches over with her right hand and pats my left, calming my anxieties. I don't think about the promise ring until Pierce finishes his story. I realize then where Brecklyn's hand is resting, and my mind immediately starts racing.

Fartknocker, I think I'm going to die right here and now.

I attempt to curl my left hand into a ball, but when I lift it slightly from my leg, Brecklyn cups it with hers, enfolding it in a delicate grasp. I'm not sure if all the blood has left my face or if it's flushed, but the sound of rushing blood is overpowering my hearing, and my vision is going fuzzy.

No! No! NO! Not now, please, not now. We haven't even had the betrothal conversation yet. I can't handle adding the 'sight' conversation on top of it!

Taking a few deep breaths, I focus on halting the transformation before the 'sight' can take hold. Opening my eyes, I find

Pierce kneeling at my feet. I don't think he noticed my near slip because his face is serene as he reaches out, grasping my hand still held in his mom's.

Stroking his thumb across our hands, Pierce says, "Mom, I'm sure you already know, you've always had an intuition about these things, but I am madly in love with Tova. There's no doubt that she's the one for me. I instantly gravitated to her the first time I saw her. I realized I would do anything for her when she was injured at the track by a rogue arrow that could have killed her. I stayed at the clinic while she was being treated, and I even sewed up her forehead and back. Feelings were swirling inside the entire time I worked on her, mixed up topsy-turvy churns and giddy flips in my stomach, then ones of nausea. It didn't take me long to recognize those were emotions of love, I vowed to myself to protect Tova and make her mine. If it were up to me, we'd already be united. We've decided to have a ceremony at her house by a lake with just close family and friends. I'm going to ask Dad if he'll do the honors of performing the service."

Well, I guess just laying it all out like that is one way of breaking the news, ripping the bandage off fast as it were.

Tears well up in Brecklyn's eyes. "I can see that you love her, dear. You've never brought a girl home to introduce to us. I recognized as soon as I saw you two approaching the porch that she's the one for you." She looks over to me, then back to Pierce. "You were admiring her the entire time you two were walking up the path. The way you were holding her so protectively and the sparkle in your eyes when I came out to meet you told me everything I needed to know. I couldn't be happier for you, son, and you, Tova."

Rising from her rocking chair, Brecklyn opens her arms for us both. We move into her embrace, and I begin to tremble from all the love and acceptance I wasn't prepared to receive.

Stepping back out of the hug, and placing her palms on my shoulders, she asks, "Oh dear, are you getting chilly?"

"No, ma'am. I'm just overjoyed that you'd embrace me and welcome me into your family so warmly," I explain. Pierce places one hand on my lower back, his touch easing my shivering.

"I'm a pretty excellent judge of character, Tova. Nevertheless, I can sense your unease. Now and then, you have to forget your fears and understand you deserve the best. There's no uncertainty in my mind that you two are perfect for each other. Pierce's father, Elon, and Kage will see it too, so please don't fret," Brecklyn soothes.

Still unsure if she's correct about Kage and Elon, I glimpse at her soft, forgiving eyes. "Thank you, Brecklyn, for being so kind, and I promise, I'll try my best."

Reaching for the door, she suggests, "It's getting close to when they should be back. Want to head inside and get things started in the kitchen?"

Pierce and I nod yes, and he states, "We'd love to."

Brecklyn leads the way inside with us close behind, Pierce escorting me with a hand at the small of my back.

24

PIERCE

The three of us made quick work of preparing dinner and are now setting the table for the meal. Dad and Kage finally got home and are just finishing getting cleaned up after cleaning the fowl for dinner.

"Tova, you sure know your way around the kitchen." Mom raves as she sets out the glasses.

"Mama and I do this before each meal. It's one of our favorite past times. The more beautiful the table setting, the better," Tova explains with a bright smile.

"Oh, I bet she and I will get along just fine. I love my old china set; it's been in the family for centuries. When we have her over, we'll break it out and use it then. Well, not literally break it." Mama laughs, waving her hand as if to dismiss her silly pun. "Oh, you know what I mean."

"She would be delighted to meet all of you!" Tova says as she folds each linen napkin and places them beside each plate. "Actually, we should plan a get together before the ceremony. Mama said she'd have my dress done in about six weeks."

"Darlin', let's make it a habit of having Sunday brunch or dinner all together. You and Pierce, your mama, and our family," Mom declares, following after Tova setting out the silverware.

"I'm sure she'd like that very much. Thank you for being so inviting." Tova beams, placing the last napkin.

"Sweetheart, please, stop thanking me. It's what family does." Mom shuffles to Tova and presses a kiss to her forehead.

Smiling at their exchange, I head to the refrigerator, grab the pitcher of tea, and bring it back out to the table. I catch Tova eyeing the pitcher and give her a wink as I cross behind her.

"Where are you sitting? I'll fill your glass with water," I whisper as I pass.

Looking over the table, she whispers back, "Umm, beside you. So, wherever you're sitting, just fill the one next to it."

"What are you two whispering about?" Kage asks, appearing in the entry between the kitchen and living room with a teasing smirk.

Tova jumps, and I snap, "We're discussing where we're going to sit if that's okay with you, you nosey asshole."

"Oh, well, if that's all it is, let's get to sittin' and eatin'," he laughs, walking towards the table and pounds me on the shoulder as he passes.

Dad comes in shortly after Kage, and we each take our seats at the table. Having already introduced Dad when they got back with their catch, we all sit down, Mom and Dad at each end, Tova and I on one bench, and Kage on the other directly across from me. We pass the food around, filling our plates, and devour the delicious meal. While we're eating, we enjoy small talk about Dad and Kage's hunt and our journey here on the horses. We still haven't mentioned anything about mine and Tova's plans or her sight transformation, but we're getting to that. I figured everyone having food in their bellies first would ease the news.

"Well, Dad, Kage. I have some exciting news to share with y'all," I say as everyone gets close to finishing their meal.

Dad pushes his back into his chair, ready to listen, as Kage leans in and places his elbows on the table. Oh no, that's not intimidating, not at all, but I don't care. I'm not changing my mind whether he likes it or not.

Tova reaches for my hand underneath the table, weaving our fingers together and holding on tightly, a clear sign her anxiety is through the roof at the moment. Attempting to soothe her, I rub my thumb across the back of her hand softly as I speak.

"I'll get straight to the point. Tova and I have grown very close over these past few weeks. It's easy to see we're attracted to each other, but it's much more than that. We can't deny our connection and love for each other. I've asked Tova if she'll be mine. I choose her. There's no one else for me."

"And I choose him. There's no one else for me either," Tova utters, barely audible, as she looks adoringly up at me.

175

Dad exhales and clasps his hands together as he leans forward with a wide grin. "Son, I'm thrilled for you two."

"Thanks, Dad. I was actually wondering if you'd perform the ceremony?" I turn to look his way.

"I wouldn't have it any other way," Dad responds, his eyes gleaming with delight and pride.

Mom is the first to move, jumping from her seat and dragging Tova and me in a warm hug with Dad and Kage following quickly after offering congratulations. Even Kage admits to me he's happy for us. With another round of hugs, Mom ushers all of us into the living room. As we settle comfortably in the living room, Mom, oh so casually, mentions the sun is sinking much too close to the horizon for us to make it safely back to Tova's farm before dark. She insists we stay the night with them, assuring we'll have plenty of time to return Shenan's horses after our regular training in the morning.

Knowing there is no use in arguing with her, Tova and I settle on the loveseat with her tucked close against me and my arm around her waist. Mom and Dad sit side by side on the couch across from us while Kage wanders to the glass door, staring out of it deep in thought for a moment.

After a minute or two, he turns to observe us; then he motions towards our spot and summons, "Tova, would you mind if I speak with you a moment?"

Gripping her side, I stare him down and lean over to tell her, "You don't have to."

She dismisses me. "It'll be fine," she assures me and turns to face him. "I don't mind at all, Kage."

She stands and walks out the back door, Kage close on her heels as they exit. It's easy to see them through the glass door, but I don't like that I can't hear what they're discussing. My palms start to steam reflexively.

Mom and Dad seem to think it'll be alright because Dad

chuckles as he chides, "Pierce! Kage isn't going to steal your girl. Calm down."

Jerking my head toward Dad, I snap, "What the hell, Dad? I wasn't even thinking that! I don't want him to say anything to make Tova feel uncomfortable or try to drive her away, is all."

"Why would you think he'd do that?" Dad asks, clearly skeptical of my concern.

I shove my fingers into tousling my hair and lean forward in my seat, holding my forehead in my palms. "Well, he's been tough on her at training, even opened her wound back up by shooting her with rubber bullets in the arena. He knew damn well she was just barely healed from a stray arrow that shot her shoulder, slicing her back while we were at the track." Frustration edges my voice.

Dad rubs the scruff on his chin in thought before he responds, "Hmmm, I see. I think he's taken special consideration in trying to train her right. He probably sees that she'll make a fantastic Superior Protector one day and wants to get her ready for that. Plus, he'll make sure she's more than ready for when y'all go on your first hunt this fall."

Gesturing toward the porch, I notice my hands are all but glowing from my intense emotions as I say, "I told Tova the same thing. That he sees potential in her, but Dad, I was so pissed when I saw the blood seeping from her wound he reopened. I would have pounded Kage if I could have gotten my hands on him."

Leaning back into the couch, Dad affirms, "Son, that's just the Protector coming out of you. You're doing a fine job guarding and being a good man to her. I'm not sure what her story is, but she's lucky to have you."

Mimicking his position, I relax back into the loveseat, but my hands are still smoldering. "Thanks, Dad. I reckon I just need to simmer down."

"Just take some deep breaths, like I showed you when you first found your gift, and you'll calm down quickly," Dad advises.

"Yes, sir."

I get up to go back into the kitchen, needing a distraction because seeing them without hearing them is about to drive me crazy.

"I'm getting more pecan pie. Do y'all want any?"

Mom and Dad say they're good and don't want any, so I go ahead and bounce toward the delicious goodness that awaits me.

25

TOVA

S itting down in a rocker beside Kage, he turns to face me; I still have a clear view back inside the house as I angle to face him. I try to focus on Kage, but it's apparent, even at this distance, that Pierce is visibly upset. Redirecting my attention to Kage, I declare, "This conversation had better start with an apology."

Grinning from ear to ear, Kage asks, "Now, what would I go and do that for?"

"Oh, I don't know...for being an asshole!" I glare back at him.

"I'm the nicest asshole you'll ever meet," Kage laughs with a cocky grin.

"Okay, asshole, why do you hate me so much?" I cross my arms in defiance of his attitude.

Looking baffled, Kage chuckles, "What on God's green earth makes you think I hate you?"

"Are you kidding me right now, Kage? Are you freaking kidding me?" I ask incredulously, scrunching my eyebrows together.

"Seriously, why do you think that?"

I release my folded arms and gesture with both arms flailing. I all but shout, "Because! I'm busting my butt during training, and you make it your mission to see that I fail!"

Kage attempts to cover a smirk with his hand, "Ha, I'm not seeing to it that you fail. Not at all. I'm sorry I ruptured your shoulder back open. I truly am. But you need to know that you're one of the strongest, most stealthy students I have. You move so fast and so quiet that it's like you've already perfected the 'step of the cat' or 'pas de chat' that I teach the Protectors, and some guys can take years, if ever, to get it."

I laugh a little on the inside. If he only knew why I'd seemed to have mastered this "step of the cat" maneuver, he'd probably laugh too. Snapping out of my train of thought I continue to listen.

"You're difficult to track, that's for sure. You keep me on my toes, but that's not why I'm hard on you. I'm pushing you and teaching you what you can expect from outside that stone wall. One day I see you taking over as the Superior Protector for the women's training. I'm confident that you'll be ready for that by the time you graduate. One thing that you need to work on the most is not leaving your group. That's when you're most vulnerable. I need you to listen to your surroundings and not stay focused on just taking out training targets. Listen for others approaching you, trying to find you and take you out. Once you get that, you'll be unstoppable. I hope you're healed enough to join us tomorrow. But none of this is why I wanted to talk with you."

Now I'm the baffled one. "Uh, okay. What is it?"

Kage's soft smile turns into a stern stare in a matter of seconds. "I see the way Pierce looks at you. He'd give his life for you, in a second. I don't know if you know this or not, but Pierce is loyal to the core. When we were younger, I fell out of the barn's rafters, and he wouldn't leave my side. I was injured pretty bad, but he saw to it that I was mended the best he could manage and then hobbled me back up to the house so Mama could take me to the clinic." Kage pauses to ensure I'm fully attentive then resumes, "He's labored away on this farm his entire life. He's a damn hard worker. He's proud of where he comes from and stands up for what he believes. He's like Mom and wears his heart on his sleeve, but most importantly, he's the best damn brother anyone could hope for. All I ask is that you don't break his heart."

I go to interrupt him, "Kage..."

But before I can finish, he continues, "I don't know you all that well, only what I've observed over the past year of you pulverizing the pavement at the track. You've always been in your head, ignoring every other guy that has approached you out there, but for some reason, you've taken kindly to Pierce."

Hesitatingly, he stammers, "I... I have already mangled his body with scars that will forever be my reminder. I can't undo that. So, if there's anything I can do, I will. I'll do my dead level best to make sure he doesn't get hurt unnecessarily ever again. He deserves love. Please, Tova, for the love of God, promise me you won't crush his heart."

Trying to calm him down, I place a hand on his shoulder. "Okay, Kage, now it's my turn. I appreciate your concern for Pierce. But let me be the first to tell you, I never intend on crushing Pierce's heart. I want to protect it with every fiber of my being. I never in a million years thought I'd have what I have with him, and I don't intend to let it go. He's one of the good ones. He thinks with his heart, not with his head. I also asked him about all the scars on his arms, and he told me what happened. It's not your fault the Dust has changed you. And, while you may see mangled scars on Pierce's body, I see beauty. Those scars mean that he's lived life and has something to show for it." I remove my hand and carry on. "Pierce is a wonderful man. I'm so glad you see that he deserves love, and I can't believe I'm saying this, but doesn't everyone?"

Looking down at the well-honed wooden planks creaking beneath our rockers, Kage admits, "I'd like to think everyone deserves love, but I just don't know."

Seeing the hurt in his eyes, I stretch out and set my hand on his knee with a gentle pat. "Kage, you have to forgive yourself. You never meant for Pierce to get hurt. I know that, you know that, and he knows that. Don't miss out on the opportunity to love and be loved if it comes to you because you're afraid of accidentally hurting them."

Clearing his voice, Pierce squeaks the outside door open just to a crack and asks, "Everything okay out here?"

I push off of Kage's knee to stand and glace down at him.

"Kage, everything's going to be alright. And thanks for the bode of confidence," I smirk, then I stroll over to Pierce.

Walking inside, Pierce loops his arm around my back. "Y'all were out there long enough. What in Sam Hell did y'all talk about for so long?"

Slanting my head up at him, I smile softly. "It's a long story. I'll fill you in tonight after we get ready for bed. I'm emotionally exhausted."

"Okay, babe, we can tell everyone good night," Pierce concedes, pressing a soft kiss to the top of my head.

After saying our goodnights to his family, I jump into the biggest, fluffiest bed I've ever seen and yank the covers up to my neck, snuggling into the warmth of it all. "Oh, this is so much better than the hay bed in the loft! It's so soft!"

Crawling into the bed next to me, Pierce steals a little bit of my covers and, to his credit, lasts all of five seconds before questioning, "So...inquiring minds want to know..."

Twisting onto my side to face him, I offer an indulgent smile. "Yes, love, I know. And as promised, I'll tell you. Kage was being an overprotective brother bear, making me promise not to crush your heart. I told him I had no intention of doing so. He still struggles with the pain and scars he's caused you; you know that? I told him he needed to forgive himself and allow himself to love and be loved when the time comes. Oh, and I may have gotten an apology out of him for being an asshole."

"My, my, my how the tables have turned. I guess you'd better heed to your own advice and realize that you are worthy of love," Pierce teases, tugging me close.

"Haha. I'm here, aren't I? Not alone in the girls' cabin or

alone in the loft. I'm with you, and that's where I plan to stay. Forever."

I plant a big ol' sloppy kiss on his juicy lips and flip over so he's behind me, molding his body to mine. The way we fit together is a perfect fit. Dozing off tonight will be even easier than when we sleep in the loft.

26

PIERCE

Silencing the blaring alarm, I roll over and peck Tova on the cheek, "Rise and shine, baby."

Not wanting to wake up at the crack of dawn, Tova grumbles and tosses her pillow at my head. "Mondays should be optional."

"You know you want to show me up on the track today," I tease, pitching the pillow to the foot of the bed.

"That may be so, but I want another few hours of sleep more." Sighing, she stretches her arms over her head and arches her back.

"Come on, bleary eyes. We've got this."

Approaching the track, Kage notices the two of us walking toward the grassy patch off to the side where we can stretch when he yells, "Well, butter my butt and call me a biscuit. Look who decided to train with us today. You feel up for it, Campbell?"

Kage rotates his body as he stands in the middle of the track while he continues to watch the other trainee's jog.

Tova hollers back as we sit to change and lace up our shoes. "Underestimate me; that'll be fun."

"Well, stop hem-hawing around and hit the pavement," he declares, turning back toward the rest of his troops. Tova sticks her tongue out at his back.

Laughing at her, I pat her thigh while rising to stand. "Give 'em hell, babe."

"Oh, I plan on giving him more than that, like a punch to the throat," she grumbles.

"Y'all's love-hate relationship is brutal," Adi sneers, lacing up her sneakers.

"Yeah, I love to hate him," Tova says, frowning in Kage's direction.

"Ready, babe?" I ask when she bounces to her feet at my side.

"I was born ready," she affirms.

As we sprint side by side, she expresses, "I've never run with someone before. Not sure I'll be good at conversing or not. I usually just admire the wildlife and scenery."

"Babe, we don't have to talk while we jog. We can run in silence; it won't bother me. It just feels good to train with you." I do my best to match her stride.

After completing our two hours of running, we do a cooldown lap. Adi and Dani Jo catch up to us.

Adi catches her breath. "It's hot as hell out here. Air... I... need... air..." She purses her lips while breathing deeply.

Dani Jo, on the other hand, is scheming as she twists her hands together with an evil smile as she suggests, "Want to seek out Kage and his tormentors today and show them they've messed with the wrong group of trainees?"

Tova belly laughs, "Absolutely."

Glancing at the determined trio, I remind them, "Girls, y'all know that he's the absolute best at this cat-and-mouse game, right?"

Dani Jo places her right hand on her hip, cocking her knee out at an angle. "Yeah, but you've lived with him all of your life, and we have you on our side. He won't even see us coming." Dani Jo looks entirely too proud of herself.

Eyeballing her, I scoff, "This is true, but it'll be damn near impossible to beat these guys. If Tova doesn't go wandering off on her own, then Kage will stay with his team. It'll be easier to defeat him and induce as much pain as we can if he's alone. We'd better come up with a damn good plan before we go in guns a-blazin' because if we don't have our shit together, he'll make examples out of all of us, and we'll be crawling out of that arena today."

Looking at her comrades, Dani Jo asserts, "I'm up for a challenge, y'all?"

Finally able to breathe, Adi exclaims while high-fiving her, "Hell yeah!"

"You had me at 'seek out Kage.' Girl, it's on."

Shaking my head in disbelief, we walk over to our towels and wipe sweat from our dripping brows., "Okay, we've got our work cut out for us. Let's head that way now and come up with a plan," I say, resigned to helping them with this foolhardy mission.

W e let Jace, Kole, and Kaden in on the plan on the way over to the arena. Scaling some trees, trying our best to scan the arena before we're allowed in, we get the best vantage point on the east side of the wall. We can see several places that Kage would likely hide and the best place to get him alone.

God, he's going to kill me for this. Oh well, it's too late to back out now. All of us are situated on branches in large oak trees near each other as we try to memorize the arena. Climbing down, we gather together and conspire.

"Okay, guys, our best bet is to take him out near the falls," I explain. I turn to squint at Tova. "I know Kage told you never to leave your group, but today that's exactly what you need to do. We need to get him away from Larson and the other Superior Protectors. He knows that I'll likely follow you; so, he'll wait and watch for my lead, then take off in the same direction. That's how we track deer when we're on a hunt."

Swiveling my head to Jace, I coach, "I want you with me. We work well together. Plus, there's safety in numbers. Not to mention, your skin is so dark, Kage most likely won't see you with me, and he will only think it's me going after Tova. If he attacks me, we both can take him on and have a better chance at overcoming him." Jace gives me a nod in affirmation, and I continue, "Kage will be on the east, waiting for Tova." I, then, turn to Adi and Dani Jo. "I want you two to head to the top of the falls before she leaves the group. Sneak off together. He won't be focused on y'all. Kole and Kaden are tall enough to hide you two as you head off. We'll give you a five-minute lead, then I'll signal for Tova to high-tail it off on her own."

"What weapons do you think will work best for taking him down?" Kole asks.

Staring at him, I chuckle, then scan each member of our circle briefly. "Y'all, it's crucial that you take more than one weapon." I pause for a slight second. "I know we're supposed to only take one each week, trying to master it first, but I want us to hide guns and rubber bullets in our pockets. I want some of y'all to grab crossbows with rubber-tipped bolts, and a couple of small rubber axes, and shove them anywhere in your clothes that's not visible, just to be safe. When he gets wind that his Protectors can't find us all together, he'll call them all together. When that happens, we'll be walking into a shitstorm, and I promise..." I stop for a moment, pinning each of them with a solemn stare, then emphasize, "We. Will. Not. Walk. Out. Of. Here. We'll barely be able to crawl."

"What do Kole and I do after y'all take off?" Kaden questions.

"You two head straight for the top of the falls as well, right above where Tova will be. She'll be at the bottom where it's loudest, hiding in the brush at the bottom of one of the trees." I explain, turning in the twins' direction.

Next, I focus my attention to Adi and Dani-Jo. "You two, when you get there, stay out of sight. Once I get to the pine across from Tova, I'll give a whippoorwill call. That'll be your cue to start down toward us. By the time we all meet up, we'll either have Kage all to ourselves or be against his entire team. Be prepared for the worst. If it's just Kage, Tova will distract him by scurrying out of hiding toward the next oak about thirty feet away. It has a hollow groove in it where she'll remain hiding as the rest of us sneak over the downed log near the base of the falls. Do not fall off of the log! The falls have enough power to either drown your ass, or if you're lucky enough, wash you a mile or more downriver before it calms down enough for you to drag your battered body to shore."

Giving everyone a once over, I emphasize, "This is no joke. These waters are a force to be reckoned with. Once we reach the other side, we will sneak up behind Kage and take him down. If it's the worst-case scenario, then we'll meet our doom, get intercepted, and ambushed by his team, and it'll be every man for himself at that point. Everyone got it?"

They all mumble their agreement, and we walk as a group to the entrance of the arena.

After we all grab our weapons and suit up, we go inside and wait for the buzzer to sound. I clutch Tova's hand and pull her close to me, whispering, "Be safe, Spitfire."

She reaches up on her tip-toes, giving me a quick kiss. "I will, you be safe too. I'll see you on the other side." With a downright evil glint in her eyes, she smiles and declares, "He's going down."

The buzzer sounds. We all glance at each other, then Kaden and Kole form a human wall hiding Adi and Dani-Jo. Once they head off, the rest of us sneak into the forest, slinking around for a good five minutes. While we're giving them their head start, we shoot at some random targets appearing to be in normal training mode.

After about five minutes, our team shifts our focus to a group of faux Lynxwolves. That's when I motion for Tova to take off. At my gesture, she tears through the woods toward the falls.

I hold up my right hand to gesture the guys to stop walking. Coming to a halt, I close my eyes, listening to her tracks. As if on cue, I hear another set of padded feet. With my eyes closed, I twist my body toward the sound of the second pair of footsteps. Snapping my eyes open, I catch a glimpse of Kage dashing after her.

I motion for Jace to follow me and nod for the twins to head to the falls. Hot on Kage's trail, we stay on the opposite side of the sounds of Tova's running. She's stealthy, so Kage has to stop and listen now and again to see if he can stay on her trail, but we know exactly where she's going. He already knows I'm on her trail; that's just how we work, one benefit of growing up with the 'Tormentor' as the girls call him. However, though he knows I'm going after her, he doesn't know that we already know her plans. So, when his steps falter, we stop as well.

A good forty-five minutes into him tracking her, we end up at the base of the falls. Water is rushing so loudly it's almost deafening. When I told them I'd send up a call to let them know when to head down, I should have considered that.

What am I going to do now without giving away our positions? Considering for a moment, I need to belly crawl to Tova and see if she can send an actual whippoorwill up to them on the ridge. I tell Jace my plan, and at first, he looks at me skeptically, then after I tell him I'll explain later, he nods in agreement.

Crawling low to the ground, I make my way to Tova in the brush. She peers out of the leaves and furrows her brows demanding, as low as she can but loud enough for me to hear, "What the hell are you doing?"

"The falls are too loud; they'll drown out my call. There are several birds here. Can you tap into your gift and see if it's possible to send one up as the signal?" I whisper yell in response.

"Oh my God, Pierce, you have got to be kidding me!" she demands, flabbergasted.

With pleading eyes, I push, "Wish I were, babe. Can you do it?"

"Well, I don't have a choice, now do I?" she barks, smacking her forehead.

Removing her hand from her head, she closes her eyes, and within a matter of minutes, birds scatter everywhere, all but one, that one ascends to the area where the rest of the crew should be. I lean back and peer up and see some branches rustling, and I know they got the message, but the birds scattering must have startled Dani-Jo, or the single one that went up scared her, because her form descends our way.

Son of a...!

Tova gasps as she lifts her hand to her mouth.

Oh No!

If Dani-Jo falls thirty or forty feet, she'll either die or wish she had because breaking every bone in her body will hurt like hell.

Wait... What the hell?

About a third of the way through her descent, Dani-Jo sprouts... *are those wings?* Stretching from her arms to her sides like a wingsuit, but attached to her body. They're not gigantic wings from her back like a bird's would be, but more like a sugar glider, just enough to keep her from plummeting to her death. Spreading both arms out, catching the wind, she lands without a sound. Not realizing I was holding my breath, I let out a deep huff.

Focusing back on Tova, the horror dissipates from her face,

and peck her on the cheek. "You're awesome, babe. I don't know how you did that, but you just saved our hides."

Shoving me backward, she says, "Thank God my adrenaline is pumping. Check on Dani-Jo, then get back to Jace and let me know when I need to get to that other tree."

Back on my belly, I head toward Jace. The rest of the group is with me, Jace, and Dani-Jo in less than ten minutes. Once we are all settled, I motion for Tova to move.

Just as she reveals her position, the sharp pop of shots rings out through the trees.

Damn it!

Kage is firing at her. Keeping her in my sights, I check; she's not hit. Thank God. I motion for our team to get to the log.

Creeping through the brush, staying well-hidden, we make it to the tree that bridges each side. We fix our concentration on our target, watching for Kage or any of the other Superiors.

Shit, this log is slippery.

I'm doing my best to go as fast as I can while not losing my balance when the log suddenly bounces underneath me. When I look back, I see that Adi is barely holding onto the log with her arms. She doesn't scream, but you can see it is a struggle for her to stay on.

Rushing to get to her, Kole reaches down, but as soon as she lifts her hand to grasp his, she plunges into the rushing white water below.

Shit. Shit. Shit.

Tova must have been watching from her hideout because I see her running as fast as possible to get to our location. Hesitating, she waits a minute, then looks at me in desperation. I point my two fingers at my eyes then back to her. Getting the hint, she dives in.

If I'm right and pray to God I am, her cat vision should help her. They have excellent night vision. Scooting to the other side of the falls, we forget our task of taking out Kage and hide behind trees, waiting to see if Adi and Tova surface. After what seemed to be the longest minute in my life, Tova's head pops up. None of us see Adi, though.

Holy hell!

Come on, Tova, you can find her.

She gets a gulp of air and submerges back into the depths below. Damn it, my nerves are getting the best of me as my hands begin to glow. Shit. I can't give away our position, so I have to just breathe, pray, and calm down.

Another minute passes, and Tova resurfaces, again empty-handed. Refusing to leave without Adi, she searches for her four more times before she tires and climbs out of the water onto the banks on the other side.

Collapsing onto her back, breathing heavily, she rests for a couple of minutes. Once she has her energy back, she looks our way then points downstream.

Maybe Adi got pushed downstream by the force of the water. Ok, I see what she's thinking and where she's going with this, but we still have to worry about Kage attacking or his team charging us.

Lifting my index finger, I motion for the crew to head down the river. We stay close to the water to drown out our footsteps, but far enough away that no one will find our trail.

On our way to where the river calms down, we hear no more gunshots or get ambushed. I figure Tova hasn't been shot, but I just pray she hasn't been hit by anything else or captured by Kage.

Roaring waters seem to cease as we step into a clearing and see a small pebble beach. Searching the area, we are greeted with the most superb sight. I gasp and rush to the small beach Tova and Adi are at.

"What the hell happened, Adi? You scared the shit out of

us!" I scold, landing at their sides. Everyone else is bustling to get at her side.

"Well, dip shit, you saw that I lost my balance and tumbled into the water, but the force was too much. I couldn't resurface, so I decided not to fight it and just go with the flow," Adi explains.

Tears fall on to Dani-Jo's cheeks. "But we never saw you come up for air. I thought you were dead. Tova dove in after you and searched for you for five to six minutes before deciding to look for you down here."

Adi hugs Dani-Jo. "I'm so sorry I scared you, but the weirdest thing happened," Adi explains, embracing Dani-Jo. "I was terrified to fall into the raging river, but I realized that I wasn't struggling to breathe once I was submerged. In fact, it was quite the opposite. My lungs weren't burning or starving for air like they do when I run. I could breathe underwater. So, I decided to stalk Kage. I could see that he took off toward his side of the arena. When the water was calm, I surfaced at this beach and hid."

She pauses, pointing to the forest behind us. "When I saw Tova, I waved furiously to get her attention. When I caught her eye, she flew into the river to get to me. We haven't been here long. I just got done telling her about my mermaid-like ability right before you all showed up."

"You can breathe underwater! That's flipping awesome. I want superpowers like that," Kole says, with no small amount of jealousy, as he gawks at Adi.

Kaden wallops his brother on the back. "And Dani-Jo, you can fly? Hell Yeah!" Looking back at Kole, he affirms, "I sure hope we have freaking amazing abilities."

"Adi, I'm glad you're okay, but there's still thirty minutes left in this training, and Kage and his team are still at large. We need to hustle and find him before he finds us," Jace states calmly, scooting closer to Adi.

Straightening from my hunkered down position, I concur, "I hate to admit it, but Jace is right. We're almost to their entrance of the arena. Let's travel that way and see if we can find him, because in this clearing...we're sitting ducks."

27

TOVA

We all head through the woods, not knowing where Kage ran off to, only that it was toward his side of the arena. I can only assume when we find him, we'll be ambushed by his team. Dreading the worst, we are all on high alert, prepared for anything. I mean, where did he run off to? I was so engrossed in saving Adi that I didn't think twice about Kage.

Creeping around, careful not to give up our positions, we end up all the way to their entrance gate, with none of them in sight. We can't have more than twenty minutes left to go in the training when the hair stands up on the back of my neck, and adrenaline floods my veins. I jerk my head toward Pierce and the team to let them know something's up. Getting the hint, each of us ready our weapons, crouch down, and wait.

Fifteen minutes left.

Ten minutes left.

My blood is pumping, adrenaline coursing when at five minutes left, we hear Kole yell in pain. Gripping his hamstring, we see he's been struck with an arrow. Even though it's a rubber ball, it incapacitates him, bringing him to his knees.

Kaden immediately shoots up into the trees where the arrow originated from when abruptly, one of the Superior Protectors falls to the ground grasping his chest. He couldn't have been over ten to fifteen feet up in the tree, so he didn't get hurt badly from the fall.

Then the ambush begins.

They hammer down on all of us from the surrounding trees. We're hit with rubber bullets, axes, knives, and arrows.

I shift my eyes to my newfound vision and notice movement in the trees. Our team has assembled in a circle with our backs facing each other. I yell the opposing team's whereabouts, and each of our team unloads their weapon in that direction.

A minute before the buzzer sounds, our time is up; we have their entire team downed... all but Kage. *Where the hell is he?* I close my eyes and listen. A few seconds later, the sound of rustling leaves in an oak straight above me has my eyes opening, and I fire my gun, unloading every bullet left in the clip.

Kage falls down fifteen feet, gripping his chest. Heaving, he pants, "Damn girl, that aim is flawless."

After a few minutes of writhing in pain, he gets his wits about him and declares, "I was about to thrash you with my ax, but you nailed me. Well done, Tova. Well done. Now I'm going to exit with my team while I still have a little dignity left."

Hooting and hollering our accomplishment, our team leaves the arena.

Wiping the sweat off of my brow, I address the group, "I don't know about y'all, but I need to clean up before we go eat lunch."

They all agree, so I tell Pierce I'll go back to the girls' cabin with Adi and Dani-Jo to get ready. He heads off toward the men's cabin with Jace to do the same, and we all plan to meet up at the cafeteria.

Once the girls and I are all cleaned up, we start the hike up to the common area. I can't seem to let go of the idea that Adi can apparently breathe underwater, and Dani-Jo can basically fly.

"Ummm Adi, Dani-Jo...either of y'all care to elaborate on your newfound abilities?" I ask, no longer able to resist.

Dani-Jo bounces up and down on the balls of her feet clapping her hands in excitement. "I know, right? I had no freaking clue I could sprout webbed wings! I was so scared when I fell, out of habit, I just outstretched my arms to catch myself. The next thing I knew, they appeared. It was so liberating, exciting, and frightening. I think I'm going to have to free fall from trees and jump off of cliffs more often."

"Yeah, you free fall, and I'll swim," Adi laughs. "I was completely taken aback when I realized that I didn't need to come up for air. I knew then, that was how I was going to escape Kage." Looking at us sympathetically, she continues, "I'm so sorry I scared you. It was impulsive and selfish, and I won't do it again." Changing the subject, she turns toward me. "Though, Tova, I need to ask...what did you think you were going to accomplish by diving into and searching for me in the depths of that raging water?"

Mischievously, I let my lips curl up into a grin. "You know how cats are great at seeing in the dark?"

Both reply, "Yes."

It takes a moment, but they gasp, stopping dead in their tracks and turning toward me they take in my stunning cat eyes that I've shifted them to.

Adi sputters, dumbfounded, "What the what? When? How?"

Dani-Jo teases, "Okay, cool cat, you've got a lot of explaining to do, and I don't mean only your eyes. I want to know the story about how that ring has mysteriously found its way back on your finger."

Feeling the heat creep up my neck, I rub at my nape and transition my eyes to normal then explain, "Uh, yeah, about that…that's actually how I found out about my feline senses. Pierce went to get the ring out of his pocket. When I noticed it, my emotions got the best of me, my vision went haywire. Since then, I've been practicing changing my vision back and forth. I also have this keen ability to connect with wildlife. It's so surreal."

Throwing her head back laughing, Adi wisecracks, "See, was I right or was I right? I told you he was a good guy, Tova. I knew it from the get-go. I'm glad you're going to tie the knot and not a slip knot like all your other 'no strings attached relationships.' With those guys, after you called it off, your heart didn't miss a beat."

She eyes me enviously before continuing, "But I'll tell you one thing…Larson had better make it a romantic gesture when he gives *me* a promise ring."

"You two have been together for a while now. When do you think he'll do it?" Dani-Jo asks,

"Well, I know he wants to wait until he tests out of Protector training so he can have a steady income, and we can have our own cabin to ourselves. I mean, we talk about it, but he hasn't hinted when or where he'll do it," Adi laments. "He's already asked Mama for permission and Daddy for my hand. He doesn't know I know, but Mama let it slip at dinner a few months ago. He didn't tell her when just that it'd be after his testing."

"Isn't his testing time in the next month or so?" I ask, knowing it usually occurs only a few weeks after the newest batch of recruits make their Decisions.

"Why yes, it is!" She says in a high-pitched tone before skipping off ahead.

"He had better live up to her expectations. If he doesn't...it's going to be a miserable time for both of us. You know we'll never hear the end of it," Dani-Jo grumbles next to me.

"Oh, girl, I'm not about to have a miserable friend. I think this Friday at the bonfire, we take it upon ourselves to give Larson some pointers. What do you say?" I ask with a conspiratorial wink as I hold the door open for her.

"I say you've got yourself a deal," she laughs, giving me a high-five as she passes.

Looking around the cafeteria, we see the guys have already positioned themselves at the table with a few extra seats waiting for us. We make our way through the line quickly, grabbing our food and heading to the table. Adi sits down next to Larson. Once seated, he leans over and presses a tender, affectionate kiss to the top of her head.

I sit down next to Pierce, and he possessively wraps his arm around my waist, pulling me close to him. Dani-Jo sits on the other side of me, next to Kage.

"Good to see you again, ladies," Kage pipes up with a grin.

"Don't lie. You can barely walk. Admit it," I retort sarcastically.

Rubbing his sternum, he smirks, "Yeah, I'll be sore for a few days, that's for sure. You would have thought you were planning on taking out some sort of revenge on me for some odd reason."

"Yeah, bro, she's a badass," Pierce quips, a grin tugging at his lips.

Rolling my eyes, I refuse to acknowledge Pierce's comment in the current company. "Ha, ha. Revenge, payback, settling scores; whatever you want to call it...that was the goal," I say with a smug smile. Shoulder bumping Dain-Jo, I gloat, "Goal achieved, and man does revenge taste sweet."

"At this rate, you'll all be going on your first hunt and barter trip in the next few weeks. Venison supplies are getting low anyway, so going early won't be a bad idea." Kage explains, almost hiding the begrudging acceptance in his tone. Almost.

Fear stricken, I stiffen my back and take a deep breath and what little bites I've ingested start to creep up the back of my throat. Pierce and Adi both pick up on my tension.

Adi mouths, "You okay?" While Pierce leans over and whispers, "I've got you, babe."

Good thing, too, because I'm about to puke for fear of possibly running into Cladec out there. I know he could very well be dead, but I can't be for sure. Oh gosh, my breaths are coming quickly, and I'm about to freak out.

Pierce places his hand on my thigh, "Babe, slow your breathing. Come on, I know you can do it. Take intentional breaths. Close your eyes: Inhale for four counts...hold your breath for four counts...exhale for four counts. Good job, love. Keep that rhythm up. Just know that you're going to be more than prepared to defend yourself, and we'll be there every step of the way. I won't leave your side. I'll die before I let anything happen to you."

Now that my hyperventilating has ceased, I feel like I can function somewhat again. "Thank you, Pierce. I know you'd lay your life down for me, but that's not what I want anyone to do or even think about doing because of that psychopath." I swallow hard, not wanting to give voice to my fears.

Kage, having watched my turmoil unfold, must get the hint that I may not be as "ready" as he may have thought. He leans back behind Dani-Jo and asks me, "Everything okay? Is there something out there we need to be concerned about? Do you think someone really is out to kill you?"

Not wanting to discuss this in front of everyone, I just shake my head. I know I've got to tell him what we could be walking into out there. With all of the suspicious activity going on having me with them will put a giant target on their backs, too. But if I talk about it, I'll lose my lunch right here and now. I'll just have Pierce fill him in, or I may muster up the courage and tell him a little about the rage my father had in his eyes the day he was banished for abusing my mom and me. I just can't make myself do it at this moment. Pierce sends his brother a silent warning, shaking his head with a meaningful stare to let him know we're not having this discussion right now.

Needing to get out of here, I grab my tray with the rest of my untouched food and rise. Then the rest of the table does the same. I hate that I ruined their lunch, but I need to be outdoors, where the walls don't seem like they're crashing in on me, causing me to panic again.

I know what I need. I need to ride my horse. The horses are still at Pierce's family's house, so we have to go get them and take them back to my mom's anyway.

Once we are all standing outside, I hang my head, trying to hide the shame and panic on my face as I say, "Y'all, I'm so very sorry for freaking out in there. I wasn't expecting Kage to think we'd be ready to go outside the wall any sooner than planned. I knew it was coming, but just not that fast. I know I have to get over the fear of going outside those walls but it's just very close to the surface right now with everything else going on."

I have no clue how to even begin to get over that deep-seated fear. Knowing there is nothing to be done right now, I change the subject. Stammering and stumbling over my words, "I… I have to get the horses from Pierce's house and get them home. I'll miss the lecture this evening, but I'll see y'all in the morning, okay?"

"Okay, but you know we're here for you if you need us for anything," Adi assures, pulling me into a tight hug.

"You always have been, and I appreciate that more than you'll ever know."

"You've always been the strong one. You have guts of steel; never forget that. I love you so much." Taking hold of my shoulders, staring me straight in the eyes, Dani-Jo stresses, "You're fearless; you just don't know it. That's what I always loved about you. I always thought, 'If she will be my friend, if I can just be near that strength, maybe it'll rub off on me.' You've been a light to me my entire life. You'll figure out how to overcome this panic. I know it."

Not very sure of myself, I sigh, "Thank you. You're right. I will. I just have to figure it out."

Pierce enfolds me in his arms, wrapping them around my middle and tugging me close. He brushes his lips across my cheek as he assures, "We'll figure it out together. Now let's go get those horses."

"Awe, you two are perfect for each other," Adi coos.

I glance up at her and force a smile as Pierce threads his fingers with mine. Departing for Pierce's parent's farm, we turn from the girls. We step toward the solid oaks that appear to be welcoming us with their arms waving us inward. For the first few minutes, we walk in silence. My mind is whirling in fifty million directions. I have no earthly idea what I need to do to conquer this fear.

Stopping my train of thought, Pierce interjects, "Baby, I see those wheels turning again. You know you don't have to move that mountain by yourself. You're not one to ask for help, but I'm going to help you. Come hell or high water, I'll make sure you're mentally and physically ready to go outside those walls before you ever step foot out there. We've worked aimlessly at mastering weapons, but we've only touched the surface on physical self-defense. I truly think if you feel you can stand on your own two feet, defending yourself, in the unlikely chance that you're alone with Cladec, then your fears will subside somewhat. When we get back to your barn, would you like to kick my ass while learning how to defend yourself?"

Feeling more at peace, I can't hold in a snicker and slant my eyes at him. "I'd like nothing better."

His pearly whites greet me back. "I bet."

28

PIERCE

B ack at Tova's barn, we settle the horses into their stalls before I turn to her and ask, "Alright, babe, you ready to do this?"

Assuredly she takes a fighting stance. "Absolutely!"

"Alright, there are seven essential moves we're going to practice. I'll step through them with you and explain as I go. Then you can beat the crap out of me. Sound good? I'll come from different angles, surprise attacks, and some full-on frontal attacks. The key for you…is to figure out which tactic will be most beneficial at escaping each one."

I clear a space for our training in the middle of the barn before turning back to her. "Ready?"

"I was born ready!" Excitement gleams in her eyes.

Smooching her soft lips, I say, "I love your tenacity!"

I grab for her hand and bring her to the barn's center, the place I cleared for us.

Turning to face her, I begin, "First and foremost, always be sure of your awareness. You need to be completely cognizant of your environment. Minimize distractions as best you can. It's important to ensure you can hear everything around you." She nods in understanding and I begin to demonstrate, "The first move is a Hammer Strike. Using a stick or sharp object is one of the easiest ways to defend yourself. You can also use this move in a swinging motion. To perform it, hold your stick or sharp object like a jagged rock, or whatever you can find, in a tight fist, like holding a hammer, hold one arm in front of your chest. At the same time, you use your other hand to 'hammer' that object at the offender's face."

Practicing this with various objects lying around the barn, she comes at me repeatedly until she feels confident.

"You picked that one up quickly. Let's move on to the groin kick. This sounds simple for you, but please, go easy on me. Our future children are at stake, after all," I joke nervously.

Still, after seeing her commitment with the last move, I am honestly more than a little worried about my poor, innocent manhood.

Smirking, she tilts her head. "Yes, love, I'll go easy on you and the family jewels."

"Thank you," I say and kiss her forehead. "Now, suppose it's a frontal attack. In that case, a groin strike could produce adequate strength to incapacitate the assailant, enabling you to get away. To best do this, steady yourself, so you don't fall over, then hoist your right leg upward and drive your shin into the person's nuts." Demonstrating the move, I counter, "On the other hand, if he's too close, use your knee instead."

Pausing, I take a deep breath and brace myself for what comes next. "Okay, show me what you've got."

I stalk toward her in my most aggressive posture; her eyes are fixed on mine. She crouches down, and no sooner do I get within three feet of her, her right foot nicks my nut-sack.

Damn it!

My vision goes blurry, and I'm on the ground rolling and clutching my groin protectively. Ugh, I can't breathe. Coughing, "I thought you were going to go easy?"

Tova rushes to my side and drops down beside me, apologizing, "That was easy! I only lightly grazed you! I promise I didn't mean to hurt you. I'm so sorry, baby. Please forgive me."

Heaving up to my knees and forearms, I groan. "It's okay, babe, but if our kids come out with three eyes and four arms, it's on you."

"You knew what was coming. You could have protected yourself." She helps me to a standing position.

Tilting my head from side to side, I sarcastically gabble, "Ha. Ha."

Once I'm able to get my wits about me, we continue.

"All joking aside, the next maneuver is a hand-palm strike." I explain, "The trick is to hurt the nose or esophagus. Be sure to be in front of the enemy. If you strike the cheek or forehead, that's okay too, but you want to hit the most vulnerable parts if you can."

Grabbing her dominant hand, I help her through the move. "Take your right hand, bend at the wrist and aim for their face." Holding her hand out, I move it in an upward thrusting motion. "Aim for either here or here." Our hands aim at the middle of a pretend face or neck. "Ensure there's enough force to snap their head backward but withdraw your hit promptly. You don't want that person to grab your arm, trying to steady themselves, and then counter-attack. If you can't get directly in front of them, you can always slam your open hands to both of their ears, causing pain and stupefying them."

Practicing this over and over, Tova directs, "Okay, I think I'm comfortable with this. What's next?"

"Babe, you're doing great. I just want you to know that."

She grins, then nods her acknowledgment. That's my cue to keep going. "Okay, the next move is the elbow clash. Again, have a sturdy stance. For this move, your attacker is going to be very close to you, and he may even have you in a hold. "Crook your arm, bend it at the elbow, and shift your body forward, smacking your elbow into their throat, mouth, eyes, or any weak area you can reach. If you're in a hold, try this... raise your right elbow toward your shoulder. Swivel on your right foot and spin, hitting any part of their face with the back of your elbow."

Having practiced that several times, Tova wipes sweat from her temple with the back of her hand. "I never knew learning to protect myself could be so exhilarating."

"I'm so glad you're adrenaline-charged and feeling better. The more we practice, the better you'll get, and the less you will have to think about which move to use. The reaction will become second nature."

"I'm getting a different mindset. The more I'm learning, the more I'm confident I can stand against, not only my sperm donor but anyone who tries to hurt me." She widens her smile. "Show me more." She motions for me to keep teaching, a new hunger in her eyes.

"You got it, babe. Next is escaping from a Bear Hug

embrace." I coach while crouching down, "You need to get low and create some space from the hug. For this move, bend headfirst at the stomach. Twist backward with your arm, allowing your elbow to strike the attacker, then twist to the other side and do it again. Keep doing this until his grip loosens, allowing you to rotate completely. As you're facing the attacker, punch their face, and then sock his nards. Once he's down, run."

My gaze rakes over her slight frame, and I lose my train of thought, taking in her sweat-soaked figure as she moves effortlessly around the space. *Damn, she's hot!*

Brandishing that thought, I refocus, "I'm going to come behind you, but please, for the love of God, go easy this time. Think of our future children."

Putting her right hand on her hip, she sasses, "Babe, I swear I didn't mean to hurt you. I'll go as easy as I can. I promise."

I proceed with caution, shaking off the thought of getting injured again. "Okay, this next tactic is how to get away from a bear hug with your hands confined. When someone comes from behind and pins down your arms, this is the best thing to execute: Do not let the person's arms go from your waist to your neck, putting you into a headlock. Twist your waist to one side. You should have enough room to punch them in the groin with your fist. Retrieve your hand while lifting the other elbow to turn into the grasp. Hold your arms snug to your torso as you're rotating to face him. Continue to attack back until you're released. Once you're out of his grasp, knee him in the groin and side-kick him in the stomach with your shin. Then get away while he's down."

Approaching her from behind, she tenses up as I grab her waist in a firm hold. Struggling to step to the side, allowing access to my groin, she just drops to the ground causing me to lose my balance. Taking her left shoulder, she dips under my left arm and, with all her might, thrusts me forward in a front flip.

The air is completely knocked out of my lungs when I land. As I'm gasping for air, Tova scrambles to me, hovering over me upside down as she assesses me. "Holy crap, are you okay?" she asks, panic in her voice.

Sucking wind, I'm finally able to grunt, "Never better."

Her eyes are wide with dread. So, I gently pull her down to me, her nose brushing my chin as our lips meet.

Once she relaxes, she pulls back, sitting her bottom on the heels of her feet, and she suggests, "Why don't we work on the last skill?"

Flipping onto my stomach, I push myself onto my knees, mirroring her posture. "Deal! This last move is to get you out of a headlock should your attacker manage this maneuver. If the aggressor clenches an arm circling your throat, the first thing you need to ensure is that you don't get choked. Twist into that person's side as best as you can, bring your chin into their ribs, avoiding being strangled. While in this position, use your free hand and sock his manhood until you can free your head from his grasp entirely." Rising to a standing position, she mimics me. Locking eyes, I rally, "Ready?"

Wiggling her head up and down, I charge her, taking her into a headlock. She stumbles backward. I squeeze harder, keeping her from backing out of my grip. Not being able to inhale all the way, she panics, clawing at my arm and back.

"Remember, the maneuver I taught you. Don't panic when you can't breathe. Focus. I'm not going to smother you. I promise," I coax, not releasing my hold.

Closing her eyes, she redirects her attention to my ribcage. Jamming her chin into my side, she's able to loosen my hold slightly. Grabbing the inside of my leg, careful not to do more damage there, she pinches the blood out of my inner thigh. I yell, "Damn it, Tova," and immediately drop her out of the hold.

Collapsing to the ground on her back, inhaling rapidly, she spouts, "How was that?"

Bending over rubbing my thigh, I compliment, "Woman, you're a beast. You know that? Thank you for going easy on my manhood, but I'm pretty sure I'm going to have a nasty bruise on the inside of my leg."

Panting, she peers up at me and mocks, "Beast mode…" and uses her index finger, motioning a check mark, "on."

29

TOVA

Feeling better after my self-defense lessons, sweating like a pig, I roll over in the dirt, pushing myself to my knees then up to my feet.

I stroll over to Pierce as he's rubbing his inner thigh. "Sorry babe, I didn't want to hurt the goods." Pointing at his groin, I smirk, "Therefore, I went with the next best thing." Pouting, he rubs his inner thigh in response.

"I'll kiss it and make it better tonight," I say with a seductive wink as I saunter toward him.

"I guess I'll have to get hurt more often. You know…just so you can kiss it and make it better." Smirking, he sits up and pulls me into a firm embrace, "I love you, Spitfire."

Perspiration is beading on my brow. Dirt and hay is scattered in my untamed hair while my shirt's sucked to my body, saturated with sweat.

"I love you too. But I look and smell awful. Let's shower and get ready for dinner."

Walking up to the front door of my mom's house, I intertwine my fingers with Pierce's. Goodness, it feels so wonderful to finally have some peace of mind knowing how to fight for myself. Crossing the threshold to the kitchen, I beam up at Pierce with hope and promise in my eyes. "I'm so thankful for you, Pierce. I don't know what I've done to deserve you. I feel at peace when you're around. I have this absolute trust that you won't hurt me, and I know you'd do anything to ensure my safety. I never knew that love could be like this."

"Baby, I just wished I'd been here for you sooner. I wish like hell that I could have saved you from all the torture you went through growing up, but I swear on my life that I'll die before anything like that happens to you ever again."

Tugging his arm toward the bathroom, my gaze pierces his soul. I don't need to say anything, he can feel my love for him, and I'm keenly aware of how he feels too. His arm is raging with heat. My hands are starting to sweat from the warmth he's emitting from his palms and from my intense feelings for him. Shoving the shower curtain back to turn on the water, I release his hand.

Looking from the bathroom door to me, he raises his eyebrows. "When's your mom coming home?"

Using my index finger in the come here motion provocatively. "Not for a couple of hours. Don't worry. I wouldn't drag you in here if I knew she'd be home anytime soon. I'd never do anything to jeopardize her believing you hung the moon. We're just showering off. That's all."

Standing to meet him with a satisfied smirk, he places both of his simmering hands on my cheeks. As I wrap my arms around him, he anxiously holds my stare. Ravishing my lips once more, he mouths, "Fair enough."

Once we're done washing up, and the waters run cold, we towel off and head to the kitchen. "Mama will be so happy that we'll have supper cooked when she gets here. She's always taken care of others. It'll be nice for her to be taken care of for once."

Cooking in the oven is sweet potato souffle, green bean casserole, squash casserole, and barbeque pork chops. We set the table for the three of us, and just as the food is finished, my precious mother whisks through the front door.

Completely taken by surprise, she gasps, "Oh my gosh, what is that wonderful smell?"

Gliding over to her, I take her hand, leading her to the dinner table. "Mama, you're always taking care of others…it's about time someone caters to you. I hope you like what we've concocted."

Kissing my cheek, she croons, "I'm sure it's perfect, whatever it is."

The timer goes off, indicating the food is done. Pierce takes it out of the oven and places it on potholders on the table. I grab the utensils for each entrée, then pour everyone something to drink. Appreciating my current circumstances, I stop and admire the scene.

Gosh, I love this sight—both of the people I love the most sitting right here with me. I never dreamed this would happen. I don't want this moment to end.

H aving finished eating, mama wipes her mouth with her napkin and surprises me. "You know, I had a slow day at work today, and I got to work on your dress almost all day. At this rate, I'll be done with it in a few of weeks instead of six."

Bug-eyed, I gape, "Really? That's fantastic. When do you think I'll be able to try it on?"

Stars gleam in her eyes. "I bet by next Saturday."

Pierce chimes in, "That's fantastic." Then eagerly, he leans forward and asks, "That means we can have the ceremony sooner?"

Unsure if he's ready for it to happen so soon, I tilt my head toward him skeptically, "Um, is that what you want?"

Pierces all but shouts, "Hell yeah, the sooner, the better." Wide-eyed, he covers his mouth and gives an awkward chuckle, "Sorry Ms. Campbell, I'm just so excited."

Patting his hand, she assures, "It's okay, Pierce. I'm glad my little girl has found someone as good as you."

Rolling my eyes, I point out. "See Pierce, I told you she thinks you hung the moon."

All of us bellow in laughter.

Man, this feels like heaven.

30

PIERCE

The sun's rays strike my eyelids as I pull Tova close, snuggling her body into mine and nipping the back of her neck. "Rise and shine, beautiful. It's another day in paradise. We get to go show everyone your new ass-kicking skills."

Grumbling, she flips over to face me. "Okay, but only

because I might get to actually do some damage to your ruthless brother."

"As long as it's not me, I'm good with it." I nibble her luscious lips.

She nuzzles into my bare chest with a laugh. "I just love sleeping next to you and waking up in your arms. I want to always be in your embrace. Can't we just stay like this all day?"

Pressing a kiss to the crown of her head, I say, "After our ceremony, we'll get an entire week off of training, and I swear if this is all you want to do, then that's what we'll do. I don't need an elaborate place to escape to that I've never seen before, like some people do after they say their vows. I don't even need food or water. I just need you."

"You know, I wouldn't mind seeing the coast. I've never been outside these walls. I've been told there's nothing like the vast sea, crashing waves, and soft sandy beaches."

Raising up, I prop myself up on my arm. "If you want, we can go there. One territory that we barter with is along the shore. Kage has been there a few times and always raves about how stunning it is."

"I'd love to go one day." Hesitancy fills her voice, "But I don't want my first time outside the protection wall to be for our pleasure, though. I want to get a little more familiar with the surroundings on the other side, and maybe when we go to an exchange, we can venture out to see the ocean. I'd rather spend our week here, not traveling, just you and me..." Scanning the loft below, she adds, "and the horses."

I admire her blue-green eyes. "I'll go wherever you want, babe, and do whatever you want."

"Mmm, I love you, Pierce. You were made for me, you know that?" she murmurs and closes her eyes.

"Yes, baby, and you were made for me."

I kiss her once more before we drag our bodies up, forcing ourselves to get prepared for today's training.

Hitting the track with the guys, we fill them in on Tova's new self-defense skills while we run. Once we've completed two hours of running, we're all soaked with perspiration. Tova's friends are on the track's outskirts, and we meet up with them and stretch, getting ready to head to the arena.

"Tova, it looks like you're in much better spirits than you were yesterday," Adi observes.

Tova counters, "I am, thanks to Pierce."

Adi eyes me up and down suspiciously. "Oh really...?" Closing her eyes, she shakes her head. "Nope, I'm afraid to ask...not going there."

Tickled, Tova responds, "No! Nothing like that. Gosh Adi, does your mind always go to the gutters?"

"Tova, you know it does," Dani-Jo teases.

Tova sneers and pulls her arms behind her back, tugging on them in a stretch. "Ugh, Adi. Pierce and I had a one on one..."

Interjecting, Adi jams her fingers into her ears, belting, "La la la la la la! I can't hear this! My virgin ears will bleed."

Tova yanks Adi's arms away from her ears. "Stop it! Let me finish. I was saying that he taught me some bad-ass self-defense skills, that's all!" Glaring over at Kage, she spitefully hints, "Given the right opportunity, I'll unleash my newfound skills on him."

I call attention to her vengeance, wiping the sweat from my brow. "You really have it out for him, don't you, babe?"

"Well, if he didn't have it out for me, then I might not be as bitter. But as it is, I'm just ready for payback." She twists her hands together and taunts, "Let's get this party started."

Enthusiastically, she grabs my wrist, tugging me toward the

exit. I caution, barely able to keep up with her, "Babe, you know he's the one who taught me all of those moves. He'll be ready to counterattack without a thought. If you two end up brawling it out, don't forget to focus. Don't let him get inside your head. Don't let your guard down. Anticipate his move before he does it. He's trained to bring out your weakness so you can get stronger in that area. It's not personal. He's a great guy, a wonderful brother, but a brutal mentor." I stress every word, "He. Will. Not. Go. Easy. On. You."

"Pierce you don't think I know that? My freaking back is living proof of his ruthlessness, but I'm not afraid, and you shouldn't be either. And don't think for a moment you can intervene. I have to figure this out on my own," she threatens.

"Babe, you can't expect me to sit back and watch my brother mistreat you."

"I just have to remember that and focus on perfecting my skills. If I get to a point where it's too much, I'm sure he'll let up," she says, attempting to reassure me.

I snatch my wrist out of her hold. "Ha, that's where you're wrong. He'll take you down and not think twice about it, and he'll never apologize either. He's hard-wired to instruct, using whatever it takes to make you better. If he doesn't single you out, don't go looking for trouble. Promise me."

Flinging her head back, she groans, "Uh, okay. I promise. Now can we go get ready for the arena?"

She sulks toward me and I take her by the waist. "Of course."

Now that we're all in camouflage and prepared to enter the arena, I quickly scan our group, reminding them, "No pajamas this Friday, only steak, now let's kick some ass."

All together in a circle, hands in the middle, we chant, "Superiors are Losers!"

The buzzer sounds, and we haul ass inside, our adrenaline surging. We equip ourselves and seek out the Superiors. Quickly we make a beeline toward the other side where we know they're entering. Stealthy as possible, we sneak onto the other side of the arena and circle up, our backs together toward the middle. We're in a heavily wooded area, so these guys could be hiding anywhere. Crouching down, we hold our stance, prepared for an attack on any side, or even above, like before. A good thirty minutes pass by without so much as a sound from the opposing team. Not relinquishing our position, we hunker down and wait them out.

Kole hisses, "I guess they're trying to tire us out."

"They should know by now we're not easily exhausted," Jace scoffs.

"Yeah, they should know we're a force to be reckoned with," Kaden agrees.

"They're up to something. I don't know what it is, but the hair is rising on the back of my neck. When they pounce, it's going to be rough," Tova warns.

"Bullets will be hard-pressed to reach us through this thicket. They'll have to come in on us hot and heavy, forcing close contact," I acknowledge.

No sooner than I finish my sentence, the brush in front of Adi rustles, and she's immediately taken from our circle. Dani-Jo lets out a squeal, then she's next. All of us rise from our crouched positions and ready our weapons.

Kole is prepared to shoot into the bushes where they were taken, but before he can unload, Jace shoves his arm down. "You could hit the girls. We need to follow them and go from there."

I nod at the two, letting them know that Kaden, Tova, and I

are okay with their plan. They rush through foliage and disappear.

"They're not done, Pierce. I can still feel it," Tova says in a low voice.

"Focus, babe, don't let fear overcome you."

"Okay, I'm trying my best."

"Let's put our backs together and slowly circle around. The Superiors will have a harder time snatching anyone if we're not directly in their line of fire." I look over my shoulder at Tova. "You know you're next, right? Kage is probably just waiting for the right moment."

"Yea, I'm aware," she sighs.

"If this was real, we'd be climbing trees to get a better vantage point, but you want to get revenge, right?"

"More than you know."

"Alright, be prepared for..." Before I can finish my sentence, she's snatched from our circle. Kaden and I wait a minute or two before we both tear through the bush after her.

We can't hear a peep. They must have her gagged.

Shit!

Now, I'm the one panicking. Kaden places his hands on my shoulder, pressing us down. "Look at the grass...how it's snapped. We need to follow the trail." Reading me like a book, he breathes, "Don't let your emotions get the best of you. She's going to be okay."

I inhale deeply. "Yeah, okay. Let's get moving." "Where did they disappear so fast? This is ridiculous! I can't hear them or see movement anywhere." I deliberate, thrusting my fingers through my hair.

"Not sure, but we need to give Tova time to escape on her own. That's what she wanted. Remember what we were all talking about this morning while jogging on the track?"

"Yeah, but I hate the thought of anyone hurting her."

"I know, man, but just trust that you taught her the skills necessary to free herself without our help. Now is the perfect time to let her build her confidence. This is a controlled environment. The Superiors will make sure she's not hurt... severely." Kaden's attempts at calming my anxiety are less than spectacular, but I know he has a point.

"That's just it! I don't want her hurt *at all.*"

Lowering closer to the ground, I spot footprints leading toward another path. Flashing my eyes up at Kaden, I nod my head in that direction. We creep in the tracks' direction, rising to an upright position, and follow it for at least ten minutes.

We approach a nearby oak and stand still as we glimpse rustling in some brush. Looking at each other, we creep toward the movement. Almost to the base of the tree, Adi rolls out in front of us, gagged, hands and feet bound. She's visibly pissed. We rush to her side as she huffs and squirms, trying to free herself. Kaden and I slip our hands under her arms, placing her on her rump. She glares at the two of us with a flushed face as sweat pours down the side of her temples. I snatch off the gag while Kaden loosens her hands and feet.

Shifting the loosened ropes, Adi snarls, "God, I'm going to kill him. Just wait until I get my hands on him. His life, as you now know it, is over...soooooo over." She brushes off the leaves and dirt from her clothes, asking. "Did y'all see which way he went?"

"Which way who went? We only saw the bush rustling, and then you popped out," Kaden explains.

Adi rolls her eyes. "Ugh, Larson." She swerves her head in all directions, looking for Larson. "I swear on my grandmother's grave, the next time I see him, he's going to wish he'd never been born."

Kaden chuckles. "Oh, I can't wait to see that. A small package of dynamite like you exploding on a brute like him..."

Rubbing his hand together, he adds, "I'd pay money for that show."

I remind her, "Looks like he didn't hurt you. Plus, I thought you two were an item, you know...in love."

Growling, she snaps, "Oh Pierce, there's a fine line between love and hate. And yeah, he hurt me, well...my pride, anyway." Changing the subject, she notices it's just us and asks, "Where's the rest of the crew?"

I report, "Dani-Jo and Tova were taken. Kole and Jace went after you and Dani-Jo, and we were following a path hoping to find Tova."

Adi shoos us with her hands. "Well, let's get a move on it. Hopefully, we'll find the other two before time's up."

Kaden proposes, "I say we take out a few fake targets as we search. The more we take out, the better our chances are at humiliating them when they lose and have to wear their pj's to the bonfire Friday. I mean, we're grown-ass adults. Enough of this embarrassment of wearing pj's in front of everyone. I'm over that shit!"

"Okay, just don't make a large commotion when we do it. We don't want to draw attention to our whereabouts," I warn.

We take down at least twenty targets and are now almost in the center of the arena. Glimpsing a couple forms out of the corner of my eye, I ready my ax to throw until I realize that Jace, Kole, and Dani-Jo are together quickly running toward us. Lowering my weapon, I take a deep breath in.

Thank God!

"No shit, you found Dani-Jo," Kaden praises as he fist pumps the air.

Kole high fives him. "Yeah, she was all bound up and tossed into the thicket close to the river."

"Those assholes dared to manhandle me like I was a rag doll and had me bound in ropes before I even knew what was going on, then just left me. Why the hell did they do that? Did they think I'd miraculously escape on my own? Thank God they found me," Dani-Jo vents, pointing to Kole and Jace, "or I'd still be there screaming into the gag until I lost my voice."

Adi seethes, "Oh, don't worry, Dani-Jo, we'll get them back…if it's the last thing I do. Those heifers did the same thing to me. Except you know who was behind my abduction?"

"Seeing how mad you are, I'm going to guess Larson," Dani-Jo chuckles.

"Yes, and when I get my hands on him, he's going to be begging for mercy."

Jace guffaws, "I sure do feel sorry for him."

Noticing Tova isn't with us, Dani-Jo stammers, "Oh—Oh no, where's Tova?"

Kaden replies, "She was taken shortly after they got you. We waited a couple of minutes to give her time to free herself, but we've seen no trace of her or any of the other Superiors. We've been randomly taking down targets while we look for her to add to our target count."

I point out, "Now that we're all together, we can span out six breaths wide and search a larger perimeter."

Jace speaks up, "I wouldn't put it past them to tie her up in some tree thinking we'd only be looking on the ground for her."

"You have a point, Jace, only I'd hoped she'd have freed herself by now." I bow my head in defeat.

Jace pats me on the back. "Don't look so downhearted we can still hope. Don't discount her determination. We'll find her. But I still say we look everywhere."

Lifting my eyes to meet his with a little more fire in my bones, I reply, "Okay, let's do this."

31

TOVA

Crap! Kage has managed to wrap one of his muscled arms around my waist and carry me off. His buddy here is covering my eyes and gagging me with some fabric. Why? I have no idea because I'm not even trying to scream. My feet are dangling off the ground. I'm waiting for some footing before I counter-attack. I know he can't carry me forever. As I'm bouncing around like a limp noodle, another person takes my wrists and wraps them with rope.

Oh, hell, no. I don't think so, buddy. I may have played the damsel in distress, but now someone's about to pay.

Yanking my arms free from the other person, I manage to fling my inside leg in front of Kage's, causing him to stumble. He catches himself from completely falling, and he loosens his grip on me. Immediately, the other guy rushes to me as I'm bent over. He throws his arm around my neck, and I go into defense mode. I jam my chin into his side, take my outside arm, and thrust my fist into his gonads. Yelling obscenities, he lets me go and drops to the ground, grabbing his manhood. I rip off my blindfold and the gag, but Kage doesn't miss a beat and proceeds to bear hug me from behind. I sidestep him enough to allow my inside arm to deliver a blow to his groin.

Refusing to loosen his grip, Kage, barely able to talk, grumbles, "Tova, you don't play nice."

"Oh, like you do?"

He's still holding me, but we're more crunched over, so I take my head, pushing it as far as I can away from Kage's face, then fling my head back, delivering the worst head blow I can manage. Seeing stars, I squeeze my eyes shut.

"Damn it, Tova. You busted my nose," Kage bellows.

"Well, let me go!"

"Ha, you have to do better than this. Some Superior Protectors overheard you and your team talking about wanting to use new self-defense skills. Show me what you got!" he taunts.

"Be careful what you wish for; you just might get it."

By this time, I've already figured I'm going to groin punch him again, then unleash all of my energy into defeating him. Sidestepping one more time, I pound my fist into his gonads. He loosens his grip, but not entirely. I rotate to face him, then open both of my hands. Flat palmed, I smack his ears simultaneously, stunning him.

He lets me go while he grabs his ears and closes his eyes,

yelling in shock and pain. While he's still bent over, I place both of my hands on his back to steady myself. I lift my right leg back and thrust my knee into his gut.

Down to the ground, he goes.

Oh, but I'm not done. I take my right leg again, lifting it back to get momentum, I ram my shin into his guts once more. I leave him gasping for air, his nose bleeding all over the place and rush to the guy still rolling on the ground, moaning in pain.

"You didn't think I was done with you, did you?"

Peeking up at me, I repeat the same maneuver and kick him with my shin in his gut as well.

Now that both of my captors are incapacitated, I take off toward the sound of the river, knowing that it's near the middle of the forest. Hopefully, I'll find my team there.

I tune into my feline senses and listen for any of them talking. Climbing up this last hill before I can see the water, I hear a few footsteps coming in my direction.

God, I pray it's not more Superiors.

I jump back behind a tree and into some shrubs, waiting for the footsteps to get closer. Hearing a female voice, I realize it's Adi. I leap from my position, scaring the hell out of them.

Kole hollers, "What the hell Tova? We were worried about you, and you retaliate against us?"

I throw my hands up in surrender. "I didn't mean to scare you. I didn't know if you were friend or foe when I heard your footsteps. So I hid, but when I heard Adi, I got excited."

"Whoa, your eyes!" Jace exclaims.

Transitioning my eyes back, I say, "Oh, sorry about that. I was just trying to tune in a little deeper to my ability, so I could find y'all."

"You found us alright, and now some of us may need to

change our undies because you scared the shit out of us," Kaden scoffs.

Pierce rushes to my side, hugging me tightly. But as his hand closes around my neck in embrace, he notices a matted dried crusty substance. "What the...? Is this blood?"

"No?" I answer, unsure if it is or not.

"That's not a question you answer with a question, Tova. Why is there blood in your hair? My God, did someone hit you upside the head?" Pierce growls.

I shake my head, but Pierce counters, "I swear when I get my hands on him..."

I place my palm on his chest and explain, "No, Pierce. No one hit me. I head-butted Kage when he took me into a bear hug. I busted his nose. If it's blood, then it's his blood. He's a sight to see. He may not be my friend anymore after today. Just saying."

Pierce, holding my shoulders, looks at me suspiciously. "What? You mean to tell me you kicked his ass?"

I point my thumb behind me. "Oh, not just his. I kicked his dumb partner's ass, too. Let's just say they won't underestimate me again." As I finish my statement, the buzzer sounds. Laughing, I ask, "Can we go get cleaned up? I'm a mess."

Everyone yammers that showering is a great plan. We all head back to the cabins because they're closer. After we've all cleaned up, we all walk to the cafeteria together. Adi and Dani-Jo fill me in on their kidnapping. The guys boast about how many additional targets they acquired. Pushing the door open for me, Pierce steps aside, allowing me and everyone else in our group to enter inside. The Superiors have beaten us here. They're currently in line filling their trays. Kage glances in the direction of the door, and we all take in raccoon eyes and a swollen nose.

Jace grips my shoulders. "Holy Hell, Tova. You did that?"

"Un-huh. And see the guy behind him? He may have a hard time bearing children."

Letting loose of his grip, Jace teases as he takes a step back, "Damn girl, remind me to never piss you off."

———

Sitting down to eat, Pierce taunts Kage, "Say, old man, you gonna be able to eat alright, or do we need to mush it up so you can swallow?"

Kage waffles, "Ha, ha. She didn't bust my mouth or throat-punch me."

"Yeah, well, by the looks of it, she beat the shit out of you," Pierce mocks, unphased.

Kage admits, "I may have asked for it. So, no hard feelings."

My eyes widen in shock and I snap my head at him, "What? You're just going to forgive me, just like that?"

"Yeah, I am. You proved yourself out there. You are one badass woman," Kage admits, shoveling food in his mouth.

Pecking me on the cheek, Pierce commends, "that's my little Spitfire."

Adi fumes and points her butter knife at Larson, giving him an 'eat shit and die' look. "Well, I do not forgive you that easy! Buddy, you have some explaining to do."

Larson attempting to explain, "Look, babe…"

Not letting him get another word in edgewise, Adi unleashes on him, "Don't you 'babe' me, honey. Where do you get off thinking you can just snatch me, gag and bind me up and throw me into some bush?"

Larson opens his mouth to speak, but Adi continues, "Nope, you don't get to talk right now. I'm not some piece of trash you can just haul over your shoulder and leave out for the takin'. I'm your freaking girlfriend. I don't care what Kage or any of the other Superiors have instructed you to do. YOU DO NOT EVER DO THAT AGAIN! Do I make myself clear? Because if you do, I'll cut your penis off in your sleep."

"Babe, that's a bit harsh, don't you think? I didn't hurt you... physically, that is. Now you know we had to do this exercise. What if someone outside those walls decides they like you and want you for themselves? They're not going to just tie you up and leave you for dead. Oh no. Those people out there rape women, then kill them and cook them for dinner. So, don't get so freaking pissed off that I caught you off guard. I want you to be as prepared as you can be before we leave these walls, or I'm going to suggest you stay behind because I could never live with myself if something bad happened to you. You are my everything. Don't you see that? I was doing this to help you."

I have never seen Larson, so beside himself, it's truly eye-opening to see this level of emotion from him.

"Grrrrr, oh okay...fine then. I'll forgive you." She peeks over at Kage and asks, "Do you think we can all take self-defense lessons soon if it really is as dangerous out there as you all say it is?"

"Oh, it is, and then some. We'll make it a priority to do that," he says with a firm tone.

Smiling, she affirms, "Okay, it's settled then."

We all finish our food and leave for the learning commons, to brush up on history and naturopathy. After our lessons, we hug out our goodbyes and head off to our destinations so we can rest up.

32

TOVA

A few days have passed, and we're all getting ready for the bonfire. Once again, we lost to the Superior Protectors, getting the most targets for the week in training. Not by many, but nonetheless, a loss is a loss. With my fingers twisted with Pierce's, we hike to the bonfire with Adi and Dani-jo walking beside us. I'm in my most atrocious sleepwear. When we're closer to the fire, I notice Larson sitting on a log alone on the outside of the circle where everyone else has gathered to either roast marshmallows or hotdogs. I side-eye Dani-Jo, hinting that now's our time to fill Larson in on his proposal plans. Now we just have to figure out a way to talk to him without Adi around.

Striding to where Larson is, we all plop down around him on different logs. Adi snuggles into his side as he wraps his arm around her back.

"Larson, you not hungry?" I ask.

Shaking his head no, "Nah, not right now. I was waiting for y'all to get here before I roasted any dogs."

Adi nuzzles him and says, "That was awful kind of you. But if It's okay with you, I'm going to go cook one. I'm starving. Practice today has my tummy grumbling like crazy."

"I'll get it, babe, you just stay here," Larson insists.

Reaching back and tapping Dani-Jo's arm, I nod in the direction of the bonfire. Taking my hint, she rises to her feet. I lean over a whisper to Pierce, "Dani-Jo and I are going to go talk to him about Adi. I'll cook us some food."

He eyes me suspiciously before replying, "Okay, Spitfire, but I'd rather be the one to cook the food. I need to take care of you like he is her."

"Love, I can cook for us. No one will judge you for sitting back and relaxing."

Placing his hands on the tree, he pushes up. "Yeah, that's going to be a no from me. I won't eavesdrop. I'll cook, you chat."

I shove my elbow into Pierce's side. "Stubborn!"

"You're the pot calling the kettle black." He's able to catch his balance.

Dani-Jo, Pierce, and I all walk over to where Larson is standing. I'm now roasting a marshmallow because Pierce demands to cook the food.

Dani-Jo stands on one side, and me on the other side of Larson.

Larson gives us the once over. "Oh great, I smell double trouble."

Letting a half-smile slip, I prod, "So, when do you plan on giving Adi a promise ring?"

Surprised, Larson coughs, "Ummm, what?"

"You heard me," I declare.

Larson babbles, "Ugh, what if she doesn't want to spend the rest of her life with me anymore? I pissed her off really bad the other day. I mean... I love her with all of my heart but I feel like I screwed up royally."

Dani-Jo spouts, "Yeah... you did! But after you explained yourself, she calmed down. I'm pretty sure there's nothing you could do to ever change her mind about you."

I reaffirm, "Don't doubt yourself. I see the way she still looks at you even after two years. You've got her...hook, line, and sinker."

Larson grunts, "Ok, ok. I'll ask her soon."

"How soon?" Dani-Jo asks.

"Ladies, I don't want y'all to tell Adi. So, I'm just going to keep the details to myself."

Balling my fist up, I slam it onto my hip. "Ok, fine. Don't tell us when, but have you thought about how you're going to ask her?"

"Kinda," he responds sheepishly.

Glaring at him, I snort, "Kinda? What the hell does that mean?"

"Y'all, I'm a guy, I'm not fluent in romantic gestures. I thought about asking her at dinner. I'll cook supper and put the ring inside a dark-colored glass of tea, so when she drinks, she won't see it until she's done."

Dani-Jo suggests, "That sounds like a fun idea. Can I recommend maybe a sunset picnic that you make food for?"

I contribute, "Also, she loves flowers. Pierce's mom has these gorgeous fields of the biggest sunflowers you've ever seen. I can go ahead of you and set everything up, scatter rose petals across the blanket and put a small vase of flowers in the center. Just keep that ring in your pocket. Do not lose it. Sneak it into the glass and after she finds it, pop the question."

Pierce lets one of his lips curl up on one side. *Ha!* He *is* eavesdropping, but that smile lets me know he approves of our meddling.

"Y'all, that sounds like a fantastic idea. When the time gets closer, I'll let you two know. I just don't want you to let it slip before then." Larson gives us a wink.

Jumping up and down, I clap my hands. "Eeeekkkk. I'm so excited for you."

I've burned and dropped the marshmallow off of my stick, but I don't even care. I'm so freaking excited for my friends.

We're currently padding back to our seats as our food has successfully cooked over the open flames. Adi eyes us suspiciously. I just grin back at her, not letting her in on our conversation with Larson.

Once we're done eating and socializing, Adi weighs in, "Hey, so since y'all are going to be attached at the hip soon, I say we steal Tova this weekend for a girls outing."

Dani-Jo seconds the idea.

I look up at Pierce to see his reaction. He places a small kiss on the top of my head. "Go on, babe. I just hope you actually get some sleep."

I pucker up and plant one on his soft lips. "Thank you. I'll do my best to sleep at least a couple of hours."

33

PIERCE

Watching the girls disappear into the woods, I turn to the guys. "Ok, now that they're gone. I need to ask y'all something. Actually, I really need a huge favor."

Kage joins our little rendezvous, stroking his jaw with his finger and thumb like Dad does. "What is it, Pierce?"

"I'm going to transform the loft of Tova's mom's barn for us into a living space. I need to build a hay shed first to clear the loft, then run some wire for electricity, plumbing for water, and make an area for the kitchen, bedroom, and bathroom. It'll be like a barn-dominium. Do you think we can rummage up enough Protectors to join in so we can get it all done this weekend?"

Kage declares, thumping me on the back. "Think? I know! I'll have all the guys up at the barn by seven AM. That work for you?"

"Absolutely, I'll go to Mom and Dad's tonight and update them on the new plans," I state.

"I'll head to the guys' cabin and alert them of their new tasks for this weekend," Kage informs.

Kole bellyaches, "Awe man, so no late-night howling at the moon, then?"

I give him a sympathetic look. "Sorry, man, not tonight. I've got a long haul, but I'll see you numbnuts in the morning."

Kaden doesn't miss a beat. "See ya, Flamethrower."

Chuckling, I march in the direction of the ranch.

Getting up at five AM is not my kind of Saturday. That two-hour trek on the back of a horse in the dark was hellish; I'm pretty sure I dozed off a couple of times. I yawn, rubbing my blurry eyes and stand before the barn holding the horse's reins.

"Guys, y'all ready to sweat?"

A few of them yell in unison, "Born ready."

All the guys are wearing tool belts with all the equipment for the job at hand. They even brought piping, wires, switches, faucets, a toilet, wood for separating the living spaces, you name it… they have it.

"Thank you, guys, for hauling all of this stuff here. I sure appreciate it. Hold on a second, I'll be right back. I'm going to put up Ace; he lugged my ass for two hours straight. I'm sure he's tuckered out."

"That's what friends are for." Jace thumps me on the back.

After Ace, my stud, is stowed away, I plod back to the guys. "We need to divvy out into groups if we're going to get this done in time. Whoever is skilled in plumbing step to my left, those proficient at electricity step to my right. Those who want to hammer away, stay right in front of me."

The guys shift in all different directions and after everyone has been given their assignments, we get to work.

The shed is almost complete, I see, when I stand to wipe my brow. I catch a glimpse of Shenan out of the corner of my eye. She's placing tablecloths along picnic tables where the farmers eat during the week. I keep hammering away but notice she makes multiple trips to the picnic tables with food and drinks, playing such a good hostess.

Turning my attention back to the shed, I'm almost done building, swinging my hammer to drive a nail in when she sneaks up on me.

"Pierce, hon..."

I jump out of my skin, dropping the nail to the ground.

She apologizes, "Sorry, dear, I just thought you and the guys might like to take a break and have some lunch."

Picking up the nail, I respond, "Oh, how kind, Shenan. You didn't have to do that."

Swiping her hand in an 'it was no bother,' fashion, Shenan replies with, "I know, son. I wanted to do it to show my appreciation. Y'all have got a lot accomplished. How much more you got to go?"

I tuck my hammer into my belt. "There are some guys running plumbing and electricity upstairs in the loft. They may be close to being done. The others are building partitions to separate the living spaces into living areas. Then we just have to put in appliances, toilet, shower, bed...then we'll be finished."

"That sounds like a huge feat, but I know you boys can do it. I'll plan on making y'all lunch tomorrow, too. I bet y'all will be done by tomorrow afternoon if you keep going at this pace."

Leaning my head down to my shoulder I use my shirt to wipe away sweat from dripping into my eyes. "Yes ma'am, that's the goal."

Shenan motions her hands for us to come on, insisting, "Why don't y'all take a break and come eat? I've got sandwiches, water, tea, and fruit. Plus, y'all can cool off for a minute."

Taking off my tool belt, I place it on the top of a pile of wood. "I'll round everyone up. Thank you again for everything."

Looking pleased, she responds, "No problem at all. Happy to do it. If y'all need more to drink, just holler at me, Ok?"

"Yes, ma'am, will do."

34

TOVA

I cough up the remaining blood that's choking me and grasp at the floor. The shadow steps closer to me and straddles me as I dig my nails into the wooden floor, gritting my teeth through the pain. "I won't let you touch them," I scream as I look to the corner of my dark room where Adi and Dani-Jo are cowered down.

Another shadow appears at my side and crouches down beside me, taunting, "Look at you, tears streaming down your face and blood oozing from your mouth. Y'all won't survive this."

Both shadows stand and loom toward my best friends, and I scream, "NOOOOOOOOOOOOO!"

I vaguely hear Adi's voice at a distance as she cries, "Tova, wake up! Wake up!"

My eyelids feel weighted down with iron and lined with sandpaper. Forcing my heavy lids open, I see a blurry Dani-Jo standing nervously in front of me, visibly upset. She's biting her trembling bottom lip, and I feel Adi at my side, stroking my back. I blink my eyelids, attempting to clear my hazy vision, my limbs can barely function as my muscles shake like Jell-O when I reach for them.

Realizing it was only a dream, I begin to weep and wobble up to a sitting position in my bed. "Oh my God, you're ok! You're both ok."

Dani-Jo is unable to contain her emotions and speaks through her sobs. "Tova, those nightmares are torture. I'm so sorry you deal with this every night. You're screaming scared me so badly, I thought you were dying."

"Yeah, they are, but honestly, as bad as they get, I'm glad they're only dreams and not reality." I reach for both girls and embrace them.

Adi voice is scratchy as she declares, "We're all three sleeping in this bed tonight. It's only two AM, and I want you to know we're here with you."

"Ok, we'll all be burritos, exactly like we used to be when we were little. That may help me sleep better, knowing y'all are right beside me." I remove the covers, letting them slide under with me.

It can't be any later than seven AM. Adi and Dani-Jo are hounding me to get up already, "Good gravy, after last night's escapade and the fact that it's Saturday morning, you girls want to rise and grind? What's wrong with y'all?"

Dani-Jo teases, "Haha. What do you mean, what's wrong with us? We just want to get this day started already. Now get up, Sleeping Beauty."

Adi insists, "Yeah, we want to spend as much time with you as we can before you're no longer an unattached woman. So, get up."

Grumbling, I sling my legs over to the side of the bed, "Fine." I stand elongating my arms and arching my back in a stretch, I ask, "What do you girls have up your sleeves that requires me getting up so dang early?"

Dani-Jo squints while rubbing her hands together. "Oh, you'll see."

I pout. "Ugh, I hate surprises."

Adi mocks, "We know, that's why we're not telling you anything, but we need to bring a towel, pack food for lunch and dinner, and wear some good hiking shoes."

Raising one eyebrow, I counter, "Um, a towel? What about a bathing suit or a change of clothes?"

Dani-Jo jests, "Unnecessary."

Rolling my eyes, I stand to get ready. "If you say so."

Everything's packed and ready to go. All three of us don backpacks full of the necessities they instructed me to bring. Trudging down a path leading to who knows where, we walk down memory lane.

Adi reminisces, "Remember when we were all about twelve

or thirteen, and hiked up to the highest point that we could on this mountain, just to test how far we could see?"

I grimace, "Oh yeah, I remember. How could I forget? We had to cross that dang river to get to the other side, and I fell off of it three times because my balance sucks. I should've just swum to the other side after that third backflip off that dumb tree."

Dani-Jo chuckles, "Oh, but not you. You and your determined self were going to cross that tree, come hell or high water."

Rubbing my temples in a circular motion, I wish I could forget. "Yeah, but even though I finally got to the other side, with the help of a tree branch balancing me, I still fell at the very end of the log, trying to get onto land..." I then slap my palm to my forehead at the memory. "I face-planted into the bank and blacked out for a split second."

Dani-Jo marvels, "One thing's for sure, if there's ever an obstacle presented before you, you'll go over, around, or under it, just to conquer it. That's what I love about you. You never see an impossibility. You always see a way."

I burst out laughing, "I just hope and pray that my relentless ways aren't the death of me."

Adi cracks, "Are you kidding me? You'd stare at death straight in the eyes and say, 'You can take my lungs, you can take my heart when you pry it from my cold dead hands,' and you know it."

"You're probably right. I'm too stubborn to die."

Adi flatters, herself. "Probably? Yeah, right! It's a fact."

Almost missing the path I had no idea we were supposed to take, Adi falters, "Oh... Oops, turn here."

Slipping from the mushy mud as I twist to go in the right direction we were supposed to be traveling, I beg, "Where exactly are we going?"

Dani-Jo answers, "Girl, you've got to learn patience."

"So, a simple inquiry is impatience? Good to know." I watch my footsteps, trying not to stumble again, and dig, "It's damp in these woods from the morning dew and lack of sun rays beaming through. If I knew where we were going, I wouldn't have almost busted my ass trying to get back on the correct path."

Adi stops for a minute and places a fist on her hip. "Oh, if you fall, you'll just get back up again, dust yourself off, and keep right on going. So, stop trying to get me to tell you where we're going."

Crossing my hands over my chest. "Ha, and y'all say I'm bullheaded. I may have learned it from y'all."

Looping her arm in mine, Dani-Jo nudges, "Maybe we all have a stubborn streak. It's not a character flaw."

"I never said it was. It's probably why we're all best friends because we're all so similar."

"Ain't that the truth." Adi encourages us forward.

Climbing another thirty to forty minutes, we finally near a clearing in the woods. Taking in the most beautiful meadow of wildflowers I've ever seen, I let out a deep exhale, "How in the world did y'all know about this place? It's spectacular."

"When you were out with your injury, Adi and I ventured out here with Larson, Kage, and a couple of other guys. This isn't even the best part." Dani-Jo beams, tugging me into the field.

Closing my eyes, I take in the fragrant aroma. "Really?"

"Really."

She guides me through the field of flowers until we get to the clearest cirque tarn. It has three different streams running into it from the mountains. Letting my arm go, she plops down her backpack.

"This is our destination for the day."

"Girls, I have to say you may have outdone yourselves." I say, dropping my bag to the ground.

Pleased with herself, Dani-Jo straightens out her towel on the ground. "Right? It's the perfect place for a picnic. You're still in for another surprise. This still isn't the best part yet. We brought supper for a reason."

"Hmmm, let me guess," I ponder, tapping my finger to my bottom lip, "the sunset is going to be breathtaking, too?"

Laying out her food on her towel, Adi retorts, "You guessed it. We know how you relish lovely sunrises and sunsets."

Once our lunch has been consumed, Adi stands and removes her shirt and pants.

Stunned, I cover my eyes. "What the heck are you doing, Adi?"

"Oh girl, you didn't think we were coming up here without swimming, did you?"

"Well, I didn't think we were going to because you said no swimsuit was needed before we left the cabin."

"What kind of fun would we have if we didn't go skinny dipping at least once in our lifetime? We're not holding anything back. You only live once. Not to mention, there's not a male in sight that would see us."

Giving in to her peer pressure, I shimmy off my pants and top as I grunt, "Oh, alright."

Dani-Jo, doffing her attire, adds, "Fair warning, it's colder than a witch's boob in there."

Huffing, I say, "Just fanflippingtastic. We have no clothes to change into. I'd better not catch pneumonia right before our vows. I will not miss out on my first sexy, steamy, lovemaking sesh because I'm sick."

Wide-eyed, Adi delves, "You mean to tell me that you two haven't had sex yet? Even with him staying with you all this time?"

I shake my head. "Nope, we sure haven't. He's chivalrous and wants to wait. We've done other things, just not that."

Dani-Jo shoves her fingers into her ears. "I don't need the details."

I grab her forearms and pull her hands away. "Oh stop, I'm not giving you insight on our love life." Turning to take a plunge into the pond, I ask, "How deep does this go? I can see clear to the bottom."

"It's at least twelve feet deep. You can dive if you want," Dani-Jo offers.

Alone in the middle of a picturesque meadow with my best friends, all of us in our birthday suits, I take in a big gulp of air. "You must have read my mind because the only way to get into frigidly cold water is just to do it and get it over with."

I dive into the freezing pool, then scurry to the surface. Pushing up above the water, I rasp, "Cheese and rice! This is worse than bathing in ice water."

Both Adi and Dani-Jo leap in. Rising to the surface, I wallop water at Dani-Jo's face.

"Hey, that's no way to show gratitude to your friend for a fun-filled day," she sputters.

Laughing and giggling, we dash, spray and splatter, soaking each other. I nod in Adi's direction in the center of the pool where she's still immersed underwater. "Show off."

Starting to shiver, Dani-Jo and I retreat from the pond. Dani-Jo deliberates as she grabs her towel, "I wonder how long she can stay submerged?"

Wrapping my towel around myself and stuffing the corner between my breasts to secure it, I answer, "If she can breathe under there, then probably a while, or at least until she's a prune and wants to surface. But with as cold as this water is... I'm guessing only a few minutes. I bet we're about to find out."

We sit at the water's edge, both of us admiring Adi and her blissful underwater pirouetting. I lean back onto my hands, propping myself up. "She looks so peaceful."

Dani-Jo agrees, "She really does, doesn't she?"

Dani-Jo peers up to the clouds as she lays back onto the grass, and points up "Look! An elephant."

Resting my head close to hers, I reply, "Gosh, I've not made objects out of clouds since we were kids."

"I know, I miss the simple life."

Furrowing my brows, I say, "Me too, but I'd never go back to those days."

Turning her head toward mine, she answers, "Tova, I'd never wish that on you. I'm so sorry you went through hell growing up. I'm so glad you've found your happy place."

"Thanks, Dani-Jo. Speaking of a happy place... inquiring minds want to know, what's the deal with you and Kage? You two sure have been hanging out a lot lately."

Heat flushes her cheeks. "Oh, I'm not sure it's anything. I'm not expecting him to see me as more than friends. He sees you with Pierce, Adi with Larson, and I think he feels sorry for me. He's just being a friend and doesn't want me to feel like a third wheel."

I tilt my head upward to meet her eyes. "Do you feel like a third wheel?"

She shakes her head. "No, not really. But if Kage wants to be nice, then who am I to stop him."

I grin. "You two make a cute couple. I know you're shy, but don't let that stop you from allowing yourself to be vulnerable to falling in love."

She rolls onto her side, props herself up on her elbow and rests her head in her palm, careful not to let her towel come unwrapped. "He's gorgeous Tova, I'm sure he could have anyone he wants. Not sure that's me. I mean, have you seen me? I just don't want to shrug him off and have him think I'm a jerk. I don't have any expectations for this to develop into anything."

Mirroring her, I prop myself up too. "Dani-Jo, you understand that you're only one decision away from a totally different life. You don't have to end up lonely. That doesn't have to be your destiny. You are in control of your future. Now take pleasure in the ride and stop thinking that you're not 'pretty enough' for him. Girl, you're beautiful. Any guy would be blessed to have you."

Springing up from the water, Adi moseys toward us, water cascading down her body. I joke as I throw her a towel. "I thought you'd never come up for air."

"It's not the air I came up for. I could stay underwater for days, at least I think I could. I came up because it's so freaking cold." She dries herself off, her quivering lips barely moving, "Are my lips blue? I feel like they're blue."

I have to bite mine together to keep from laughing. "Actually, they're kind of purple."

"Ha. I knew it." Finally getting the last drops off of her trembling body, she slowly lowers down to face us. "What were y'all talking about so intently?"

I glance at Dani-Jo to see if she will answer, and she glances back, questioning the same. I widen my stare to hint for her to say something, anything. If she doesn't want to discuss Kage, then that's up to her. I'm not going to tell if she doesn't want me to.

Fed up with the silence and awkward stares, Adi sarcastically claims, "Are you two keeping secrets?" Again Dani-Jo clams up, and I'm about to say something when Adi comes back with, "Your stunning silence is very reassuring."

If Dani-Jo isn't going to talk, then I'll have to come up with something. We've never been one to keep secrets from each other, but she's apparently not comfortable letting Adi know she's interested in Kage. She can at least let Adi know there's a potential someone.

As I finally open my mouth to speak, Dani-Jo interjects, "I might like a guy, but I'm not sure he's into me."

Adi squeals, "Really? Do I know this someone?"

Dani-Jo looks to me, pleading for help, and I shrug my shoulders, acknowledging that this is her story to tell. Hesitantly, she speaks quietly, "Maybe. But it could be nothing. I don't want rumors flying for nothing. Can we just forget about me and focus on Tova? This is her last weekend as a free woman."

"Girl, I may be going to tie the knot, but rest assured, I'll always make time to hang out with y'all with or without Pierce." The determination in my eyes glows toward Dani-Jo. "Now don't change the subject, and let's talk about this guy."

Adi scooches up closer to us. "Yes, I need all the juicy details."

Tearing off a blade of grass, and refusing to look at either of us, Dani-Jo says, "There are no details. Right now, we're just friends, and I'd say *barely* friends at that."

Putting her two index fingers together and touching her lips, Adi taps out a cadence. She looks like a mad scientist trying to figure out a potion. "Let me get this straight. You like a guy who may like you back, but you're not sure. Right now, you two are just in the 'friend zone,' but you want to figure out if he wants more? Does that sound about right?"

"I don't want to know, right now at least, if he wants to be more. I think that'd just scare him off."

Adi, with a long face, sincerely pats Dani-Jo's leg. "You've always been bashful, never letting your emotions show. Life is too short not to act upon feelings, not expose yourself to love. Don't be afraid to risk your heart. I feel like we're all so afraid of being hurt that we don't allow ourselves the chance to experience love. We need to forget all the 'what ifs.' I never want to look back and say, 'If only I had done this, or said that, or went there.' I want to love with no regrets. Remember, people who avoid disappointments never experience triumphs. You deserve much more than a mundane life. We all do. Take action toward your dreams. You'll never know how far you can fly until you fall, literally and figuratively."

Blinking her eyes rapidly, twining her fingers through both of her hands in a begging fashion, Dani-Jo clowns, "Oh wise one, if we could all be as courageous as you. You and Larson have such a wonderful relationship. We'd all be blessed if we could experience that in life."

Smiling, Adi encourages, "You can. Just have a little faith in the process and watch it flourish."

Feeling a slight breeze, I shudder. "I don't know about you two, but I'm done swimming for the day. I'm going to get dressed."

Both of them following my lead, proceed to put their clothes on. After buttoning my jeans, I reach for my bra and stop when I hear Dani-Jo whistle, "Oh my word. I didn't realize how bad that scar is on your back. Does it hurt at all?"

I reach for my shoulder blade. "No, not at all. I'm pretty sure if it hurt, it'd be so numb from the water I wouldn't feel it, anyway." I shrug my shirt on, feeling a sudden quickening in my gut.

I snap upright, scanning the forest opposite the pond, looking for any movement.

Noting my odd behavior, Adi tentatively interrogates, "Tova, what's wrong?"

Becoming astute to my sixth sense, I investigate the woods. "Did we go outside the protection wall when we came here?"

Dani-Jo reassures, "No. We haven't crossed the perimeter. Why?"

"I just have the impression that we're being watched."

Adi states, aghast, "Gosh, you're freaking me out now. Do you see anything?"

"No, I just have the hair standing up on the back of my neck. I'm looking for any signs of movement, but I don't see anything. I don't know about staying to watch the sunset and us traveling back in the dark. What do y'all say about us heading back now?"

Dani-Jo is on edge, gnawing her fingernails. "I say we listen to your gut instincts. We can always come back and watch the sunset later when the guys are with us."

We all gather our belongings quickly, shoving everything in our packs and throwing them on our backs. We make a beeline in the direction we came, which thankfully is the opposite of where I perceived the potential threat.

Crinkling her forehead, Adi declares, "Dani-Jo, I don't know about you, but those self-defense classes can't come soon enough."

"I couldn't agree more. Let's pick up the pace," Dani-Jo adds, shuffling faster down the narrow path.

All of us are on high alert, expediting our pace back toward the cabin. Not knowing how long we have to hike back, I ask in a hushed tone, "Hey, how long will it take us to get back to the cabin? I wasn't paying attention on the way here because I was busy pestering y'all about where we were going."

Adi says, "Maybe an hour and a half at a leisurely pace. But we're high-tailing it out of here, so, I'd say an hour tops."

The tree next to Adi sprays bark everywhere around her.

I slam my body into her, forcing her to the ground while screaming at Dani-Jo to, "GET DOWN!"

Diving behind a large pine tree, she hides while we crawl to her on our hands and knees. Frantically, I comb over Adi. "Are you hit anywhere?"

"No, I'm not. I'm fine. We've got to go. Now."

"Ok, but we can't outrun a gun. If this person is seeking us out and thinks we'll be on this path, we need to get back another way and fast. Dani-Jo, do you think you can see like a bird? I know we discovered you have bird-like appendages, but what about distance visions? I can see really well up close and in my peripheral. I can notice movement but not clearly defined images from far away. We just need to know what direction the threat is in so we can go the opposite way."

"Tova, I'm terrified that if I poke my head around this tree, then I'll be shot. I'm not immortal. I know that."

"I know, I know. I thought you could sprout your wings, or climb and get high enough to see. Do you think you can do that and do it quickly?" Visibly shaken, she nods. "Come on, Dani-Jo, you've got this. Take a deep breath, pick yourself up, dust off your legs, and get moving."

Dani-Jo leaps from branch to branch until she's about thirty feet off the ground, obtaining a good vantage point and peering down at us then back in the attacker's direction. Understanding the importance of us leaving immediately, she flaps down swiftly and quietly, completely uninjured.

"I didn't get a good look at the person, but he's alone. He's about one hundred yards away, Northeast. We need to go southwest. I saw a much smaller path that will lead us in the right direction to the cabin." She waves her hand toward the alternative path. "Follow me."

Adi and I scramble up, dust ourselves off, and scamper behind Dani-Jo. We sprint like we've never run before, veering off of the path we were on in an attempt to confuse the attacker of our whereabouts. After about thirty minutes of dashing through the woods, we arrive at the clearing where the cabins are. Panting as we come to a slower pace, we frantically search the guys' cabins for anyone to let them know about what happened. To our dismay, none of them are around. Since we're the only females in training to be Protectors, there's no one to alert.

Dani-Jo hollers, bending over and placing her hands on her knees, "Dang-it! Where is everyone?"

Adi infers, "I guess they're all giving Pierce a farewell party."

Dani-Jo furiously blows, "Well, where the hell is this party because we're about to crash it?"

Looking around for anyone, I acknowledge, "It's got to be close to dinnertime. Let's go to the cafeteria and see if they're there."

Dani-Jo wheezes, "Good idea."

Adi pats her on the back. "You going to be okay there?"

Taking deep breaths in and out, Dani-Jo enlightens us, "Of course. My adrenaline is crashing. I'm tired and pissed off, but I'm ok. I promise."

We hike up to the cafeteria, entering the common grounds and searching for our crew. None of them are here. Where are they? Good God. My stomach growls at the smell of food while we continue our search.

Adi looks at me. "Hungry much?"

"We did just run our tails off. So, yeah, I may have worked up an appetite. While we're here, we should eat."

Dani-Jo, looking green, sits at our designated table. "Y'all go on and eat. I think I might throw up if I do. I'll save us seats."

Pausing at the table, Adi bends forward to suggest, "Want

us to bring you a small snack, just in case you get hungry later?"

Dani-Jo places her elbows on the table, resting her head in her hands. "Sure, but more like a granola bar, or banana, nothing heavy, please. Oh, and extra napkins…so we can wipe up all of our sweat while we cool down."

Giving the thumbs up, I affirm, "You got it."

After Adi and I make our trays, I plop down next to Dani-Jo, and Adi sits in front of her. Handing her some napkins, I cross-examine her, "You sure you're ok?"

"Yeah, I've never been on the run for my life. I think I may have gotten too upset."

"I'll make you a glass of water and put some ginger in it. That may help your nausea." That's a remedy we've used for as long as I can remember for queasiness. I hope it helps settle Dani-Jo's stomach. Feeling nauseated is horrible.

"Thanks. That'd be great. I wished I'd just throw up. Maybe it'd make me feel better."

"We'll go back to the cabin after we eat, there you can get some rest. I'm sure the guys will come back later. We can update them then. I mean, if you're comfortable going there."

"It'll be fine. I'll be fine. I'm sure I'll get to feeling better after I clean up and rest."

Finishing up my food, I toss my trash then head back through the line, making Dani-Jo some water with ginger.

Once Adi is done eating, we all get up and head back to the cabin. It's dusk now, and I hear some rumblings up ahead at the guy's cabins. Looking in the distance, I notice an army of guys heading our way.

Dani-Jo exclaims, "It's about time! Where have y'all been?"

Kage is the first one that reaches us, Pierce not far behind him rushes to my side, while Kage demands, "What happened to y'all? Y'all look like death warmed over."

Adi sasses, "Thanks for noticing! I almost got shot by some moron in the woods where the flower meadow and natural spring is."

Drawing his brows together, Kage asks, "Y'all almost got shot at the place we went to a couple of weeks ago?"

Dani-Jo verifies, "Yeah, the same place. I climbed a tree to see if I could tell who it was, but I couldn't. I could only see that it was one person. We ran like a bad out of Cain, but when we got here, to our surprise, no one was here for us to tell or call on for help."

"From now on, I don't want y'all going anywhere without one of us with you." Seeing the disgruntled look on my face, he amends, "at least not until we neutralize the threat. We'll take shifts watching over your cabin again."

I'm a little frustrated because I know that these guys will protect us at all costs. Still, I'd rather be armed and ready for a confrontation instead of a bodyguard. Maybe both would suffice for a week or two, but good lord, when is this going to end?

Pierce's hands begin to roast, heating my side. I peek up at him and breathe, "We're ok, calm down, babe." He glints down at me with fire reigning in his eyes and coursing through his veins. "Babe, you can't tell me that this isn't the same person who injured you earlier this summer. I can't calm down."

"No, I can't. However, we can be equipped with our own guns, bows, axes, and self-defense skills, and you guys don't have to be responsible for our safety 24/7."

"We'll make sure you're well equipped, that's for damn sure." Scratching the scruff on his chin, Pierce continues, "What's bizarre, though, is the first assault seemed to come from outside the perimeter, and this one was inside it."

"Maybe the first time was a fluke. A stray arrow, like I thought."

"I guess anything is possible, but that doesn't explain the alert you got from the animals. I just want us to all be on the lookout until we figure out what the hell is going on."

"Ok, babe. So, what's the plan?"

Pierce rounds up everyone. All gathered in the middle of the cabins, Kage barks orders, "Two men will take four hours shifts watching the cabin until we figure out who is harassing the girls." Looking at me, Adi, and Dani-Jo, he states, "You three will have weapons on you at all times, even when you sleep. I want a gun at your bedside." Kage glances back into the crowd. "We have unfinished business that we need to complete tomorrow, but I want six guys to stay back and monitor the surroundings, stay with the girls at all times, and do whatever it takes to keep them safe. Do I make myself clear?"

All the guys say in unison, "Yes, sir."

Rubbing his hand up and down his forehead, flattening out the worry lines, Pierce says, "I have to go with Kage tomorrow, but I trust that the guys who stay back will watch over y'all like a hawk."

Pecking Pierce on the cheek, I reply, "That's fine. I don't want to alter y'alls plans. I appreciate you watching out for us. I love you so much. I'll miss you tonight."

He kisses me back. "I love you, and I'll miss you too. We'll sort this out. I promise."

"I know, love. I know. I'll see you tomorrow."

I turn, with the girls, and we walk to our cabin.

35

PIERCE

L aying in the twin bed next to Jace in a shared room, I can't help but let my mind roam to all the essential questions.

Who the hell is this trying to hurt or even kill Tova or one of the girls? They're now inside Iron Mountain. Where is that ass hiding?

God, I'm never going to sleep tonight if I can't put the puzzle pieces together.

Rustling in his bed, Jace faces me. "Hey man, I know you've got a million things going through your mind. Just know that we're going to do everything in our power to protect these girls. Now, get to sleep so you can finish that loft. You're close to being done. Just a few more hours and it'll be complete. When it's done, we can head back here. But, if you want, I'll stay back with them while you guys work to finish the loft."

"I appreciate it, man. I trust that the guys who stay back will protect them. You'll keep my mind off of not being here if you come. I'd rather you be with me."

"Ok, I'll be there." He moves onto his back. "I'm surprised Tova didn't ask what you had to help Kage do tomorrow."

"I was a little stunned too, but I'm glad she didn't pry because I can't lie to her and if I told her it was a gift for her, she might spy and follow me."

"I think it's a great thing, man…making this living space for the two of you. She's fortunate to have you as her partner for life."

"Thanks, man, but I'm the lucky one."

After a few hours mulling over all the what-ifs, I'm able to drift off to sleep only to be awakened by the most terrifying scream I've ever heard. Jolted out of my sleep, I jump out of bed and jet out of the cabin with Jace, Kage, Larson, and the twins behind me.

Running over to the girl's cabin that's being watched by a couple of Superior Protectors, I ask, "Was that scream from here? Did y'all see anyone enter the cabin?"

The guy's answer as the lights are turned on inside, and the screaming ceases.

"The scream came from inside. We ran up to the porch and

knocked. But no one has answered. We didn't see anyone enter the cabin," the guard explains.

"They may not have heard the knocking because of the screaming." I proceed, knocking on the door once more but with force.

Adi answers promptly, reassuring us, "It was just a nightmare. Tova's okay. We're okay."

Not happy with just, 'Tova's okay,' I press, "Can I come inside and check on her?"

Adi steps aside, allowing room for me to enter. "Absolutely. That may actually calm her."

I rush inside, looking to Adi for which way to go.

She points and discloses, "Second door on the right. Dani-Jo is with her."

I waste no more time as I burst through the door, but the sight of Tova stops me completely in my tracks. She's as pale as a ghost and trembling like a leaf on a tree while Dani-Jo is doing her best to soothe her, handing her a glass of water to sip on.

Slowly approaching Tova, I ask, "Spitfire, are you ok?"

She dips her head low, answering, "I'm fine. I'm sorry I woke everyone."

Carefully lowering myself on her bed beside her, I wrap my arm around her waist. "Don't apologize."

Tova merely leans into my chest and whispers, "Thank you for coming to check on me. I don't know if I can go back to sleep."

Knowing the rules, that no guy can sleepover in a girl's cabin and vice versa, I suggest, "There are a few empty cabins for future betrothed Protectors to live in. I'm sure Kage will let us stay in one tonight. I'll go ask him. After tonight, we'll stay in the loft if the cabin is out of the question."

Her trembling eases up as she raises to a sitting position. She rasps, "I need some fresh air."

Dani-Jo, kneeling at Tova's bed, pats her leg. "Do you think you have the strength to walk? You're pretty shaken up."

Tova pulls the cover from her legs. "I think so."

She's wobbly on her feet at first as she collides into me. I put my arm underneath her shoulders so she can steady herself.

"The rest of the guys from my cabin are outside on the porch. I don't want you to be alarmed when you see them."

Turning to face me, she asks through sober eyes, "Oh ok, thank you. Are they upset?"

I take her hand in mine and declare, "No. Why would they be? They're just worried. We had no idea what happened. We just heard screaming. We envisioned the worst. I hate to admit it, but I'm glad it was only a nightmare and not a physical injury to one of y'all. I'd never forgive myself if something happened to you."

Standing on the deck with Tova, I inform the guys what happened and about Tova's nightmare. Then I pull Kage aside and request that Tova, and I sleep in one of the vacant cabins; he's quick to oblige.

The guys all pat us on the back, grateful everyone's ok. The two scouts are still manning their positions to watch over Adi and Dani-Jo while Tova and I head to the nearest available one-bedroom chalet.

Once inside, I lock the deadbolt and fasten the chain lock. Pilfering through a drawer near the bed, I find and light a candle. Now that I can see better, I pull the covers back for Tova and me. She crawls into bed first and scooches over to let me in. I scoot up behind her, draping my arm over her middle.

Inching her back into my chest, she sighs. "I think it's safe to say that you're my only peace and comfort. I knew those guys were watching over us, but I had the worst dream as soon as I dozed off. I feel horrible that I woke everyone up. I wished all the tormenting dreams would vanish forever."

"Do you want to talk about it?" I ask as I pull her closer to me.

"I normally don't like talking about them; they don't feel fictitious. It's as if they're really happening," Tova utters as she places her right hand over her forehead.

"Perhaps if you talk about it, it'll help you overcome your fear. Do you want to try and see?"

"I guess... I'm willing to try anything at this point," Tova proclaims.

"I'm listening whenever you're ready," I coax.

As Tova is pressed against my chest, she begins trembling. Through a quivering voice, she begins, "Well, I'm running through the woods. Then I notice the trees are reaching out, grabbing my jacket, but as I'm being grabbed, I notice it's not the trees reaching for me. It's the shadows looming in the nightmares. They're always out to hurt me. I'm thrown to the ground, and as my face pounds into the dirt, my mouth is split open from the force of the blow. As my mouth fills with blood, the shadow pounces on top of me, binding my hands and feet. As I lay on the ground with my hands and feet bound, the rain is stinging my skin hammering down on me. And after the shadow tightens my bindings, it retreats to go get another figure lurking behind the trees.

"I struggle to free myself from ropes cutting into my flesh. Unable to free myself, I scream and cry as both of the shadows prowl toward me, one waving a machete while the other fans a dagger at me."

"Holy Shit! That's one hell of a nightmare. I feel like if you knew Cladec was, in fact, dead and it didn't seem you were actively pursued, then maybe you'd sleep without terror, and these nightmares might actually go away." I brush her cheek with my lips and reassure her "We'll get to the bottom of this. I'm here now. Try and get some sleep."

Resting her head on my arm for a pillow, her shaking stops, and she mumbles, "Mmm-k."

There's no way in hell I'm going to sleep tonight. So, I simply watch over Tova for the next couple of hours.

There's a little daylight outside when I hear a small rap on the door. Slipping my arm from under Tova's head, I sneak out of the cover and head to the door. When I open it, Kage is standing there, all ready to go.

"We still on for today to complete the loft?"

I push my unruly hair to the side with my hand. "Yeah, let me tell Tova I'm going with you. Are the guys still watching over the cabins and girls?"

"Of course. I think we'll be done with your loft in a few hours. You'll be back here in no time. I'll be waiting for you to get ready, then we'll all go."

"Ok, just give me a few minutes."

Kage nods, and I close the door. Walking over to a literal sleeping beauty, I tap Tova on the shoulder. "Tova, love, I'm going to head out with Kage to finish a project. We'll be gone for a few hours, but I'll be back soon. Are you okay with that?"

Tova grumbles, rubbing her eyes when she rolls over to face me. "Mmm, yeah. I'll get up and go stay with the girls." She tosses the covers aside. "Don't rush whatever y'all are doing. We'll be ok. I'm going to make sure we stay around here today."

Stepping outside, I see Kage is already back at the guys' cabin, so I walk Tova over to join the girls.

R eady and out the door, we all trudge to the loft. Most of the walk there is in silence. All of us are still on edge about yesterday's shooting and the terrifying scream that woke most of us in the middle of the night has us even more tired and on high alert. Looking to my left, then to my right, I reflect, *these guys are so loyal and hardworking. I'm very fortunate to have them in my life.*

Unlocking the gate for us to enter, Kage stands beside me, waiting for everyone to come in before I close and lock it back. I guess that big brother watching out for me will always be a part of who he is. After all the guys are in, we meander up to the barn. Everything has been wired, and plumbing is completed. Now, all we have to do is finish the appliances and minor details.

Jace and I grab the toilet and assemble the bathroom together as Kage heads up putting the kitchen together. Jace gives me a silent but hard stare.

"What's on your mind, Jace?" I ask.

"We got to find who this maniac is. I don't know about you, but I say no training tomorrow, and we search for this asshole. We have Superior Protectors with mad tracking skills. They may even find the bullet and see what kind of gun shot at them, and we can narrow it down to people owning guns. Few people in our territory actually carry guns aside from us Protectors. Just a few farmers and those who hunt for food."

"Sounds like a plan to me, but do you think some Superiors wouldn't mind staying back? I know that the other girls wanted to learn self-defense skills."

"Well, after we're done here today, we can teach them. It won't take us but a few hours here."

"You're brilliant. Let's haul ass and get this job done."

The loft is complete, and it's only lunchtime. I'm pretty sure that's record-breaking time for us to put together a living space. Looking around the completed area, it's quaint yet simple. I sure hope Tova likes it.

Climbing down the ladder, I round the corner of the barn to see a lovely display of food for all of us. Shenan strolls up, dusting her apron off. "You fine gentleman, eat all you want. I'll come to clean it up when you're done."

I answer, "Thank you so much. We've been at it all day. It's finally complete. Once we're done eating, we're heading back to the girls, but I don't want you cleaning all this up by yourself. We'll make sure to clean up after ourselves. Do you want to go see how the area looks? Make sure you think Tova will like it?"

Beholding all of us, Shenan grins from ear to ear. "Oh, Pierce, I'd love to. I can't believe you all got done so quickly."

Jace hints, "We've had a little more motivation today to complete the task early, Ms. Campbell."

Eyeing us suspiciously, she crosses her arms across her chest. "Guys, what drummed up this insistent motivation?"

Kage is the one to infer, "Ma'am, no one got hurt, if that's what you're thinking, but when the girls went on a hike yesterday… They were shot at."

Clutching her chest in shock, she stresses, "Oh my gracious alive. Are they ok? I know you said they weren't physically hurt, but I bet they're shaken up."

"Yes, ma'am, they were yesterday when we got back to the cabins. However, we didn't leave them alone. There are several Superior Protector's there keeping an eye on them."

"What are y'all going to do about this? How do you think

you'll find the perpetrator? Do you have anyone in mind that would do such a thing?"

Pointing to our circle of guys, Kage informs her, "All of us discussed it while we were working up in the loft. We're going to go back and teach them self-defense skills. The girls are already armed with weapons.

"Tomorrow several of us will go to the area where the attack happened. We'll drum up clues and put the puzzle pieces together. We'll get to the bottom of this. I promise. Don't worry, we're going to take care of Tova, Adi, and Dani-Jo."

Shenan folds her hands together in front of her. "I know they're in excellent hands. I guess I'll go see what you all worked so hard on. Thank you all for taking the time to gift my sweet little girl and Pierce this nice loft."

Kage tips his head. "It was our pleasure."

F inishing our lunch, we clean the tables off and throw out our trash.

Shenan comes down from the loft.

"Oh guys, it's lovely. Tova's going to love it."

I mention, "Thank you. It's a labor of love, that's for sure."

She hugs me, her head barely coming to my chest, uttering, "I know it was, son. I can't wait until next Saturday."

I sure hope Tova likes it. I'm a guy with no interior design experience. Still, it's not like Tova has to have fresh-cut flowers on the table every day or a perfect quilt on the bed with the perfect little throw pillows that have been hand sewn. Looking back at the barn as we walk toward the gate, I convince myself.

She'll like it. She takes pleasure in the simple things.

Hiking back to the cabins, Kage walks alongside me, deep in thought. I've been mulling over how to get the attacker to reveal himself. One way that I think will work makes my stomach turn, but it's almost a sure-fire guarantee. So, I put my thoughts to words and suggest, "I think we need to bait the assailant."

Kage looks at me, bewildered. "Yeah, how do you propose we do that? It seems that it's two different people. The arrow came from outside the wall, and the bullet came from inside. Unless it's someone that comes in and out or someone who has breached the wall, then we may have two different people."

"Well, we can do one or two things. First, we can let the girls have every afternoon off from class and let the stalker learn their new routine. We stay away from them, appearing to let our guard down, but really, we're just all hiding in plain sight. But honestly, I think the second idea I have will work faster."

Kage has a glint in his eyes. "What is it?"

"We go outside the border pretending to quail hunt for a few days because it's not deer hunting season. We appear to leave the girls alone in a tent while we're 'hunting,' but we'll all hide in the woods. When the attacker comes, we make his life a living hell."

Massaging the back of his neck, Kage replies, "I think I like the second plan better myself. So, let's hash out the plans... For today, we're going to do hands-on self-defense training. Then tonight, we'll pack up and get ready to go camping on a fake hunt and bait the idiot. So I guess we need to leave out at dawn tomorrow?"

"That works for me."

We are almost to the common grounds, when Kage prompts, "I think it's best if you and Tova stay in the same cabin again tonight. Then we'll all be camping this week. Good thing we got the loft done this weekend because this week is going to be crazy with us leaving." He slaps his hand to my back. "Perhaps this additional living space can be a wedding gift. She'll be able to appreciate it more after the moron is taken care of."

"That'll probably be best. I appreciate you letting us stay there. I know it's essentially breaking the rules."

Kage chuckles, "Man, after that scream Tova let out last night, I'd let y'all *have* the place."

36

PIERCE

O nce we're back in the common area, we meet up with the girls. They've obviously hung around here all day. When we hike up the hill to greet them, Adi hops out of her rocking chair.

"You guys have fun this morning working away?"

Larson heads up the steps and grabs her by the waist, spinning her around in the air, kissing her neck. Adi pretends like she doesn't like it and pushes him away the best she can. "Ew, you're gross and sweaty."

Larson sets her down and cynically points out, "Well, we had a mission to complete. We couldn't stay at the cabin and lounge around in rockers all day."

Attempting to escape his grasp, Adi cries, "Ha, ha! Someone thinks he has jokes."

I interrupt their reunion, easing over to Tova. "Have y'all had any suspicious activity today?"

Rising from the rocking chair, she tucks a few stray blonde hairs behind her ears. "No. These goons wouldn't leave the cabin until y'all got back. I tried to get them to go to the gym with me, but nooooo. They said it was better to wait... So, we've been playing cards, charades, and been bored out of our minds. I'm so glad you're back, and so soon. I wasn't expecting you until later."

"I told you we'd only be a few hours. Did you not believe me?" I ask, a teasing light in my eyes.

"Yes, but a few can mean three or more, so I just didn't know. I'm just happy to see you," she admits with a soft smile.

"You still want to go to the gym?" I ask.

Jumping up and down, she exclaims, "Yes!"

"Good. Actually, Adi, Dani-Jo, can y'all get ready to go to the gym as well. We were discussing on the way back here that we need to teach y'all self-defense."

Adi looks confused. "Aren't Sundays free days?"

"Yes, technically they are. However, we've devised a plan that's going to trap the idiot trying to hurt y'all. That's going to require our training today."

Placing her hand on her hip, Tova sternly demands, "And just how exactly do you suggest we trap the attacker?"

Gathering everyone around, I explain, "We will pack up tonight and leave out early tomorrow to go on a fake hunt." I give the girls stern looks., "You girls are going to have to trust us. We're going to leave you three alone in a tent as all of us leave on this bogus hunt."

Dani-Jo shouts, "What? NO! No way am I going to be a sitting target for some idiot to kill."

Raising my hand to stop her rant, I insist, "I never said we were going to let the attacker kill y'all. You three will have weapons on you at all times. They'll just be concealed. We'll be staked out in the forest, waiting for him to rear his ugly head. He'll be stalking y'all... Well, all of us really. He'll learn our routine, when we leave, come back, every move we all make... he'll commit to memory. That's why I believe it'll take a few days." I scratch the scruff on my chin. "It may not be only one person either. We just don't know yet."

Tova takes my hand in hers, and I know my palm is searing hot from my anticipation, but she doesn't seem to be bothered by the heat. Tova gives me a reassuring look. "We'll be fine. I trust you guys. Plus, we'll all have weapons and self-defense skills."

Kage steps forward, clapping his hands and rubbing them together, looking at everyone. "Alrighty then. We'll all meet in the gym in thirty minutes."

Crossing the threshold of the gym door, I set my sights on Tova. Noticing my arrival, she leaves Adi and Dani-Jo's side and treads my way, sizing me up and down. "Looking good in that tank and running shorts, Pierce. Ready to get your butt kicked again?"

"Hahaha. That's what you think. You knew what tactic I

was going to use. Today's a different story. You're not going to know which of us will attack, what maneuver we'll use, or what direction we'll be coming from. Today you will be blindfolded."

Her posture stiffens and she crosses her arms over her chest. "Seriously? What about Dani-Jo and Adi?"

They obviously hear us talking about them and stride over to us.

I speak up, addressing all of them. "First off, you'll just learn the skills, then as y'all progress, we'll blindfold y'all too." I turn my gaze to Tova. "You're going to have to tune out all the commotion going on around you. It echoes like crazy in here."

Tova's hands move to her hips. "Challenge accepted!" She shifts her weight to her left leg and cocks her right knee out, slanting me a sidelong glance. "Can I use my ability?"

"Of course! When we're out there, I want everyone to use their gifts. We have them, might as well use them to our advantage."

Hearing a slamming door resonating a low rumble throughout the gymnasium, we all turn to see Kage strutting in our direction. He's definitely a man on a mission. Taking charge of the session, he requests everyone to meet in the center of the hardwood floor. He divides us into three groups —one girl to each group of about ten guys. Once we're subdivided, he instructs us on how to proceed through the training.

Larson is heading up Adi's group, which I'm not sure is the best idea because she will absolutely hold a grudge if he accidentally hurts her or allows one of the guys to hurt her.

Kage is taking responsibility for Dani-Jo's group, and he's left me in control of Tova's group.

I pull out a few mats for us to run through drills on, hopefully preventing too much pain from the blows I know we're all about to sustain. Next, I place a tight blindfold over Tova's eyes and instruct her to plug her ears until I let her know we're done discussing our strategy. I gather my group of men, walk to the other ends of the room, and discuss quietly what assaults we are to execute. Apologizing in advance, I'm sure to give them some inclination of her powers. With any luck, they won't get maimed too severely.

Removing Tova's fingers from her ears, I inform, "There are a group of intruders approaching the camp. You don't know how many. Tune in your ears to hear in every direction around you. Drown out what's going on with the other groups. Focus on the noises about ten to fifteen feet around you."

Tova bobs her head up and down. "Got it."

I motion for my men to proceed.

Kaden and Kole are the first to creep toward Tova to assault. Snaking her head slowly back and forth, I'm confident she senses something is about to happen. Kaden is about two feet from grabbing her when she sideswipes his legs out from under him. She jumps upright and bends her arm at the elbow. Not seeing what she's about to hammer down on, she jumps down with her elbow and delivers a full-force blow to his ribs, knocking the breath out of him completely. He scrambles to his side, gasping for air, but she doesn't let that distract her.

Kole is next to reach for her. She must have heard the movement to know what direction he was coming from because she jolts to the left as he goes for her right arm. Crouching down, she keeps her arms bent but close to her chest. Kole regroups then comes at her from the front again, but this time she delivers an open hand strike to his cheekbone right below his right eye, knocking him off balance. She lunges forward and pushes him all the way to the ground, then kicks him in the gut.

Two more men set off to capture her. One of them rushes in and grabs her from behind. He's so forceful he lifts her feet off of the ground, and he's squeezing her pretty hard. I'm about to intervene, but she smashes his head with hers, causing blood to gush down his face. She's busted his mouth and nose open. He immediately drops her, and she falls to her hands and knees, catching herself.

The next guy is a little more cautious. Now that she's on the ground, he takes advantage of her in this position. He sneaks up, grabbing her around the neck. She backpedals on all fours to get out of his grasp. He clutches harder, and her face turns red; unsure if she's able to breathe, I start to interfere again. You'd think I'd know by now that she's got this, but I can't stand to see her struggling. Right when I'm about to yank the guy off of her, she jams her chin into his ribs, forcing a grunt out of him. Lifting her inside arm off of the ground, she delivers a backhanded blow to his cock. He instantaneously lets go of her as he falls to the ground guarding his manhood, moaning, and she falls to the ground gasping for air.

She reaches for the blindfold to take it off, but I grab her wrists, preventing her from removing it.

"Leave it on, baby. You are kicking these guy's asses. You've only got six more to go, and you're done."

Splaying out on her back with all four limbs spread out, she protests, "Are you freaking kidding me? I've only fought four, and I'm about to die."

"No, you're not. You're listening better than I knew you could…with all the yelling and other mêlées going on in here, there's no way I'd be doing as good as you. Keep up the excellent work."

"Oh, for all the love that is good in this world, can't we be done now?"

Reaching down, I grab her hand to help her up. "Come on, Spitfire. You've got this."

The other guys aren't as brave as the first four. They quickly get put out of commission. Tova, sweat beading down her face, and all the Protectors who are entirely worn out in our group are now sitting on the floor watching Adi and Dani-Jo hash out their drills. It's dark outside, indicating that we've been preparing for a good half day.

After everyone's completed their coaching, we grab our towels and water bottles. Tova throws her towel around her shoulders under her ponytail, drying the wetness underneath. Adi takes her water bottle and drenches herself with it from head to toe. Dani-Jo guzzles hers between panting for air. Now that everyone has their belongings, we amble toward the lodges.

Understanding that everyone has missed dinner, I ask, "Does anyone want to grab a bite to eat before we go back? We walk right past the cafeteria on our way."

Dani-Jo is the first to speak up, "If I eat now, I'll throw up. I just want to shower, pack up, and hit the bed."

Adi concurs with her, "I agree."

Tova mentions, "I'm not that hungry, but if you guys want to go grab something, I'll go with you."

Most of the guys say they want a small snack, so we make a pit stop by the cafeteria and let them grab some fruit, granola bars, and nuts to munch on.

Arriving back at the cabins, we drop off Adi and Dani-Jo first. There are two Superior Protectors already there outside, prepared to keep watch for the night.

Moseying over to our chalet, we wave bye to the guys as we depart the group. Once inside, I lock the door and ask, "How do you feel things went tonight?"

Dabbing the dampness from her neck, she answers, "I feel like it went great. Even Dani-Jo and Adi did fantastically."

I walk over and take her soggy towel, giving her a dry one. "Are you nervous about luring the attacker this week?"

She gives me a stern look, as if I should know the answer. "Of course. But I know that I'll be much better off once everything is done and over." Peeling off her sodden tank over her head, she muffles, "We'll all be able to sleep better, that's for sure." Now struggling to take off of her saturated pants, she hops out of them, steadying herself on the footboard. "At least I know I will. What about you; what's your take on this?"

"I'm ready for it to be all over with as well. I'm not looking forward to putting you girls in harm's way, but like I said before, come hell or high water, we're taking this asshole down."

Looking at the door, she takes in all the food, weapons, tent, and other camping supplies. "I'm guessing the other Protectors gathered all of this up for us already?"

"Yeah, Kage had some of the guys stay back and put together all the things we'd need so we can load up the backpack in the morning."

"Sounds good. I'm going to shower and get ready for bed."

Reaching for my pajama bottoms, I say, "Okay, angel, I'm getting ready for bed now. I'll be waiting for you." I already showered before we went to practice because I was pretty disgusting when we got back from finishing up the loft, and I didn't really break a sweat watching her kick those guys' asses.

Hearing the water flow in the bathroom, I turn out the lights and crawl under the covers.

I'm almost completely asleep when Tova bounces onto the bed to my right, scaring the shit out of me. Jolting my arms out, my eyes fly open. "Babe, you trying to give me a heart attack?"

Leaning over to kiss me, she cackles, "No love, but you have to admit that was pretty funny."

Turning over to her side, she asks, "You know you're pretty cute when you're half asleep like this?"

Spooning in behind her, I mumble, "Good to know." I begin caressing her arm idly. God, she feels so soft. I can't believe that we've come so far in our relationship. Fantasizing how our future will look, it's not long before I'm out like a light.

37

TOVA

Hearing that blasted alarm, I grab my pillow and throw it over my ears. The sun's not even out yet. Pierce removes his arm from my side and turns away to silence the alarm. He tosses his cover aside but refusing to move, I complain, "No, you can't get up. You're so warm."

"Believe me, babe, I'd stay in bed with you all day every day if I could. After this Saturday, we have an entire week that we can sleep in and cuddle." Reaching over nudging my shoulder, Pierce urges, "C'mon baby, let's get the show on the road."

Kicking the covers off, I gripe, "Ugh, fine."

After we've tidied up the cabin and packed our camping supplies, we exit. Standing on the porch, the sun finally peeking over the mountain, we scan the area and walk to the center of the circle of log cabins toward the other Protectors. Once everyone is gathered, Kage instructs where we'll hike to and camp for the next few days. It'll take most of the day to arrive at our destination. Taking in a deep breath, I close my eyes and tell myself, it's going to be ok, everyone will be okay, we're going to end this bastard and make it back here safe and sound.

Sensing my tension, Pierce steps close to me and takes my hand in his, twining our fingers and reaffirms, "Baby, just breathe. Don't fret. We're all on your side. Remember, you're not in this alone." Squeezing his steaming hand, I open my eyes, staring at the pathway before us.

Arriving at the Iron Gate that separates the outside world from our territory, two Protectors unlock and open it, allowing us to exit. They've got their eyes peeled on any suspicious activity outside the opening. Careful not allowing anyone or anything in behind us, they slam the gate closed, locking it after we exit.

Walking into the unknown, I begin to tremble. I clutch Pierce's hand tightly. Leaning over, he pecks my cheek. "I've got you, babe."

Practicing my breathing techniques, I do my best not to hyperventilate. I can't let my nerves get the best of me. Hearing some rustling leaves behind me, I glance back, noticing Adi and Dani-Jo are hurrying to get to me.

Dani-Jo pats me on the back. "Girl, I'm scared too, but you know I'd do anything for you. Right?"

Unable to speak, I hum, "Mmm-hmm."

Adi steps to my other side and takes my left hand. "We're all in this together."

At this point, I curl my fingers into the sleeve of my shirt and close my eyes, fighting back the burning tears from erupting in my dreaded fear and anticipation of possibly seeing the attacker, whoever that may be. My mind is processing a thousand different scenarios all at once, causing my emotions to run wild. My breathing is coming in fast, shallow breaths, and my entire body tingles all over. I can feel the blood draining from my face. Forcing my eyes open, the ground beneath me sways, and so do I. My legs barely function as I try to put one foot in front of the other. My eyelids are heavy, too heavy as I try to redirect my attention to the foot-path in front of me.

Unable to focus on my surroundings, my feet falter, as everything tunnels, I stammer, "I think I'm gonna…".

38

PIERCE

S hit! Shit! Shit!

Tova's gone completely limp. Adi and I grab her under her arms, preventing her from face planting in the rocky terrain. Whistling to Kage to stop walking, Adi and I remove her backpack then place her on her back on the ground. Dani-Jo tosses me a water bottle to give to Tova when she comes to.

Holy shit, she looks as white as a sheet. Patting her cheeks, I plead, "Tova, babe. Wake up. Please wake up."

Adi shakes her shoulders. "Tova. Come on now. It's ok. We're all here."

Tova turns her head slightly with leaves and pine needles stuck in her hair and blinks slowly. "Wha... what happened?"

Cupping her face, I sooth, "Baby, you passed out on us. Can you drink some water for me?"

Adi and I give her our hands, helping her to a sitting position. She reaches for the canteen and sips some ice-cold water. Placing her hands on her forehead and rubbing down to her cheeks, she recalls, "I blacked out. I'm so sorry. I... I just haven't been outside these walls, and all I was thinking about was what could go wrong." Tears forming in her eyes, she peers into my soul, beseeching, "Pierce, please... no one can die out here, please not because of me."

"This person or persons will not stop until we stop them. I can't promise that no one will get hurt. I'll do whatever it takes to protect you."

"I know, and that's what scares me the most. I can't live with myself if something happens to you or anyone."

Adi looking sympathetically, tries to console, "Tova, we all took the position of Protector with the understanding that at some point we're going to be put into harm's way. There are no promises that nothing bad will or will not happen. We take the risk, do our best at what we're trained to do, and go from there." Pulling her hand, she helps Tova stand, "Now let's get going. I want to set up camp before it gets dark. Those wild beasts prowl at night, you know?" Reaching over, Tova takes her backpack from Dani-Jo.

M ost of the hike to our destination is made up of crunching leaves as we march, squirrels scampering from tree to tree, and birds chirping as they fly in the canopy above us.

As we come up on a clearing, the sun is setting behind a mountain to our west. While there's still a little sunlight left, we pitch our tents in a circle. Once our tents are erected, we gather stones to make a circle in the center for a fire pit, then we collect kindling and logs for a fire tonight. Once the fire is going, Kage assembles us all together around it to discuss the plan to lure the attacker.

Kage addresses all of us, "Each night we will have six guards rotating watch over the campsite. There will be two men taking watch for three hours at a time, between the hours of nine PM and six AM. Every man will be awake at 6 AM to prepare for the fake hunt. After we eat, we will pack our guns and get ready for the hunt. Around seven AM we will dispersion in different directions. A few men will go in search for quail and vegetation to give the impression that we really are on a hunt. This will also ensure we have dinner each night. The guys that aren't hunting will stay within one-hundred yards of the campsite. We need to be hidden in trees, in the underbrush and staked out in various locations as we wait for whoever is causing the threat." Looking at the men sternly, he continues, "Do not reveal your position until the attackers raid our camp. If you have an ability that you can use on the attacker, then by all means, do so."

Larson asserts, wrapping his arm around Adi's shoulders. "When the person assaults our girls, I hope you know we're going to start an extremely hostile defense tactic to protect them."

Kage places his hand on Dani-Jo's knee and consents, "I'd expect nothing less."

Tova glances at Kage's gesture, then looks back at me. I'm doing my best not to squeeze her as my arm encircles her waist. I can see that Tova is trying to process what his body language is expressing. I candidly shrug my shoulders. I have no idea what's going on, but if he's into Dani-Jo, then obviously that makes this mission more personal for him as well, and that means... no matter what may come our way, this fucker is going down. Understanding that now three of us men are sorely protective over these girls, I let a mischievous smile creep up my face.

Tova pries as she slits her eyes at me in a half-smile, "Hm, I've seen that look before. What are you thinking?"

Looking pleased, I inform her, "Oh, just that I'm damn glad that at least three of us see this as a personal mission to eradicate this asshole."

She glances at Kage, then back to me. "Three, huh?"

Nodding in Kage's direction, I point out, "You and I both know that whether or not Kage admits it, he likes Dani-Jo, and I know him well enough to know that he takes his position seriously. No one in our group is going to let any of you girls get seriously injured, not on our watch."

"Well, I hope y'alls plan works," she says, wringing her hands together. "Like Adi said, y'all can't promise anything. We just have to trust that we possess the skills and knowledge we need to fight and defend ourselves against the invader."

Trying not to look antsy, she leans back, propping up on her elbow and forearms, and tilts her head up to the clear night sky. Mimicking her position, I lay beside her. She points out with despondency, "You know the stars always shine brightest in the darkest nights."

I flip onto my side and mention, "That goes for life too, you know? Without the darkness, we'd never fully appreciate the stars."

Letting out a deep sigh, she turns to face me and reflects sorrowfully, "You know the stars that are shining the brightest are the ones about to burn out?"

The full moon above breaks the blanket of darkness and illuminates Tova's sticking features. The dejection in her voice and the deep set sadness behind her eyes is tearing my heart in two. I have to help her see that she's a fierce fighter and is unstoppable. I gently lay my hand on the side of her face and look sincerely into her gaze. "Tova, you've been beaten, violated, and shattered into a million pieces. But there's nothing you can't do. Day after day, year after year, you've always found a way to pick yourself up, stare fear in the face and prove you're indestructible."

Dropping her head low, she dissolves back onto the grass saying nothing at all. She only stares upward into the dark abyss watching with heart-wrenching eyes, the delicate dance of the infinite stars that sweep the sky.

Kage stands, instructing everyone to call it a night except for those that'll be keeping watch. They're to keep the fire going throughout the night as well as warding off any animals.

I heave myself up to a standing position, bend over and reach out a hand pulling Tova up as well. We crawl inside our tent, get our sleeping bags out, spreading one down to lie on and the other to cover up with. Getting situated on the ground, I open my arms up to her and she curls up against me. I hold her close and graze the hair on the top of her head with my lips. She snuggles in closer to me. I slowly stroke her arm and chill bumps cover her as I lean over, kissing her neck while whispering, "You make me so unbelievably happy. I can't believe I got so lucky to have you in my life."

Tilting her head to peek at me, she says, "I'm glad you feel that way now. I just hope you continue to feel that way after this week."

"Nothing and no one could ever change the way I feel about you. Never forget that."

With that, she pecks my cheek and rolls back over. Draping my arm over her waist, I pull her body closer to mine.

We've been asleep a few hours when Tova sits straight up from a sound sleep. Startled, she announces, "Something's close by. I don't know what, but we need to warn the others."

Unzipping the tent, she flies outside before I can grab her. I have no idea if whatever is out there is dangerous, so I jet out of the tent after her with my gun in tow and my crossbow on my back. When I stand up outside my tent, I notice Tova and the two other Protectors standing too still as several red beady eyes stare back at us. Those eyes can only mean one thing... we're surrounded by Lynxwolves.

One of the Protectors has a large stick. Raising it, he swishes it at one of the animals yelling, "Yah, Get! Get on!"

That only provokes it. The massive beast lunges at him, snarling, and pins the Protector to the ground. I raise my gun to shoot, but Tova holds out her hand, beckoning for me to stop.

Not saying anything, she closes her eyes, and a few seconds later the beast is climbing off of the guy; it's not growling or snapping its teeth anymore either. When Tova opens her eyes, they're glowing catlike again. Glinting at me, then the animal, she carefully walks in front of me, approaching the creature. I hold my gun out, ready to shoot if it attacks, but Tova doesn't seem afraid at all.

Kneeling to a submissive position, Tova eases to her knees only three feet away from the massive black Lynxwolf. I'm about to yell for her to get away when the beast lowers itself onto its belly, crawling toward her. Now, I'm shaking, my hands are steaming hot, adrenaline-pumping, and my heart is pounding. I'm not sure what to do. Do I shoot, or do I let her do her thing?

Opting to stand down, I ease my gun to my side. I'm still not sure what this beast is going to do. I look to the other guys and use my hands, gesturing to hold their position, directing them not to intervene. Focusing my attention back on Tova, I see that she now has seven or eight Lynxwolves crawling to her side. My eyes are bulging out of my head in shock and awe. She's obviously communicating with them somehow, so I carefully back away from her, remaining as calm as I can.

Studying her, I can see that her eyes are open, but she's not staring any of them directly in the eyes. She's concentrating on her surroundings or something. Shifting from her knees to a sitting position, she crisscrosses her legs and holds her hands palm up, touching her middle finger to her thumb. Humming a soft tune that I've heard her hum before, the animals seem to relax even more. This practice goes on for several minutes until they appear under a trance. Once Tova has them in her command, she rises to a standing position, and they jump to their feet all at once. Pointing into the woods with her right arm and index finger, they take off.

Shifting her eyes back to normal right in front of me, I ask, "Umm, care to tell me what the hell just happened?"

"I just tuned into their auras and allowed them to sense that we were not a threat. They were just curious about our arrival, but when the genius over there started swinging that stick, they became defensive. I had to send off positive vibes of peace. Once they recognized that we weren't dangerous, they seemed to be less edgy. I helped them understand that we honor and respect them, then they quickly sought to trust me.

I was able to calm them down and help them understand that we're not here to hurt them."

"They really seemed to respond to that song you were humming."

"Oh, that's just something my mom did for me when I was having a nightmare or got hurt. It always seemed to help settle me down. So, I figured it might work for the Lynxwolves too." She says, shrugging her shoulders.

"Well, it sure did. Good job, babe. Now we can sleep better knowing that they shouldn't attack us." I reply, kissing her on the forehead.

Taking her by the hand, I lead her back to the tent. She glances at me, noting that my hands are a bit warmer than usual. "A bit edgy yourself, aren't ya?"

I kiss the knuckles my fingers are intertwined with.

"Considering I thought we were about to be dog food and when you approached them, and I was completely unsure of what was going to happen... Yeah, I'd say I was on edge. Nevertheless, I've managed to cool down."

We slink inside, and after we assume our canoodling positions, we quickly go back to sleep.

39

TOVA

Waking up to the smell of eggs and sausage, I unzip the entrance of the tent. Scanning the fire before me, I realize the guys have brought a cast-iron skillet to cook on. I step out and walk over to the guys.

Kole holds out a makeshift plate with food on it. "Want some?"

"Yes, thank you. Who in the world brought actual food?" I answer, graciously accepting.

Kole answers, seeming pleased himself, "I did. I brought a cooler with ice in it." He thumbs over his shoulder. "I left it in the freezing river overnight, and low and behold…all the food kept and is good to eat. Enjoy it while it lasts because I only brought enough for one day. Kage wouldn't let me bring enough for three to four days. So, it'll be dried beef from here on out unless we get some fowl today."

"Well, thank you very much. That's awful kind of you to think of us like this. Are you going to hunt for food, or are you staking out today?"

Chuckling, rubbing his hands together, mischievously, he responds, "Oh, you know I'd never miss a good fight. I'll be hiding in the woods waiting for the excitement to begin."

"Ha, I'm glad *you* see it as excitement. I see it as one of the most terrifying things I've ever agreed to."

Kole throws his arm around my shoulder and says, "We won't let anything happen to you girls. Besides, if we did, I'm pretty sure Pierce would kill us."

Managing a nervous laugh as I lift food to my face, I say, "I'm just praying that no one dies today or whenever the battle happens."

I notice Adi and Dani-Jo crawling out of their tents. Wandering over to us, Kole nods for them to get some food.

Pierce, observing us from the other side of the fire pit, makes his way over to Kole and I. Kole quickly removes his arm as Pierce walks to the opposite side of me. Kole inquires, "While we're gone, what do you girls plan on doing all day?"

Adi replies, "Oh, I'm not sure. I think I might want to go swimming."

Dani-Jo's next to respond, "I may want to try out my ability while descending from various heights."

Last, I point out as I cross my arms across my middle, "I'll do my best to keep myself occupied, trying not to think about what lurks in the forest."

Pierce furrows his brow as he looks at Adi. "I'm not sure that you leaving the campground to go swimming," his eyes then move to Dani-Jo, "and you being up in a tree somewhere away from camp is the best idea. That means that you three will essentially be alone."

Patting him on the lower back, I reassure, "I don't think anything's going down today. I'm pretty sure we'll be ok."

"I'd really like you three to stay together," he says with a severe stare.

I take my thumb and rub out the wrinkle in-between his brows and answer, "Pierce, we'll be fine. In a few days, we'll make sure to all stay together."

He covers his eyes with his right hand and says, "Damn it. I guess there's no changing a made-up mind." Taking me by the shoulders, he stares into my eyes. "Just promise me you'll have your weapons nearby at all times."

Uncrossing my arms, I elevate up onto my tiptoes and kiss his supple lips, assuring him I mouth, "Promise."

Once the guys have their weapons and necessary hunting supplies, they get ready to head off into the woods. Pierce comforts me with a kiss and reminds me, "I've got your back, Spitfire." With that, I pat him on the ass as he trails off with the other guys.

Now that they're out of sight, Adi, Dani-Jo, and I plan out our day.

Adi mentions, "Since it's still early, I think I'll wait until it gets warmer until I go for a swim." Agreeing with the fact that it'll be better to wait, I admit, "I think that'd be a good idea." Looking at Dani-Jo, I quiz, "What about you?"

Dani-Jo bolsters to her feet. "I don't want to wait. I'll go ahead and practice. You two holler if you need anything. I won't be far."

Waving her off, I assent, "Will do. Have fun, and please don't break any bones."

Sniggering, she grabs her handgun and rushes off, disappearing behind the trees.

Adi moves to sit on a log that has been positioned around the fire. Settling down onto it, she pats for me to join her. Doing as she wishes, I lower myself until I'm sitting beside her. Resting her palms down onto the tree, she looks up through the leaves to the clear blue, "Did you ever imagine we'd be out here looking to battle knowing that someone's going to get seriously hurt?"

Leaning over, placing my elbows on my knees, I answer, "Not in a million years. I always saw myself standing guard behind the walls while the men came out to do the hunting and exchange goods." Moving my knee, I bump Adi's leg, "It's funny how you don't know what you're willing to do until your friends are put in harm's way."

Adi exhales, "Girl ain't that the truth."

After our lunch has digested, Adi places her hands on her knees, pushing up to a standing position, "Well, I guess I'm going to find that river. Maybe there's a swimming hole. I won't be gone for more than a couple of hours."

I lean my back on a tree, sitting down on the ground, crossing my ankles over each other as I straighten out my legs, "Ok, just be careful."

Snatching her bow, she affirms, "I will."

A fter only a few minutes of quietness and the woods all to myself, I doze off. Clearly, I'm exhausted after waking up in the middle of the night to calm down those Lynxwolves. My head bounces to the side, startling me awake. Determining I need a nap, I stand up, dust the bottom of my pants off, and stroll to my tent.

Bringing the covers up to my chest, I rest my head on my pillow, feeling for the ax I've hidden underneath it. Yep, it's there. Sleep consumes me, it takes all of five minutes, and I'm out.

Startled out of my slumber, I hear the zipper to my tent being undone. I don't jump up because it's Pierce and the guys back for the day for all I know. I simply turn my head in the direction of the sound only to be frozen in fear.

Is this really happening, or is this a freaking nightmare?

Cladec is inside my tent, covered in dirt from head to toe. He's flashing a large knife at me, "Remember me?" he sneers.

Looking for an escape, I spit, "You're the reason, even now, six years later, I can't sleep at night. Damn, right, I remember you."

He creeps inside, stalking closer toward me. Throwing my covers off of me with his left hand, he slices my shirt open in the top left corner, cutting my flesh like a ripe tomato. Blood is now drenching my shirt, flowing all the way down my chest.

Trembling, I manage to drum up courage as he straddles me, trying to pin me down. I immediately knee him in the balls. Grunting, he grabs his sack and falls over off me. I immediately reach for my ax under my pillow, then I pounce to his right hand, stomping on it, forcing the knife out of his hand. As I'm lunging out the front of the tent, he grabs my left ankle with all his might, dragging me back in on my belly. Still clutching the ax in my right hand and the knife in my left, I wait for the opportune moment to strike.

Once he has my entire body back inside, he violently flips me over, causing my head to bounce off the ground like a ball. Opening my eyes to darkness, I realize my vision has gone black. Even though I can't see, I shove the ax underneath the covers so Cladec can't see it. Shaking my head, my vision comes back, but it's blurry.

Do not let him do this to you. Get it together, Tova.

Hovering over me with a menacing laugh, Cladec taunts, "Oh, I'm not through with you. You thought what you endured as a child was horrible, just you wait and see what this knife feels like. And when I'm done there, I'll make sure to leave you bleeding out just enough to keep you alive until lover boy gets here so he can watch you die a slow and painful death."

He's holding my legs still with his, and his arms are forcing mine down. Yet, as he lifts his right hand loosening his grip on my left hand, reaching for the knife I'm gripping with my life, I twist my right wrist toward Cladec's thumb. I manage to free my right, and without hesitation, I use the Hammer Strike and slash his face with such force with the ax I hear the bone crack. He lifts his hand to his head and yells, "You've done it now, bitch. You're gonna pay for that."

He takes his right fist and bashes my face on the left side, leaving my ear ringing and that oh so familiar copper taste of blood filling my mouth. I know now that if I don't do something else, I will die in this tent. I switch my senses to tune into the surrounding wildlife, praying they're near enough to intervene soon.

Still holding the ax in my right hand, I thrust the smaller end of it forward, piercing Cladec's gut, pushing it as hard as I can inside him. He muffles a grunt but refuses to get off of me. He drops his hand from his face, raising it to hit me again, this time, backhanding me with his left hand, hitting my right eye and slashing it open. Blood fills my vision. I withdraw the ax from his abdomen and quickly stab it even lower into his pubic area while taking the knife in my left hand and impale his right side. Causing more demonic snarls to come from him, he takes both of his hands and chokes me.

My body aches as I lay on the ground, bleeding, striving to breathe. I vaguely hear footsteps thudding toward me, accompanied by growling, shouting, and gunfire. My vision refuses to focus and is now fading quickly as air refuses to enter my body.

40

PIERCE

Noticing movement in the woods heading to our camp, the guys and I follow suit, unsure if it's the enemy or animals. All of us guys are now surrounding the campsite. They must have all noticed the movement because as we get closer, we see that about eight to ten men are searching our tents. Being as quiet as we can, we approach the intruders without so much as them knowing we were just a few feet away from them.

These guys have makeshift weapons from what appears to be used arrows from our hunts; the ones we've been unable to retrieve. One or two of them have guns; where they got those is beyond me. They're all dirt from head to toe, so it's hard to tell if we know them.

Not waiting for an introduction to these savages, we raise our firearms and begin shooting. That's when the growling starts.

The Lynxwolves are invading our camp too, but they're not focused on us. None of the men in either group seem to care. The mêlée continues with the men fist fighting, stabbing, and shooting at each other, as the wolves have their sights set on mine and Tova's tent.

Shit! Where is she?

Looking around, I realize she's nowhere to be found. She said she was just going to hang around here while the other two girls went off. Dashing my head back and forth looking for her, I hear an all too familiar voice...

"Don't worry about her boy. She's already been taken care of." Drowning out all the commotion and growling from the wolves, I twist my head in the direction of the voice. I see it's none other than my despicable uncle, Morton.

Seeing fire, I demand, "What do you mean?"

He seethes, "Oh, sonny boy, don't play dumb with me. You know who. The person she had blackballed out here to this hellhole."

Doing my best to keep my blazing ass in check, I retort, "You're telling me you've been in cahoots with that psycho manic bastard that abused her as a child?"

"How else was I going to get back at your father for everything he's stolen from me? I'm the one who snuck arrows out so Cladec could get a good shot at her on the track, only he was supposed to get you, too." He spits through a wicked smirk, "You know two for one?"

Fire now erupts from my hands. "Are you fucking kidding me? You got him weapons to use against your own family and Tova." Gesturing my hand toward our tent, I yell, "You don't even know her."

Sneering, he answers, "Yeah, boy, I did. I figured if you died, then your father might just go on and die of a heart attack or at least resign, then I'd be up for his position. And it was me shooting at them girls in the forest. I almost had 'em too. If I was in better shape, I'd a caught 'em, and they'd all be dead too." Raising a gun to my chest, he scowls, "But none of y'all were ever supposed to know it was me behind the attacks."

Not waiting for him to shoot, I stretch out my hands and force burning flames to his face. Screaming, he shoots his gun three times as he falls to the ground, fire consuming him.

I'm hit in the left shoulder, right thigh, and the third bullet hits the ground. Refusing to stop and assess my injuries, I take my fiery right hand and cauterize my left shoulder. My left hand cauterizes my right thigh as best as I can while I'm running to where our tent is. Glancing in the woods, I notice that the wolves are now on the outskirts of our camp, chomping down on some thick bloody flesh from a remaining carcass.

Getting to our tent, I'm forced to a halt at the outside of the entrance as I see the lower half of a bloody body that's been ripped into shreds. My heart is now thumping so hard I feel it in my throat. Stepping over the dead body, I duck my head inside the tent. Gasping, I fall to the ground on my knees beside a small lifeless body.

Witnessing Tova lying motionless on the ground has my hands glowing fire. I know I can't assess her pulse without scorching her. I scream for Jace. Not sure if he can hear me over the commotion outside, I slink to the opening of the tent and yell as loud as I can, "JACE!"

He butts his gun to one intruder's head, knocking him out cold, then rushes to my side.

Holding my fiery red hands out, blood drips down from my shoulder and singes as it hits my sweltering palms. I beg, "Hurry! I... I can't touch her. Please, please, can you check for a pulse?"

Seeing the dread in my eyes, Jace rushes inside. Placing his index and middle finger to Tova's neck, he gives me an alarmed look. Not saying a word, he immediately begins chest compressions.

Fuck! No! This cannot be happening!

I was supposed to protect her. The world is tunneling in on me. Looking at him, then Tova I begin to sway.

Jace yells, "Pierce, stay with me, man! Don't do this!" He screams louder. From what I can make of it, he sounds like he's demanding, "Kage, come now."

Trying my best to focus, I glimpse Kage as he enters.

Kage stoops down beside me, "Pierce, come on now. Focus! Calm down. I know you're in there. Snap out of it. We need you. Tova needs you."

The rage inside me has consumed my every fiber, and I'm not just harnessing fire with my hands. My entire arms are engulfed in flames. Kage tackles me by my waist and forces me out of our tent. Swinging at him and anything in sight, I lose myself. All the Protectors attempt to put me out of action, but they're all being charred when they get near me. I've set a lot of tents on fire and some surrounding trees in my swinging fit.

Adi and Dani-Jo run up as all the hullabaloo is going down. Letting out shrieking, ear-piercing screams as high as they can, they jolt me out of my trance, but my arms are still engulfed in flames. Stopping at two guys right in front of me, I see Larson rip the other guy completely in two with his brutal strength, then he runs toward Tova.

Slowing my arms from swinging, I swivel my head slowly, trying to focus. Coming to myself, Kage tackles me to the ground, knocking the breath out of me, dousing me with water from his palms to put out my fire.

The girls run over, screaming and crying, "What happened? Where's Tova?"

Kole and Kaden hush the girls, filling them in on the mêlée that took place.

As Kage is still holding me down, I demand, "Let me up. I need to see her."

Kage removes his tight grip from my arms and slowly gets up, assessing me as if I'm going to snap again. I throw my hands up, "I'm ok. I've got to get to her."

Still unsure if Tova is alive, we all rush to the tent she's in. Peeking inside, I see Tova, the palest blood-covered body. Jace and Larson are at her side and Larson is pressing his fingers to her neck, assessing for a pulse. I dart to her side, now able to help her in any way I can.

I drop to my knees, looking at Larson as he says, "Still no pulse."

Immediately I jump into action, performing CPR and doing mouth to mouth resuscitation. After a few more rounds of chest compressions, I notice a spark emit from Jace's hands. Looking up at him, I ask, "Can you shock her and restart her heart?"

Looking at his palms, then back up at me, he responds, "Um, I'm not sure. This is something new to me."

With pleading eyes, I beg, "Please try."

Clasping his hands together, he says, "What if I do more damage? She's still bleeding."

I assure him, "I'll cauterize her wounds while you get ready to shock, ok? If we don't try, she's not going to make it."

Closing his eyes, he rubs his hands together. I see sparks emit from them. Having cauterized Tova's wound on her chest that's now mostly closed and not bleeding anymore, I back away so Jace doesn't inadvertently shock me too.

Opening his eyes to electric hands, he informs, "I'm pretty confident that the energy is at its max. Are y'all ready?"

"Do it!" I say, not wanting to wait for a second longer.

He places both hands on her chest, closes his eyes, and shocks her. Tova's lifeless body jolts off the ground about a foot, then thuds back down. I immediately press my fingers to her neck to assess for a carotid pulse. Looking at the group surrounding us, I let out a panicked breath. "There is a faint pulse, but I don't know for how long." Turning back to her, as a tear escapes and trails down my cheek, I lean down, pressing my lips against the cool skin of her forehead. "Tova, baby, please. Please come back to me."

To be continued...

SNEAK PEEK AT DEFENDING PIERCE-BOOK 2 IN THE IRON MOUNTAIN SERIES

Tova

The bright sun is shining down on the rolling hills lavished with all kinds of colorful wildflowers. The aroma smells like heaven. As I lift my leg to begin running down the hill toward the brilliant horizon, I hear the most pleading sound. This familiar voice keeps me from going.

Turning back, I see Pierce's face desperate and so very sad. He's reaching out for my hand, begging me to come back to him. I long to touch the man I love, to ease his hurt. I reach my hand out for his and suddenly it hurts, everything hurts, my head, my chest, my entire body.

I can hear him. I can feel him. I just can't get my body to respond to him.

~Defending Pierce premieres Fall 2021~

If you enjoyed this book, please be sure to leave a review on Amazon, Goodreads, and BookBub.

ACKNOWLEDGMENTS

First of all, thank you Lord for giving me such a creative imagination. Secondly, thank you to my precious family, Jonathan, Brooklyn, London, & Cydney. You have been my biggest cheerleaders, my voice of reason, and mostly my inspiration driving me to achieve my dream of becoming an author.

And to the woman who was there any day or night I needed help...all the love to author Shanna Swenson for your patience, your kind words, your fierce editing, proof reading, coaching, hours upon hours on the phone helping me. For without you, I'm pretty sure this book would never have gotten published.

I never in a million years would have imagined how difficult, exhausting, and exciting it was to create my very own book, now series. Thank you to all of those who encouraged me to pursue my dream, never give up, and pushed me to keep going.

Chasiti, my sweet persistent sister, you got your wish. You kept pressing me to make it a series. Ha, now it is.

Tova, you'll never know how grateful I am to you for

allowing me to name my Main Character after you. I hope she did you proud.

Author C R Pugh, you wrote my first book boyfriend and inspired me to use Pierce as my man Main Character.

To my childhood best friends, much love to you because you're the inspiration for my supporting characters: Wendy, Tiffany, Steffinni.

Eva, you are such a talented artist. I'm overjoyed to feature your work in my debut novel.

Abby G., your creativity in designing my webpage and logo assembly amazing.

Thank you to all of my devoted readers who actually read my very first, very rough, rough draft and giving me pointers: Rachel, Casei, Dovie, Kellie, Kelly G., Jen, April, Amy, Karen.

And to YOU, THANK YOU for taking a chance on me and reading my very first book. I hope you love the book as much as I have loved writing it.

ABOUT HAVANA WILDER

Havana has always had a vivid imagination and is an avid dreamer. After discovering her love of fantasy romances, she decided to put her dreams into reality by becoming an author herself.

When she's not working on her next novel or reading, she enjoys wakeboarding, chasing waterfalls, four-wheeling, and roasting s'mores around her pergola/firepit that her loving husband hand crafted for her for mother's day.

Her website is: www.havanawilder.com

Find her on:

- facebook.com/havanawilder
- instagram.com/havanawilder
- amazon.com/Havana-Wilder
- bookbub.com/authors/havana-wilder
- goodreads.com/havanawilder

71432263R00190